LARKLIGHT

OR

THE REVENGE OF THE WHITE SPIDERS!

OR

TO SATURN'S RINGS AND BACK!

A Rousing Tale of Dauntless Pluck in the Farthest Reaches of Space

AS CHRONICL'D BY ART MUMBY, WITH THE AID OF
MR PHILIP REEVE

AND DECORATED THROUGHOUT BY
MR DAVID WYATT

BLOOMSBURY
CHILDREN'S
BOOKS

JFIC
4|07

Text copyright © 2006 by Philip Reeve
Illustrations copyright © 2006 by David Wyatt

Published by Bloomsbury Publishing, New York, London, and Berlin
Distributed to the trade by Holtzbrinck Publishers

Library of Congress Cataloging-in-Publication Data
Reeve, Philip.
Larklight / by Philip Reeve ; illustrations by David Wyatt. — 1st U.S. ed.
p.   cm.
Summary: In an alternate Victorian England, young Arthur and his sister Myrtle,
residents of Larklight, a floating house in one of Her Majesty's outer space territories,
uncover a spidery plot to destroy the solar system.
ISBN-10: 1-59990-020-3 • ISBN-13: 978-1-59990-020-9
[1. Science fiction.] I. Wyatt, David, ill. II. Title.
PZ7.R25576Lar 2006   [Fic]—dc22   2006004348

First U.S. Edition 2006
Typeset by Dorchester Typesetting Group Ltd.
Printed in the U.S.A. by R. R. Donnelley, Harrisonburg
2 4 6 8 10 9 7 5 3 1

Bloomsbury Publishing, Children's Books, U.S.A.
175 Fifth Avenue, New York, NY 10010

The pages of this volume are impregnated with Snagsby's Patent Folio-dubbin to preserve them
against the depradations of space moth and paper bats.

For Sarah & Sam

CONTENTS

CHAPTER ONE

IN WHICH WE RECEIVE NOTICE OF AN
IMPENDING VISITOR.

Later, while I was facing the Potter Moth, or fleeing for my life from the First Ones, or helping man a cannon aboard Jack Havock's brig *Sophronia*, I would often think back to the way my life used to be, and to that last afternoon at Larklight, before all our misfortunes began.

It was a perfectly ordinary afternoon, filled with the

usual sounds of Larklight's grumbling air pipes and hissing gas mantles, and with the usual smells of dust and mildew and boiled cabbage – smells which were so familiar to us that we no longer even noticed them. Oh, and I was having an argument with my sister, Myrtle. That was perfectly ordinary too.

I wanted to go out on to the balcony to watch the delivery boat arrive, but Myrtle was too busy playing the piano. She had been trying to teach herself how, using a large, floppy, greyish book entitled *A Young Gentlewoman's Pianoforte Primer*, and she had been practising the same piece from it over and over again, for months. It was called *Birdsong at Eventide*, and it went, 'Ting *pling* ting pling *ting,* ting tong, ting tong, ting tonggg clonk, bother!' At least, that is how it went when Myrtle played it. Myrtle said that she was a young lady now and would need accomplishments if she were one day to shine in good society, but I didn't think the pianoforte would ever be one of them. I tried telling her so, but she just slammed shut the lid of the instrument and called me a little beast.

'Oh, do come, Myrtle,' I said. 'I thought you liked to watch the delivery arrive.'

She laughed her bitter, world-weary laugh, which she

had been practising of late in the bathtub. It was supposed to sound grown-up. 'There is little enough else to do here!' she said. 'I declare Larklight must be the dullest spot in all Creation! If only we lived in England, like a civilised family, there might be balls and levees to attend! I should go about in society, and young gentlemen would offer to dance with me. Even in Bombay or Calcutta or one of the American colonies there would be visiting and so forth. But stuck here in this bleak, outlandish place . . . Oh, *why* must we live at Larklight?'

I tried reminding her that Larklight was our mother's house, and had been in Mother's family for absolute ages. Mother had loved the old place, and after she died, Father had not had the heart to leave it. But Myrtle would not listen to reason. She flung aside *The Young Gentlewoman's Pianoforte Primer*, which floated slowly up to the ceiling and hung there, rustling a little, like a disappointed bat.

'Now look!' she cried. 'The gravity generator has gone wrong again! Find a servant, Art, and send them down to the boiler room to mend it.'

In the end, she came with me to the balcony after all. I knew she would. She liked to see the delivery boat come in from Port George as much as I did, she had just grown too ladylike to admit it.

We climbed the long staircase to the balcony door, and paused there to put on our rubberised capes (to preserve us against the space damp) and slip on our lead-lined galoshes. The gravity was definitely a little patchy that afternoon, and wouldn't it have been a tragedy if one of us lost our footing and went whirling off into the boundless aether, never to be found (unless it were Myrtle, of course, in which case there would be great rejoicing and a half-holiday declared, et cetera, but ho hum.) When we were quite ready we unfastened the door and stepped outside. Space frost, which had formed thickly around the door seal, went drifting off in a bright, thinning cloud, and when it had cleared we could see the familiar view. The Moon filled the whole sky above us like a vast crescent lanthorn shining in the blackness of the high aether, and beyond it, a little off to one side, twinkled the small blue eye of the Earth.

There is a picture of Larklight overleaf, with a few points of interest marked. As you will see, it is a very old house. Nobody seems to know who built it, nor which way up it is supposed to go, but Mother used to claim it had been constructed by an ancestor of hers during the early 1700s, just a few years after Sir Isaac Newton's great discoveries had made the Conquest of Space possible. Over the century and a half since then bits and pieces have been added to it, and another of Mother's forebears had tried to improve it somewhat during the last age by adding some porticoes and things in the Classical taste, but it remains a shapeless, ramshackle, drafty, lonely sort of house, and a terribly long way from anywhere, spinning along on its remote orbit out in the deeps beyond the Moon.

→>·<←

It was peaceful up there on the balcony; the immense silence of the open aether seemed more silent still after a whole day spent listening to *Birdsong at Eventide*. In pots along the balustrade there still grew some of the delicate crystalline space flowers which our dear mother used to collect. I remembered how, when I was three or four, there used to be a pot of them upon my nursery window sill, and

~ THIS WAY UP ~

~ THIS WAY UP ~

~ THIS WAY UP ~

Father's Solar Pinet

Observation Balcony

Mother's Conservatory

Art's Bedroom

Ice Chute

Myrtle's Bedchamber

Kitchens

Main Reception Hall

Observatory & Study

Father's Drawing Room

Larklight

how they would lull me to sleep each night with their strange, wordless songs. But Mother was dead, lost aboard the packet *Semele* back in 1848, while on her way to visit an aged relative in Cambridgeshire. Neither Father nor Myrtle nor I had her skill in growing and tending the singing flowers, and over the years, one by one, their voices had fallen silent.

To distract myself from such melancholy thoughts, I snatched up a long-handled net from the basket outside the door and started trying to catch one of the fish which kept flapping past*. I hoped I might land one that would turn

---

*Father says these space fish are not really fish, but rather Aetheric Icthyomorphs. But they do look awfully like fish, except that some of their fins have grown into wings. Father has spent years and years watching them, because he says that only by studying every detail of Creation can we truly begin to appreciate the Infinite Love and Wisdom of God. Father's name is Edward Mumby, and he is the author of a useful book called *Some Undescribed Icthyomorphs of the Trans-Lunar Aether*. We have several hundred copies of it stacked up neatly in the guest wing, should you be interested in reading one. Father has even had a fish named after him by one of his colleagues in the Royal Xenological Institute. It is called *Icthyomorphus mumbii*, and here is Mr Wyatt's drawing of it.

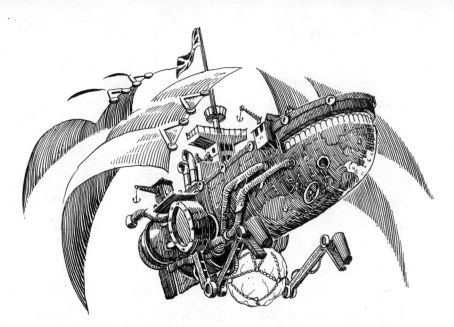

out to be of a Species Unknown to Science, and would interest Father. Alas, all I managed to net was a common or garden Red Whizzer (*Pseudomullus vulgaris*) as usual. Shoals of them often lurk about among Larklight's forest of chimney pots, seeking shelter there from prowling Grab-sharks. I wanted to keep mine for supper, but Myrtle made me throw it back.

'Look!' cried Myrtle, all of a sudden, and there was the delivery boat, far closer to Larklight than I had expected. It was a dark green boat, and from a distance it looked rather like a fish itself, except that it had a large bulge at the stern where the alchemical engines were housed. It edged up to our jetty with a few beats of its wings and quick, nervous twitches of its steering fins, moving much as the fish do. The crew were Ionians – we could not see much of them, wrapped up as they were inside tarpaulin aether-suits and tinted goggles, but you can always tell an Ionian; they are stocky little fellows with four arms. I said it would be fun to ask them in and hear what yarns they had to tell of life upon the aether, but Myrtle said primly, 'Certainly not, Arthur; they look terribly common. Why, they are not even human, let alone English.' So I contented myself with waving, and the aethernauts waved back as they unhooked the great blue-white ball of comet ice which hung in their ship's cargo-claws and manoeuvred it into the mouth of the ice chute. We could feel the vibrations all the way up on the balcony as it went

rumbling down into the ice house at the heart of Larklight.

Because the aether is not rich enough for us to breathe for very long, those of us who make our homes in the Heavens have come to rely on regular deliveries of ice, which our servants feed into special machines that extract the oxygen and pump it about inside our houses and our ships. (It also provides us with fresh water and cold stores, where meat and vegetables may be kept.) Our delivery boat brings us ice about once every three months, along with hampers of dried meat and fruit, tinned goods, preserves, and the flour and eggs and suchlike which our automatic cook uses to bake our bread and biscuits. Usually there are letters and journals aboard too.

As the boat pulled away that afternoon I raced Myrtle down the stairways to the jetty, and I won – huzzah! I opened one of the food hampers and burrowed within. Myrtle chided me for being greedy, but changed her tone quickly enough when I uncovered a jar of dried apricots. We each ate a few, and then, together, we tore open the brown paper parcel which the Ionians had left there for us, in which was bundled up all the mail forwarded to us from the Central Lunar Post Office at Port George.

There was not very much. A seed cake from our great-aunt Euphemia in Devonshire, a letter for Father, some recent editions of the London *Times* and a month-old *Illustrated London News*. The latter Myrtle snatched from me before I could catch any more than a glimpse of the engraving on the front cover, which appeared to show a giant greenhouse.

'Oh, what pretty dresses!' my sister mewed, leafing through, and stopping now and then to go all soppy over a portrait of Lady Somebody-or-other of Whatsit in a new ball gown. 'Oh, how I wish I could see London, even if it were only for one day! Look, Art! The Queen and Prince Albert are arranging a Grand Exhibition where produce from all over the Empire is to be displayed. It sounds highly illuminating. "There are to be exhibits from all over Britain, as well as from the American colonies and Her Majesty's Extraterrestrial Possessions, Mars, Jupiter and the Moon . . ."'

'Pish,' I told her. 'We do not rule Jupiter, only a handful of its satellites.'

Myrtle did not appear to have heard me. She was too busy imagining herself in a frilly frock, curtseying to the Queen. '"The Exhibition is to be held in a Crystal Palace,"' she read. '"This vast structure has been engineered by Sir

Waverley Rain* himself, and was built in his manufactories on the moons of Mars. It consists of an iron frame within which are set thousands of gigantic panes of glass crystal, specially grown in Rain & Co.'s crystal fields at the Martian North Pole." Oh, Art, how I would love to go!'

I left her daydreaming and ran off up the winding stairways to take Father his letter. Servants were clattering about in the dining-room and the kitchen, preparing dinner, and the smoke from their funnels made me sneeze as I hurried past them. Father had never been able to find human servants who were prepared to come all the way out to Larklight to look after us, so we made do with a batch of mechanical ones which we had ordered from Rain & Co. They were quite a good model, but they were getting rather

---

*Sir Waverley Rain is our greatest industrialist, and one of the wealthiest men in the Solar System. He started out as a humble cog-buffer in the spaceship yards of Liverpool, but his natural genius soon asserted itself and he made his first fortune by devising Rain's Patent Auto-Urchin, a mechanical boy who could be sent up chimneys too tall or poisonous for real orphans to sweep. He now owns vast manufactories upon the Martian moons, producing automatic servants and labourers of every type, and also engages in many other engineering ventures. He is terribly reclusive, and seldom leaves his secluded house, The Beeches, Mars.

old, and some of them smoked terribly when their furnaces had just been stoked. (Their hands overheated too. Myrtle was forever complaining of scorch marks on the household linen.)

I found Father in his observatory, almost hidden by the masses of tubes and tanks and ducts and telescopes and the teetering stacks of books. In the big vivarium at the centre of the room a few rare Icthyomorphs were drifting about with their mouths open, inhaling particles of space moss. A fearsome Grab-shark was spread open on the dissection table like a book while Father made a careful drawing of its innards. Behind him, through the observatory's big, round windows, I could see one white horn of the Moon.

'Ah, Art,' he said, looking up from his work and blinking at me in his vague, bewildered way, as if he had forgotten that I existed. Poor Father; he had never quite emerged from that cloud of sadness which enveloped us all when we heard of Mother's death. I was still sad sometimes, when I remembered her and thought about how I never was to see her again. But I was often happy too, especially when I was clambering about the roofs of Larklight or creating adventures for my lead soldiers and model aether-ships. As for Myrtle, she was concentrating too hard upon becoming a young lady to be sad all the time. But Father had given way to a sort of settled melancholy. He sought comfort in his studies, and paid little attention to anything else. Why, I believe he might have forgotten to eat if Myrtle had not sent me out on to the landing to beat the dinner-gong each evening and rouse him from his contemplation of the lesser Icthyomorphs.

He blinked again, as if he were struggling to remember

how one went about being a father. Then it came to him: he smiled his old, kind, twinkly-eyed smile at me, and set down his pencils, reaching out to tousle my hair. 'Well, what news from the great world beyond this little planetoid of ours?' he asked.

I told him about the seed cake, ('How kind of your great-aunt Euphemia,' he said.) Then I gave him the letter. He tore open the envelope, frowning slightly as he studied the enclosure. 'How intriguing. A Mr Webster, who is travelling in this quarter of the Heavens, wishes to call upon us. He will be arriving on the morning of the sixteenth. I take it that he is a scientific gentleman, like myself. See, he writes on the notepaper of the Royal Xenological Institute . . .'

Now the Royal Xenological Institute are a parcel of very learned coves whose job it is to study all the different flora and fauna of our solar realm. They have premises in Russell Square, London, where the fellows and professors work, but they are in constant correspondence with amateur botanists and natural philosophers throughout the aether. Father quite often received letters from them asking his opinion on rare aspects of Icthyomorphous Biology, or informing him of a new discovery, and very dry, dusty, dismal old gentlemen they sounded. Father, however, was quite delighted at the news of Mr Webster's intentions.

'I do not recognise the name,' he said, holding the letter up to the light and reading it again, as if he hoped that might tell him more about its author. 'I wonder if he has an interest in the lesser Icthyomorphs?'

I couldn't think of any other reason why anyone should want to visit Larklight, but I did not say so, for I had no wish to hurt Father's feelings. Instead, I ran off to find Myrtle and tell her the news. For although Father seemed unaware of it, I knew that the sixteenth was tomorrow.

CHAPTER TWO

IN WHICH MYRTLE DOES A LITTLE LIGHT DUSTING, AND
OUR AWFUL ADVENTURES COMMENCE.

What a whirlwind of cleaning and dusting, of waxing and buffing, of scrubbing and scouring and straightening overtook Larklight! We were not used to visitors, living out there as we did 'in the back of the black'. Indeed, in all my years (and I was very nearly twelve) I could not recall anyone ever troubling themselves to come and visit us before.

Myrtle was greatly excited. She wanted to know everything about this Mr Webster. Was he a very important gentleman? Was he young and handsome? What were his family connexions? Was he, perhaps, related to the Berkshire Websters? She even fetched down our dusty old copy of *Burke's Peerage* from the top shelf of Father's library, hoping to discover that Mr Webster was heir to a dukedom or a baronetcy, but a paper bat had eaten up all the entries between Vinnicombe and Whortleberry, so that was no help.

'He must be *someone*,' she said firmly. 'Why, the Royal Xenological Institute does not hand out its official notepaper to just *anybody*. We must make certain that Larklight is ready to receive this Mr Webster.'

She ordered the poor old servants to set to work and clean the whole house from top to bottom (not that Larklight really has either). When she saw that they were not up to the job, she took charge herself. She tidied away everything that could be tidied. She straightened the chairs and plumped the sopha cushions and made up a bed in the guest room. She polished the looking-glass and dusted the gas mantles, and cleaned the ornate frame of the portrait of Mother* which hangs in the drawing-room. Then she made me go down to the heart of the house and switch off the gravity generator.

I had never quite liked the heart of Larklight. When you got right down inside, away from the windows and the living quarters, it was rather sombre and spooky. Odd winds blew at you from nowhere, and sometimes strange noises issued from dusty, disused rooms. The tiles on the floors formed patterns that were too complicated to make

---

*The portrait shows Mother looking very young and beautiful, just as she must have appeared to Father when she attended the lecture he was giving at the Working Men's Institute at Cambridge in the autumn of 1832. The lecture was entitled *Some Recent Theories on the Origins of the Planets*, and I'm afraid Father made rather a hash of it, because he was put off by the charming lady sitting in the front row, who kept smiling as if his words amused her. But later she sought him out and apologised, and introduced herself as Miss Amelia Smith of Ely, whose work on song flowers Father had long admired. By Christmastide they were engaged, and the following spring they were married.

out, and seemed to change when you weren't looking. It all felt very old, somehow, as if thousands of years of time had soaked into those dank stone walls. Which was impossible, of course, for it is less than two centuries since human beings ventured into space.

The gravity generator was housed in the very centre of the house, in a chamber which we called the boiler room. It was not a proper gravity generator, alas, such as are made in dear old England by Arbuthnot & Co. or Trevithicks. Ours was a thing of antique and unearthly design, all wheels and levers and flutes and cones and giant, spinning spheres, and honestly you would not believe that a house the size of Larklight could require such an enormous and complicated machine just in order to keep everybody's feet upon the carpets. It kept going wrong too, and great portions of it seemed to do nothing at all, but sat unmoving, covered in the dust of ages. I always presumed that one of Mother's forebears must have bought it from a Jovian scrap dealer, and I dare say they paid him too much for it.

I reached out and turned the adjustor dial until the arrow pointed to zero BSG*.

* *abbr.* British Standard Gravity

The generator hissed and sighed and grumbled, and I became weightless and floated out to get enmeshed in all the tangly pipes and ducts which wriggle about the boiler room ceiling (I think they have something to do with the plumbing). By the time I had freed myself and swum back up the stairwells to the living quarters, every muffin crumb and crust of bread which we had dropped those past six months had floated out from its lurking place in the rugs and carpets and the obscurer corners of the wainscoting. Entering the dining-room was like flying through a hailstorm of stale toast. But it was all part of Myrtle's master plan. Holding down her billowing crinoline with one hand she flapped her way over to the big hutch in the corner of the pantry and let loose the hoverhogs.

Hoverhogs come from the great gas-world Jupiter, where they scoot about in the upper atmosphere and suck up insects and airborne plants. But they seem to be just as much at home in Larklight, where they scoot about our living quarters and snuffle up drifting crumbs and bits of fluff. They look rather like pigs, except that they are mauve, and about the size of hot-water bottles, and instead of legs they have flippers, which they use to steer. They propel themselves through the air by a method which Myrtle says I am not to mention because it is simply too crude, so I won't, but if you study the accompanying picture carefully I think you will see what it is.

The rotten-eggs smell of the hoverhogs' exhalations was still hanging in the air when I awoke next morning. My bedroom felt cold, but then it usually does, because that side of the house turns  away from the Sun during the night hours. For a while I snuggled down under my counterpane and tried not to think about getting up. Then I remembered. Today was the day when Mr Webster was to arrive! I leaped from my bed and tried to propel myself through mid-air to the wash-stand in the corner, forgetting that I had switched the gravity generator back on before I turned in.

As I lay there on the floor, dazed by my fall, I happened to glance up at the windows. My bedroom curtains are a bit holey where the space moths have nibbled them, and through the holes I could usually see the inky blackness of the aether. But this particular morning the blackness had been replaced by a dull greyish white.

I opened the curtains and looked out at nothing at all.

I had heard of fog, and read about it in Sir Walter Scott, et cetera, but I had never heard of fog in space. I heaved the window open and stretched out my hand to touch it. It was springy and slightly sticky to the touch. I could not push my fingers through it. I was sure that the fog Sir Walter Scott wrote about was not like that.

Suspecting that something odd had happened, I pulled on my clothes as quickly as I could and went hurrying up the stair to Myrtle's room. She was awake, and just about to break the ice on her wash-stand with a toffee hammer when I burst in on her. Her curtains are in better shape than mine (she darns the holes), so she had not yet noticed the mysterious fog. When I told her about it she said, 'Oh, what rot; whoever heard of fog in space?' Then, 'And can't you knock, you little beast?'

I threw back the curtains triumphantly, and sure enough, Myrtle's window looked out upon the same ghostly, smoky whiteness as my own. The only difference was that her room had already revolved into the sunlight, and so the fog outside glowed with a pearly sheen. It looked very pretty, but as we stood admiring it something moved past beyond it, casting a great spiky shadow.

'Eeeeeeeeeek!' exclaimed Myrtle, jumping backwards.

I felt a little like saying 'Eeeeeeeeek!' myself, but seeing Myrtle so afraid reminded me that I was British, and must be brave. I took out my penknife, which I always keep in my pocket, along with a clean handkerchief and a box of lucifers. Opening Myrtle's casement, I leaned out far enough to dig the blade into the fog. It was a little like cutting through a woollen rug. I sawed away at it while Myrtle hopped nervously from foot to foot in the room behind me, occasionally squeaking, 'Art, take care!' and 'What is happening?'

Eventually I managed to cut a triangular hole about

three inches across. I put the cut-out triangle of fog in my pocket and set my eye to the hole.

From Myrtle's window you can usually look down to the roof of my little turret bedroom, then down again, (or is it up?) to all the roofs and windows of the main living quarters. But I could not see any of them. The whole house was being wrapped up like an Egyptian mummy in thick white ropes and ravellings of the clingy fog substance. Creeping about upon these strands, plucking and weaving and spinning out yet more, were . . .

'Spiders!' I said, scrambling hastily back into the room.

'Oh, how horrid!' exclaimed Myrtle, who dislikes almost all types of creepy-crawly (although she does have a soft spot for cheesy-bugs). 'Art, you must dispose of them! Quickly, arm yourself with a well-furled newspaper . . .'

So saying, she thrust a rolled copy of the *Times* into my hand. I hadn't quite the heart to tell her that the spiders I had just glimpsed had bodies as large as elephants', and legs as long as trees.

'I am going to fetch Father,' I said manfully, closing the window tightly. 'You must stay here, Myrtle, and try to be brave.' Then I walked calmly out of her room, and ran pell-mell along the landing to my father's room. I thought I could hear scrabbling noises coming from the roof above, which made me run faster. I was in such a state of funk by the time I reached Father's door that I almost neglected to knock before I opened it.

Father was already out of bed, standing at the web-fogged window in his nightshirt and dressing-gown. 'Art,' he cried. 'Whatever is going on?'

I was too out of breath to reply at once, and before I could find my voice I heard the front doorbell ring, and the stumping footsteps of an auto-servant going to answer it. 'They mustn't open it, Father!' I gasped.

'It's quite all right, Art,' Father promised, pushing past me and out on to the landing. 'I dare say it is only Mr Webster. He is rather earlier than expected. I presume this vapour outside was generated by his ship's chemical wedding; a mist from Alchemical Space, no doubt. Fascinating . . .'

'It's not mist, Father. It's *web*,' I wailed, but Father was already hurrying away along the landing to his dressing-room. 'It's . . .'

A servant, the black-boilered auto-butler we called Raleigh, came stomping up the stairs and his mushroom-shaped tin head swung round to address me. 'A Mr Webster to see your father, master Arthur.'

I ran to join him at the top of the staircase, staring down into the hall. The front door was standing open. As I watched, an enormous, many-jointed leg reached in through it; then another. The legs were white, and looked as if they had been carved from polished bone.

'Father!' I shouted.

'Yes, yes, Arthur,' I heard him call from the dressing-room. 'I

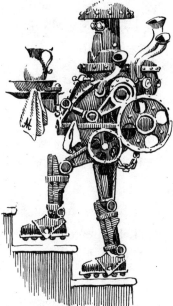

shall be there in a moment. You must ask our visitor to wait in the withdrawing-room. Perhaps he would like to join us for breakfast.'

Down in the hall, the monstrous spider squeezed its white, prickly ball of a body in through the door with a faint scraping sound. A cluster of black eyes glittered like wet grapes at the front end. Above them a shabby brown bowler hat was perched upon its spines. Beneath, hairy mouth-parts twitched and fidgeted. It tilted itself upwards, and saw me staring down at it.

'The name's Webster,' it said, lifting its hat with one huge claw. 'I'm expected.'

It spoke in a rather common way, and did not sound friendly. I looked down at the newspaper Myrtle had provided me with. It was a good, thick newspaper, but it didn't look as if it would have any effect at all on Mr Webster. I cast it aside, said to Raleigh, 'Throw him out!' and shouted again, 'Father!'

'Oh, blast these collar studs!' said Father's voice, through the half-open dressing-room door.

I waited on the top stair and watched hopefully as Raleigh clumped back down, machinery grating and clanking inside him until the wax cylinder with the correct phrase on it dropped into place. 'Excuse me, sir,' he said, 'I'm afraid I must ask you to leave . . .'

Just then, the gravity failed. Had the generator gone wrong again, or had some sneaky spider crept down into the boiler room and switched the adjustor dial to zero? I clung to the banisters and watched helplessly as Raleigh bobbed into the air like a fat metal balloon. A blow from Mr Webster's clawed forefoot slammed him against the wall, and his head fell off and went tumbling slowly through the air. Mr Webster heaved himself forwards into the hall, smashing the hat-stand into a spray of up-tumbling splinters. His black eyes were still fixed on me, glittering with triumph. He said, 'Grab 'em all, lads.'

More of the white spiders, smaller than Mr Webster but still much, much too big, came pouring into the house. The lack of gravity did not trouble them, for they were just as happy to walk on the walls or ceiling as the floor. They scuttled through the archways of their master's legs towards the stairs. I flapped my way towards the dressing-room, shouting for Father. He came floating out on to the landing,

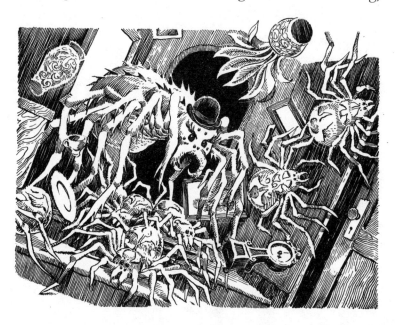

bare-legged, with his shirt-tails billowing and his collar half on.

'I say!' he cried, staring past me at the leading spider, which had not troubled itself to climb the stairs but had come straight up the wall instead, its claws digging into the wallpaper. 'What a magnificent brute! And unknown to science, unless I'm much mistaken! Quickly, Art, fetch me a net and my very largest preserving jar . . .'

'Mr Webster is a *spider*!' I exclaimed. 'There are lots more spiders downstairs!'

'Now come, Art,' Father chided, adjusting his spectacles to peer up at the beast as it came creeping towards us across the ceiling. 'It is hardly a spider. There is some superficial resemblance, to be sure, but you will observe it has at least twelve legs, whereas our earthly *arachnidae* have only eight . . .'

That was as far as he got, for at that moment the creature flung itself down upon him. I kicked it a few times, but it barely noticed, and its only reaction was to lash out with one of those twelve legs, catching me a blow which sent me tumbling back along the landing to the top of the stairs. Other spiders were coming up; I could see their black shadows jerking, all spindly in the gaslight. I heard Father shouting, 'Arthur, old chap, look to your sister! Keep Myrtle safe; I –' And then his voice was muffled into silence.

I looked back. The spider had lifted Father up inside the cage of its legs and was spinning him there like a bobbin, wrapping him from head to foot in those same white winding-sheets which had blinded Larklight's windows.

'Father!' I shouted, but there was nothing I could do, only obey his last command. I kicked and flapped and propelled myself back the way I had come, and the landing behind me was full of the skinny, dancing shadows of the spiders. Ahead, our hoverhogs blundered along in a chuffling scrum of pink bottoms and curly tails, squealing piteously. I suppose they had scented the invaders, and broken out of their hutch in a panic. They darted up an air duct, seeking safety in the shadows there, and I would have dearly loved to have hidden there too, but I had promised to save Myrtle, and so I swam onwards.

Outside the linen closet I saw two servants bobbing about, still struggling with the blankets which they must have been folding when the gravity went off. 'Spiders!' I shouted at them. 'Dust! Get rid of all those cobwebs!'

I knew they could not stop the invaders, but I hoped they might at least slow them down. As they obediently extended their broom and feather duster attachments and turned out to face the spiders I grabbed hold of the picture rail and hauled myself along it to the door of Myrtle's room.

'Oh, *knock*, Art!' she cried. 'How many times must I tell you? It is not difficult!'

Just then a great crashing and clattering came echoing along the landing. I suppose it must have been the sound of the spiders overcoming the two servants I had sent to bar their way. 'Whatever is that dreadful din?' demanded Myrtle. 'I suppose you have noticed that the generator has failed again! And where is Father?'

It was then that I realised our father was most probably dead – that the spiders had eaten him, and would eat us too if we did not make our escape.

I took Myrtle's hand. 'We must make our way to the lifeboats,' I said, as I dragged her to the door. 'I am afraid that something rather disagreeable has happened.'

CHAPTER THREE

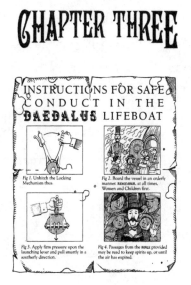

INSTRUCTIONS FOR SAFE
CONDUCT IN THE
DAEDALUS LIFEBOAT

Fig 1. Unhitch the Locking
Mechanism thus.

Fig 2. Board the vessel in an orderly
manner. REMEMBER, at all times,
Women and Children first.

Fig 3. Apply firm pressure upon the
launching lever and pull smartly in a
southerly direction.

Fig 4. Passages from the BIBLE provided
may be read to keep spirits up, or until
the air has expired.

IN WHICH WE MAKE GOOD OUR ESCAPE, BUT FIND
OURSELVES CAST ADRIFT UPON THE UNCARING AETHER.

It took me somewhat longer than I had hoped to fetch
Myrtle from her room, for she insisted upon packing a
small carpet-bag with clean linen and a hairbrush, then
going back for her diary, in which she is forever scribbling,
and then her precious locket, which Mother gave her, and
inside which there is Mother's portrait. As I waited for her
at the open doorway I could hear the sounds of the

dreadful spiders scattering and clattering the broken pieces of our auto-servants farther along the landing, and I began to realise that not all these brutes were as intelligent as their master, Mr Webster. They must have imagined the auto-servants to be living, armoured creatures, and were searching for meat inside the metal casings! It was lucky for us, otherwise they would have been upon us long before Myrtle was ready.

Of course, there was no question of going back past them and down through the hall, which was the quickest way to the lifeboat house. Luckily, I had spent many hours exploring the nooks and byways of Larklight, and I knew of an alternative route. I opened a small doorway opposite Myrtle's room and we swam quickly up a spiral of wooden stairs, strung across with the cobwebs of proper, British spiders.

Myrtle complained all the way to the top. 'Whatever are we doing in this horrible place? What has happened, Art? Where is Father?'

I could not even begin to explain, so I stayed quiet, and kept a firm hold on my sister's hand. The stairway let us out into the library. There was another stairway at the far side which I knew would take us almost to the door of the boathouse, but as we clawed our way along the bookcases towards it Myrtle gave a shriek and I looked up to see one of Mr Webster's friends scuttling across the library ceiling, having prised open a skylight to climb in. It tried to plunge upon us, but I was wise to its tricks after what had befallen poor Father, and I propelled Myrtle forcefully out of its way. It tumbled past us, all its long legs flapping and flailing, and I snatched up a great bound volume of journals from a nearby shelf and struck it as hard as I could upon its spiny head. 'Unk!' it grunted, and drifted away, curling up its legs, quite insensible.

As I started to steer Myrtle towards the stairs I noticed that the volume I had chosen was filled with bound-up back numbers of the *Times,* so I suppose she had been right after all when she told me to arm myself with a newspaper.

❧

We saw no more of the spiders as we flew down the stairs to the lifeboat house. We knew the lifeboats well, for Father had made us practise in them lest there should ever be a fire at Larklight. They were barrel-shaped objects, squatting on

spring-loaded projector plates in the middle of the shadowy boathouse. We checked about nervously for spiders before we heaved open the hatch of the nearer one and pulled ourselves inside.

'Are we to wait for Father?' wondered Myrtle, but she was looking very solemnly at me, as though she already knew the answer.

I shook my head.

'Were there a very great number of those awful creatures?' she asked.

I nodded

'And did they devour him?' Myrtle whispered.

I shrugged, and shook her away when she said, 'Poor Art! Then we are orphans!' and tried to hug me. All I knew was that Father had asked me to keep Myrtle safe, and that

I would be failing in my duty if I lingered for a moment longer in this spider-infested house. I strapped myself into one of the lifeboat's lumpy leather seats and made sure that Myrtle had done likewise before I pulled the lever marked 'Launch'.

There was a small window of reinforced Martian crystal in the nose of the lifeboat, and through it I saw the boathouse door slide open. Beyond it, where I had expected space and stars, lay only whiteness. In my eagerness to leave I had quite forgot that Larklight was entirely encased in cobwebs! But it was too late now to stop the launch. Our little vessel shook as machinery grated somewhere beneath us. Then the great coiled spring under the projector plate was released, and we felt ourselves

squashed back into our seats as the lifeboat was shot out through the open doorway like a shell from a gun. There was a faint resistance as we struck the cobwebs; then they gave way with a soft tearing sound, and we were through them, and tumbling away from Larklight in a billowing of torn threads.

I undid my straps and crept to the tiny stern-window. From there I had what I felt certain would be my last glimpse of home. Larklight was by then no more than a knobbly white parcel of cobwebs hanging in space, attached by skeins of spider silk to a strange, spiny, black ship which hung in the aether beside it.

>><<

I don't know if you have ever been aboard a lifeboat. The best I can say for it is that it is more comfortable than being trapped in a cobweb-entombed house full of hungry space spiders. There is little else to recommend it. The accommodation is cramped, the view dull, and since there is no room aboard such a tiny vessel for a chamber where the chemical wedding can occur, you are propelled through the aether by nothing but the impetus of your launching spring.

'What will happen to us now?' asked Myrtle.

'We must wait until someone picks us up,' I told her.

'And how long will that take?'

'Several hours, I expect.' But even as I spoke I had a most disagreeable thought. There had not been time to set off any emergency flares before we left Larklight. There was no way that anyone could know we were adrift out here. It was quite possible that we would perish from starvation and thirst, and our lifeless bodies tumble on for ever in the lifeboat!

I checked in the supply locker, and found little comfort there; only a keg of water, a case of fortified biscuits and a copy of the Holy Bible. But I did not want Myrtle to see how grim our prospects were, so I said, 'I am sure someone must have noticed that great black ship approaching Larklight. I dare say the Royal Navy will despatch a gunboat to investigate. I expect they are already on their way.'

→⋇←

It soon began to grow stuffy inside our tiny barrel, for although we had a small supply of comet ice aboard and a device for transmuting it into air, I did not wish to use it until the air we had started out with was quite exhausted. It seemed to me that it might be many days, or even weeks, before we were sighted by a passing ship.

It was also far too hot. We were tumbling in the full glare of the Sun, whose light came dazzling in at us through the windows. There were tinted goggles aboard, which we put on to preserve our eyes against the blinding rays, but we could do little about the heat. I took off my Norfolk jacket and unbuttoned my shirt, but Myrtle did not think it would be proper to remove her brown serge dress, and she grew hotter and hotter and more and more irritable as the long day wore on. At last she fell asleep, and I was able to think about some of the questions which had been troubling me ever since we left Larklight.

First, where had those great spiders come from? I had never seen anything like them in my schoolbooks, nor in the great thick encyclopaedias in Father's library. And how had their black ship arrived at Larklight? For everyone knows that only our Royal College of Alchemists possesses the secret of the process called the chemical wedding, which drives our aether-ships from world to world. Of course, Frenchmen and Russians and rebel Americans have all tried to steal it over the years and have even built a few shabby aether-ships of their own, but it is hundreds of centuries since any of the unearthly races were capable of sailing between the worlds.

It made me think of the legends which Captain Cook and other early spacefarers heard from the natives on Mars and Io; stories about great extra-solar ships, called Starjammers, with aether-wings as wide and white as moons, which cruise endlessly through the Milky Way and visit the worlds of our own dear Sun every millennium or so. Was it possible that our spiders had come from such a vessel as that? Were they the advance guard of some dread invasion from beyond the stars? Why, the whole Solar System might already be swathed in their webs for aught I knew!

I told myself to keep calm, and not to entertain such silly notions. The Astronomer Royal, in his observatory on Europa, would certainly have spotted a Starjammer long before it crossed the orbits of the outermost worlds, and the Royal Navy would take a firm line with any invasion fleet. Anyway, Father had told me that those old stories were a foolish superstition; the Martian and Ionian civilisations were both in a sorry state of decline, and had invented tales of travellers from other stars to explain the ruins which their own great ancestors had left behind.

It was much more likely, I decided, that the black aether-ship had belonged to the real Mr Webster, the gentleman whom we had been expecting, and that it had been attacked and overtaken by the spiders en route to Larklight. I shuddered to think of the awful fate which must have befallen poor Mr Webster and his crew at the hands (or rather claws) of the spider which had taken his name. I vowed that the first thing I would do when we were saved was to inform the authorities.

That decided, I soon grew drowsy, and fell, like Myrtle, into a troubled sleep, where great spindly shadows scuttled never-endingly through my dreams.

→>←

I was awoken by my sister poking me in the ribs. She pointed at the forward window, which I sleepily noticed was no longer filled with the star fields of the open aether, but with a lot of spiky white mountains which appeared to be drawing closer and closer.

'Art!' said Myrtle urgently, shaking me to try and rattle the sleep out of my head. 'I insist that you wake up and do something! I believe that we are about to fall upon the Moon!'

CHAPTER FOUR

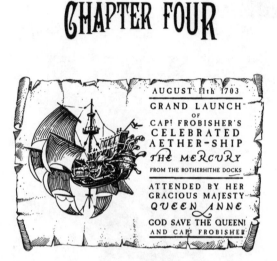

AUGUST 11th 1703
GRAND LAUNCH
OF
CAP! FROBISHER'S
CELEBRATED
AETHER-SHIP
The MERCURY
FROM THE ROTHERHITHE DOCKS

ATTENDED BY HER
GRACIOUS MAJESTY
QUEEN ANNE

GOD SAVE THE QUEEN!
AND CAP! FROBISHER

HOW WE CAME TO THE MOON, AND WHAT
BEFELL US THERE.

A ll through the history of the world, people have
looked up at the Moon and wondered what
secrets it held. All sorts of phantasies and
theories were woven about its shining seas and gleaming
mountains, and the wise and wonderful people who might
dwell among them. But in 1703 when the experimental
aether-ship *Mercury* made first moonfall in Queen Anne's

Bay, and Captain Frobisher and his merry band stepped out to plant the British flag in those white sands, they found that it was actually a bit of a dump. The seas, which had looked so enticing when viewed through telescopes from far-off England, were salt and drear. The only plants were pallid mushrooms which tasted like cardboard and grew in vast, silent groves. And the people were mushrooms too, though of a different type; they lived in the empty shells of giant lunar snails, and were so primitive that they showed no interest whatsoever in the new arrivals.

Since then, things have improved somewhat upon the Moon. Some useful mines have been dug in the hills west of Port George, and at nearby Mount Ghastly a colony for convicts has been established. These villains, transported from England for sheep-stealing and machine-breaking, soon see the error of their ways after a few years' hard work in the thin air, and their descendants may one day populate the entire Moon.

Unfortunately, apart from miners, mushrooms and convicts, nobody of any note chooses to live upon the Moon, or even visit it, and so great swathes of it lie unexplored. It was into one of these regions that Myrtle and I plummeted, bounding down a steep and rugged

mountainside in our lifeboat and coming to rest upon the floor of a deep crater, filled with fine white sand.

Luckily, the gravity on the Moon is so gentle that we were not hurt. But when I opened the lifeboat's hatch and looked out, I saw that our adventures were not yet at an end. Indeed, they might be only just beginning.

We had landed somewhere on the margin between the light and dark sides of the Moon. When I looked in one direction I could see the Sun shining brightly on a range of step white hills, while in the other all was sombre night. The crater in which our lifeboat had come to rest lay in a perpetual twilight.

We gathered up Myrtle's carpet-bag and all that we could carry of our small stock of food and water, and began walking towards the sunlight, although we both knew that there might be no human habitation for hundreds of miles.

The thin air made it hard to fill our lungs, so we did not speak much; and the sand underfoot was difficult to walk on – like walking through snow, according to Myrtle, who had once paid a visit to our great-aunt Euphemia on Earth, and never stops going on about it.

Luckily, the kindly gravity – about one-sixth British Standard – allowed us to travel some twenty feet with each step we took, which made the going somewhat easier.

Occasionally we passed through groves of spindly white fungi, like the ghosts of immense parasols. On the shady sides of rocks grew clumps of lunar puffballs, and I warned Myrtle to give them a wide berth, having read of how they had burst in the faces of luckless explorers and filled their heads with spores, which took root in their brains and sprouted new puffballs out of their eyes and ears. ('That is perfectly disgusting and I do not believe a word of it,' said

Myrtle, but I noticed she took long detours around the puffball clumps after that.)

We had been bounding along for about an hour when we saw something moving on a hilltop ahead and, drawing nearer, recognised a gaggle of the great lunar snails. They were oozing along in a sort of flock, their big mauve shells jostling and scraping one against another, and they were accompanied by a mushroom, who seemed to be acting as their shepherd – or rather as their *snail* herd, I suppose.

Myrtle, being the eldest, decided to take charge. She bounced up to the snailherd and said loudly and clearly, 'Excuse me, my good fungus, we have been shipwrecked on your horrid planet. Please direct us to the residence of the British Governor.'

The mushroom tilted his broad, spotted cap at her, and two sad, black eyes blinked out from beneath his gills. He made a bobbing motion, and said something in the whispery, sighing speech of the Moon.

'How perfectly vexing!' said Myrtle crossly. 'He does not speak English. He has probably never seen a human being before. I – oh, eek!'

She jumped backwards, covering a good forty feet of ground. The mushroom-man had reached out one of his powdery little hands to touch her locket, which he must have noticed glinting in the sunlight. 'He clearly understands the value of gold, though!' cried Myrtle, gathering herself up and brushing sand from her skirts. 'Did you see that, Art? He tried to rob me!'

'I think he was just curious,' I said. I felt sorry for the mushroom-man, who had been so startled by my sister's shrieks that he had turned pale blue and pulled his cap down tight like a folded-up umbrella. He peeked out at me after a while, and started to make little sweeping gestures with his hands, shushing and soughing at me all the time in his own strange language. It seemed almost as if he were trying to warn me of something, but I could not understand what it might be. Myrtle was already striding off haughtily towards the sunlit hills, and I knew I had to follow her. 'Sorry!' I told the mushroom.

I looked back at him as I went bounding after Myrtle. He was still motioning with his hands, pressing them against his stalk at a point where his throat would have been if he had had one. I thought he looked sad.

When I caught up with my sister she had stopped at the top of a jagged outcropping of moon rock.

'That was very rude,' I told her. 'Father always says we must be polite to all sentient creatures, even if they are only mushrooms. He says a gentleman is without prejudice . . .'

'Look!' was all that Myrtle said.

I looked, and saw at once why she had halted here. Beyond the outcrop we were standing on there stretched a plain dotted with tall towers of wind-worn rock, and between the towers, piled higgledy-piggledy one atop the next, there lay an enormous number of large, white jars. Each jar was taller than Myrtle, and roughly spherical in shape. And every single one was broken; either split completely in half, with shards and fragments littered all about, or simply pierced by a small, dark hole near the top. Broken pieces crunched under our feet as we walked down the slope, looking about us in wonderment at the mounds of jars. There must have been ten thousand of them. Who had made them? Whence came they? I forgot how tired and scared I was and began imagining how my name would become known for this great discovery: Arthur Mumby, first explorer of the Plain of Jars!

'Oh, look!' cried Myrtle, pointing.

In the bottom of one of the nearby jars, which had been so shattered that only a sort of pale bowl remained, lay a litter of white bones.

'It must be a funerary urn,' I said. 'I expect in years gone by the dead of some great, vanished, lunar race were laid to rest in these containers. I wonder who they were? Not the ancestors of our mushroom-friend, that's for sure. Mushrooms don't have bones.'

'They don't have buttons either,' said Myrtle nervously. She pointed at something lying among the bones, and I reached down and picked it up. She was right; it was a brass button with a raised design in the shape of an anchor with a coiled rope.

'The MacCallister expedition!' I gasped. 'They set out from Port George to explore the dark side of the Moon back in seventeen hundred and eighty-something. They never returned, and no one ever knew what had become of them. One of them must have ended up here . . .' But even as I spoke I had that slidy feeling which comes to you when a pet theory begins to collapse, for how would one of Captain MacCallister's men have become interred in an antique funerary urn of unknown design?

'Not just *one* of them,' whispered Myrtle, horror-struck. 'There are bones in this jar too!'

I checked another urn, and then another. More bones, more buttons, and a rusting sword. The urns themselves were made of some material which I could not identify; neither porcelain nor clay, but just as hard and shiny. In some there were no bones at all. In one I found the crumbling shell of a young lunar snail.

'Oh, Art,' said Myrtle, fingering the bright locket at her throat, which flashed in the sunlight. 'What is this dreadful place?'

There came a whirring, whirling sound; a rustling. I looked up. Nothing moved. The stars hung bright and cold above my Plain of Jars, and the lunar wind blew little flags of dust from the summits of the rock towers. I turned back to Myrtle, meaning to tell her that we should hurry on. But Myrtle had gone.

'Myrtle!' I said loudly. I did not understand where she

could have vanished to, since I had looked away only for an instant. I hunted for her among the nearer jars, and even checked inside a few, but I found only bones. I started to run, calling out as I went, 'Myrtle! Myrtle!' You can run a long way quite quickly on the Moon. Each time I pushed myself off I travelled twenty yards; each time I came down I shattered an urn to dust and fragments. In one I saw a skeleton that was fresher than the rest, with shreds of flesh and cloth still clinging to the bones. Its ankles were chained together with rusty shackles. The poor fellow must have been an escaped convict from the colony at Mount Ghastly – but however had *he* ended up in an urn?

The answer came down at me from above, in a great flapping and purring of grey wings. I had a glimpse of a huge, furry body, prism eyes, a tongue that uncurled like the spring of a broken watch. Then something stung the side of my neck, and I fell down into darkness.

CHAPTER FIVE

In Which We Find Ourselves Imprisoned on the Plain of Jars and Contemplate a Ghastly Fate (Again).

When I came to my senses I was still in darkness, and I could not move. I lay on some hard, uncomfortable surface which seemed to curve up past my face, and curved beneath me too, like a bowl, or . . .

With a terrible lurch of understanding I realised that I was *inside* one of the urns on the Plain of Jars! Someone or something must have mistaken me for dead, and I had been sealed within one of those unearthly vases, where my lonely bones would lie and whiten just like those of the poor men whose mortal remains Myrtle and I had stumbled across earlier!

'Myrtle!' I tried to shout, but my mouth would not work.

And then, down in the dark beside my feet, something moved. I was not alone in my jar. I felt the weight of a heavy body creep across my paralysed legs. I was so afraid that I finally managed to force out a sort of noise ('Eeep!', it went) and I felt the thing flinch and heard it growl, or rather sort of *warble*. It began to tug at my boot.

I tried desperately to move my legs, hoping to kick my way out of this prison. But they lay as heavy and lifeless as wet ropes. I strove to move my hands then, thinking that if I could only reach into my pocket I might at least find my matchbox, and strike a lucifer, by whose light I might see what it was that I had been entombed with. But no effort of mine would move them. The thing which had stung me, the thing with the wings and the glittering, prismatic eyes, must have injected me with a paralysing draught! It had looked, in the brief glimpse I had had of it, like a huge moth. I had expected it to eat me, not to seal me in a jar.

Why should a moth wish to seal people up in jars?

And then I understood. I was not to be food for the moth, but for its young! That thing which I could feel gnawing and nibbling at my boot must be some sort of caterpillar! The moth had made this jar out of spittle and moon dust and the chewed-up mulch of mushroom-trees and laid an egg inside, and left me in there along with it, to provide food for the hungry larva when it hatched!

Among my mother's books I had once discovered a volume of stories by a gentleman named Mr Poe, who lives in Her Majesty's American colonies. There was one, *The Premature Burial*, which gave me nightmares for weeks after I read it, and I remember thinking that there could be no fate more horrible than to be buried alive, and wondering what type of deranged and sickly mind could have invented such a tale. But as I lay there immobilised in a jar on the wrong side of the Moon with only a ravening caterpillar for company I realised that Mr Poe was actually quite a cheery, light-hearted sort of chap, and that his story had been touchingly optimistic.

With an immense effort I managed to shout, 'Help!' I did not expect any help to come, there in that unmapped corner of the Moon, but it seemed the only thing to do, and

I felt my loathsome companion recoiling slightly from the noise I made. 'Help!' I shouted again.

To my astonishment, I heard an answering cry. A moment later something struck the jar from outside. A star of hairline cracks appeared, then widened beneath the impact of a second blow. I heard voices without, shouting, 'Over here!' and, 'There's someone walled up in this one!' English voices! Hurrah, I thought, and shouted out, 'Help!' again, loud as ever I could, by way of an encouragement to my rescuers.

One whole side of the jar suddenly fell away, and as the light spilled in on us I had my first look at the creature whose breakfast I was to have been. It would have given Mr Poe himself bad dreams. A hairy maggot half as high as me, it reared up on the hindmost of its hundred legs and opened a complicated mouth full of huge teeth to hiss at me. I didn't see any eyes, though I suppose it didn't need any, living as it did in the dark inside a jar. Anyway, I had only a split second to study it; then there came an immense

There were enough knives and revolving pistols stuck
through his belt to make him look very desperate indeed.

thunderclap from somewhere close to my right ear and the top of the jar vanished in a spray of flying fragments, taking most of the caterpillar with it.

There was a smell which I supposed must be gun powder, and quite a lot of smoke. A hand gripped my shoulder and rolled me over. A face looked down at me.

I don't know what I was expecting. One of those Great White Hunters, perhaps, who are forever setting off into the wilds of Africa or Mars in search of big game, with only a few native guides and their trusty elephant gun for company. Well, my rescuer had an elephant gun all right, but otherwise he looked not one bit like the hunters I'd read of in books. He was not much more than a boy himself, for one thing; just about Myrtle's age. He wore high boots and a very ancient wideawake hat, and his face, which was the only part of him not covered by his tarpaulin space-suitings, was the brown of well-stewed tea. There were enough knives and revolving pistols stuck through his belt to make him look very desperate indeed, but I was relieved to see another human being at all, so I said, as clearly as I could through my numb lips, 'Thank you. I am Arthur Mumby. How do you do?'

The brown boy put a finger to his mouth, hushing me.

Then other figures came barging from behind him, snatching me and heaving me upright, and I might have tried to run had I been able, for these newcomers were not human at all. Fingers and tentacles rummaged in my pockets, and something like a man-sized blue lizard held a flask against my lips. Scalding liquid trickled down my throat, and I choked and panicked and spewed and fell back gasping.

'Quiet,' said the boy with the elephant gun.

'It tastes foul!' I spluttered.

'It's rum,' he replied.

'Yes, it is rather.'

'Jamaican rum. It will counteract the moth's venom.'

Sure enough, I quickly found that I could move again, although my arms and legs felt stiff and strange, and I had awful pins and needles. I started to whisper my thanks, and then had a terrible thought. 'Myrtle!' I gasped.

'What?' asked the boy, and his inhuman friends all looked at one another and shrugged and sighed and murmured.

'My sister!' I went on eagerly. 'I think that creature caught her too!'

The boy looked grim, and I could well see why. Where

we were standing, half a hundred jars lay heaped about in the shade of a rocky ridge, and although some had shattered most had no more than a small hole where infant moths must have hatched out, and looked quite intact. One of them, I knew, must still be whole, and contain poor Myrtle. But which?

I'm afraid I started to blub. It seemed so unfair to have one's father eaten by a spider and one's sister devoured by a caterpillar on the same day (though I suppose flies must put up with that sort of thing all the time and you do not hear them moaning about it). I thought how sad it was to be all alone, and felt terribly sorry that the last time I had spoken to Myrtle was to tell her off for being impolite to fungi.

'Stop piping your eye,' the boy said softly. 'That moth might still be about.' But instead of keeping quiet himself he turned to the strangest of his companions – two things that looked like walking sea anemones, with not so much as an arm or a head or a face between them, only spreading crowns of writhesome, delicate tentacles. 'There's another Earth child trapped somewhere here, boys,' he said. 'Can you sniff out her thoughts?'

The reefs of jars shifted and chinked as the weird pair set about their work, scrambling around on their soft, pad-like

feet, touching and
feeling the jars
with the tips of
their tentacles. At
last they settled on
one that seemed
more interesting
than the others, and
began to trill and coo,
their tentacles flickering
with light. The boy and his

goblin companions pulled out hatchets and set to work,
quickly staving in the side of the jar.

Inside lay Myrtle, quite whole and unharmed, still
clutching the handles of her carpet-bag. Although she had
been taken first she must have been sealed in her jar after
me, for she was still unconscious, and all that lay at her feet
was a quivering, soft-shelled egg. Our rescuer squashed it
with his boot, and his friends carried Myrtle to a flat, sandy
space between the mounds of jars and tipped their foul-
tasting liquor into her. She woke up coughing and
protesting, then started to scream when she saw the ring of
weird, inhuman faces leering down at her. 'Art! Who are

these dreadful people?'

'I'm Jack,' said the boy rather coldly, as if he didn't much like having his friends called dreadful. 'These are my crew; good shipmates, all. And you'd be wise to keep your voice down, missy, for that moth may still be about.'

'What moth?' asked Myrtle, quite mystified.

'The Potter Moth,' said Jack. 'It haunts these parts. Makes its nest on those spires of rock and swoops down on passing travellers to make a breakfast of for its larvae. A maggot would be mumbling on your bones by now, if me and my men hadn't fetched you out.'

'They are hardly men,' Myrtle pointed out pedantically.

The boy called Jack ignored her. 'The moth takes snails and mushroom-folk mostly, but it don't mind rich little Earth boys and girls when it can get 'em. Bright things draw it. I expect it saw the flashing of that pretty necklace of yours from its eyrie.'

'So that's what the mushroom-gentleman was trying to tell us!' I cried.

'Course it was,' said Jack. 'And it's a pity you didn't listen to him. Luckily, he knew our ship was moored near here, and he came and told us that two ignorant Earth children were wandering into the moth's hunting-runs. Now, hide your trinket away, so that we can start back in peace.' And he reached out and tried to stuff Myrtle's locket down inside the collar of her dress.

'How dare you touch me!' Myrtle squealed, flapping him away. The chain that held the locket broke, and it fell slowly to the ground. Myrtle stumbled backwards and sat down heavily, raising a small cloud of dust and shell fragments that might have buried the locket for ever, if yours truly had not had the presence of mind to scoop it up and pocket it. (Myrtle's brown serge dress had no pockets whatever, so I felt it my place to look after the locket until we could have the chain repaired.)

'I am a subject of Her Britannic Majesty,' announced Myrtle, who had grown very red. 'And that locket was given me by my dear, departed mama! Oh, this is intolerable! I insist that you take me and my little brother to the Governor at once!'

This outburst did not have quite the reaction Myrtle must have hoped for. Our new friends all chuckled and nudged each other, very amused I suppose by how easily we had let ourselves be turned into caterpillar food. 'They're pretty green,' I heard one of them say, but he was grey, with four arms, so who was he to talk?

Jack scowled at her, as if he wasn't used to people taking such a tone with him, nor sure quite how he should react. 'Where are you from, anyway?' he said at last. 'What brings you to the Moon?'

'Please, sir,' I said, being keen to make a good impression on our saviours before my sister could say something else to anger them, 'we are from Larklight, sir. It is a house; a sort of floating house, up there. It was attacked by monstrous spiders, and our poor father eaten up.'

This stopped the laughter of the goblin crew, at least. Jack looked at me. 'Then you are orphans?' he asked.

I nodded.

That seemed to change his opinion of us. He looked at us with a sort of grudging pity. 'Come on,' he said. 'Our ship's a few miles back. We'd best take you aboard her.'

'What ship?' asked Myrtle angrily, as he went stalking off between the heaps of jars, his gun across his shoulder. 'He is only a boy, Art. How can he have a ship?'

One of the boy's followers reached down to help her up, but Myrtle recoiled, because the creature was a type of gigantic land-crab and instead of a hand he was proffering her a hand-sized, blue-black pincer. He peeked at her from inside his shell and said earnestly, 'You'll be all right, missy. No harm comes to them as sails the aether sea with Captain Jack Havock.'

'Oh, get away from me, you horrid insect!' my sister wailed.

The blue lizard thing came close to her from the other side, and she sprang up to escape it and found herself going after the boy almost by accident, with the crabbish fellow and all the rest of the crew clustering around her, glancing at the sky behind us from time to time and keeping their cutlasses and blunderbusses ready. I ran along behind, calling out as loudly as I dared, 'He's not Jack Havock! He simply cannot be!'

CHAPTER SIX

WE BOARD THE AETHER-SHIP *SOPHRONIA*, WHERE I MAKE A
REMARKABLE DISCOVERY CONCERNING THE CHEMICAL
WEDDING.

The real Jack Havock was no boy of fifteen; of that
I felt perfectly certain. Nobody knew very much
about who he was, or where he had sprung from,
but on one thing everyone was clear; he was no mere boy.
How could he be? He was the Terror of the Aetheric Main,
a daring pirate chief who had been raiding ships of the

Royal Interplanetary Company for the past three years, and slipping away afterwards with the holds of his brig stuffed full of booty. When Dr Ptarmigan's expedition to Saturn was lost without trace, it was Jack Havock they blamed. The pictures I'd seen all showed him as a brawny buccaneer with lighted tapers blazing in his beard and a cutlass gripped between his teeth, boarding helpless merchant ships with a pistol in either hand and his gang of monstrous Callistans and armoured Ionians yowling behind him. I wondered how this slight, brown boy with his ragtag following of lizards and crustacea dared steal Jack Havock's name. What if the real Jack Havock found out, and came to claim it back?

I caught up with Myrtle and took her hand. She looked at me with wide, shocked eyes. 'We must escape from these villains, Art!' she whispered.

'Just because they look a little odd,' I said, 'it does not make them villains. They saved us from the Potter Moth, after all. They may help us to reach the authorities.'

'Perhaps you're right,' sighed Myrtle. She called out, 'Boy! When we reach your ship, I shall insist that you take us straight to the Governor's residence in Port George. We must inform his Excellency about the spiders which invaded our home, so that he can arrange for a gunboat and a few squads of redcoats to go and deal with them.'

Jack looked back at her, but he did not stop walking. 'I'm not planning to go nowhere near Port George, missy.'

'Oh, but sir,' I said, running to catch him up, 'it may be most terribly important! These spiders were like nothing I have ever heard of before! Even our father was surprised by them, and he has been studying the strange creatures of the Heavens for ever so many years! I believe they must have come from beyond the borders of known space; from Saturn or even Uranus —'

'Art!' warned Myrtle, interrupting me. 'Polite people refer to that lonely planet by its original name, Georgium Sidus. It provides less opportunity for cheap jokes.'

'Myrtle,' I cried, 'how can you worry about such trifles at a time like this? Father has been ate! The whole Empire may be under threat from these spider things!'

'All the more reason to keep up our guard against coarseness and crudity,' said Myrtle.

'Well, I'm sorry about your father,' said Jack, still walking, 'but I don't give a d—n about your Empire.'

'Oh!' squeaked Myrtle, and I could not tell if it were the boy's lack of patriotism which shocked her most or his shameless use of the d-word.

'You think it makes any odds to me and my crew?' he went on. 'Don't matter to us whether we live under the rule of Queen Victoria or a bunch of creepy-crawlies who have crept out of Ur—... Out of Georgium Sidus. We'll still be outcasts, won't we, boys? Still have to live by our wits, and hide out in the black where the writ of no law runs ...'

His followers nodded and muttered their agreement. In desperation, Myrtle tried to appeal to our new friend's mercenary instincts.

'Please take us to the Governor's residence! I shall recommend that he offers you a small reward for your assistance ...'

Jack stopped walking when she said that. He turned, raised his gun, and pointed it at Myrtle's head.

'Oh, very well, you blackguard!' she squealed, ducking. 'A *large* reward!'

The gun went off, and the echoes rumbled like rolling thunder among the silent lunar mountains. It had not really been pointing at Myrtle, of course, but at the great moth which had been gliding down on silent wings out of the sky behind her. Bits of the monster – its legs and feelers and the silvery dust from its wings – rained down about us as the gun smoke cleared.

'Told you to keep your voice down, missy,' called Jack. The recoil of his gun had carried him fifty feet away, and he stood waiting for us there beneath a spinney of mushroom-trees.

'Good shooting, Cap'n!' his goblins chorused, dancing little jigs of victory on the moth's remains, and getting slime all up their trousers. 'There's one moth as won't be snatching up poor little mushroom-people ever more! Fine shooting, Captain Jack!'

I started to wonder, as we set

off again, whether he might be the real Jack Havock after all. His crew certainly looked wild and rough enough. As we walked on, I took the opportunity to study them, and listen to their talk, and started to learn their names. There was a stocky Ionian with a chest like a barrel and four thick-fingered arms, whom the others addressed respectfully as 'Mr Munkulus', and whom I took to be the first mate. There were those two walking sea anenomes, almost identical, with crowns of gently waving arms where their heads should have been, who did not talk, but cooed and trilled like birds; they were Squidley and Yarg, the Tentacle Twins. Then there was a hobgoblin named Grindle, whose speech seemed to consist entirely of dreadful sounding curses. I saw my sister blush each time he opened his mouth, and the big crab-like thing, whose name was Nipper, kept turning round to him and saying, 'Language, Mr Grindle! Don't forget there are ladies present!'

I couldn't understand what he meant by 'ladies' at first, until I looked again at the blue, spiny-headed lizard thing. There was something rather graceful and girlish about the way it moved, and I began to suspect that it was a female – though of what species I could not imagine, for there were no blue, talking lizards in any encyclopaedia *I'd* ever read.

After we had gone a mile or so the lizard confirmed my suspicions by delicately extending a blue hand to my sister and saying, 'I'm Ssilissa, misss; it'll be nice to have another girl aboard.'

Myrtle started back, looking deeply shocked. I'm not sure what upset her more – Ssilissa's sharp teeth and flickering, pointed, jet black tongue, or the fact that she was wearing trousers.

In this strange company we walked another mile, and found ourselves passing through the fringes of a lunar forest of widely-spaced mushroom-trees, some of which towered to several hundred feet in the Moon's low gravity. We turned along a narrow, rocky defile, overhung by the spreading mushroom-tops, and there ahead of us sat an aether-ship, perched on the floor of a canyon, and quite invisible until we were almost upon her. She was only about a quarter of the size of the freighter which delivered our groceries at Larklight, and the metal bands which sheathed her timber hull were streaked with rust and speckled with space barnacles and clumps of hanging weed. She looked at least a hundred years old, and at her rear, above the bulbous exhaust-trumpets of her wedding chamber, the mullioned windows of a fine old stern gallery glinted with the light of distant Earth. There was gilded carving underneath the windows; birds and angels and a peeling, painted scroll that bore her name:

'What a filthy old ship!' exclaimed Myrtle as soon as she saw it. 'Surely you don't expect us to go aboard it? It cannot be safe!'

'She'll fly,' said Jack, turning to glower at her, and his friends glowered too, for no aethernaut likes to hear his ship disparaged, however humble she may be. Jack took a heavy key from his pocket and fitted it into the lock on the ship's big, arched hatchway. 'I'm sorry she don't meet your high standards,

Miss Mumby. Maybe you'd prefer to walk after all?'

'I did not say that,' replied Myrtle, looking prim, and then primmer still as Jack heaved the hatch open and the fuggy, musty, shipboard smell of the *Sophronia*'s innards spilled over us.

'We'll drop you near Mount Ghastly,' said Jack, turning to us again as his people started going past him through the hatch. 'You can walk to Port George easily enough from there.'

'Oh,' cried Myrtle, 'not more walking! We are so very tired of walking, and having hair's-breadth escapes from certain death. Could you not see your way to putting us down in Port George itself, preferably at some spot nice and handy for the Governor's residence?'

The others, those that heard her, all burst out laughing, but Jack just scowled. Nipper patted my sister on the shoulder with a friendly claw. 'Bless you, miss,' he said, 'Captain Jack can't go nowhere near Port George! Especially not the Governor's place, where all them guns and redcoats are! Don't you know that he's a pirate, and would be hung in chains along with the rest of us if ever he were caught?'

'A pirate?' said Myrtle in a small, whispery voice. She

looked up at the old ship's flagstaff, high above, and saw the banner that flew there; night black, with a three-eyed skull and two crossed bones done in white upon it, billowing proudly in the lunar breeze.

That was enough for her. It had been a long day, filled with spiders, moths and mushrooms, and to meet with real live pirates here at the end of it was the last straw. She gave a little moan and fainted, falling backwards into the claws of Nipper, who lifted her carefully and carried her through the open hatchway into the belly of the *Sophronia*.

The inside of the pirates' ship was a musty wooden cavern, stuffed with coiled ropes, barrels, hammocks, chests, ducts, lanterns, ladders, shadows, crates, coops, racks of tools, tethered cannon, heaps of shot, stands of swords and swabs and ramrods and a strong smell of tar and unwashed, inhuman bodies. Some underclothes had been pegged up to dry on a line, and I noticed that many of the pants had flaps in unlikely places, and several of the vests had many arms. I felt quite relieved that Myrtle was unconscious, for I did not think her delicate nerves could have withstood such an unseemly sight.

Nipper laid her down on a heap of tarpaulins in a quiet corner between two of the wooden braces which strengthened the old ship's sides, and all the other crewmen gathered round to stare at her. Seeing her laid there amid that crowd of weird forms made me think of a picture out of *Grimm's Fairy Tales*, of Snow White surrounded by her dwarves. But although they all seemed touchingly concerned for her, Jack would have none of it. 'Don't stand there gawping like you've never seen an Earthlet before,' he shouted. 'If anyone saw that lifeboat fall there will be government ships on their way here soon. And for all we know that gunboat that chased us from Mars may still be on the prowl. We don't want 'em to catch us on the ground, do we?'

The crew all scattered quickly into different quarters of the vessel and began hauling on ropes, fitting poles into capstans, and generally carrying on like experienced old space dogs, all the while bellowing out a lusty shanty called, 'Farewell and Adieu to You Ladies of Ph'Arhpuu'xxtpllsprngg'. I crouched beside Myrtle, and saw that, though pale beneath her coating of moon dust, she was sleeping peacefully. It seemed unfair to wake her, because I knew that she would simply hate the din and dirt around us, so I looked about, wondering where I should go, and noticed the blue, reptilian person called Ssilissa slipping through a small brass door at the back of the big cabin. I had a notion what might be in there, and I ran after her, catching the edge of the door as it swung shut and squeezing through without Ssilissa noticing me.

Just as I had hoped, the door led into the wedding chamber – the alchemical engine room at *Sophronia*'s stern. Pipes, tubes and ducts snaked all around me, tangling over the walls and roof in a way which reminded me dimly of Larklight's boiler room. In the heart of it all squatted the great alembic: the vessel in which the secret substances which power our aether-ships are brought together and conjoin in the chemical wedding.

Now one of the things which I remembered from those reports of Jack Havock's doings in the news-sheets was that a certain mystery surrounded his ship. The Royal College of Alchemists claimed that none of its members would stoop to perform the chemical wedding for a pirate, and yet the *Sophronia* sped about the aether quite happily in the furtherance of Jack's crimes, moving at speeds which could not be achieved without both an alchemical engine and an alchemist to operate it.

I felt giddy with excitement as I lurked behind the knots of pipework, waiting to see the rogue alchemist whom Jack Havock must employ.

But to my surprise, blue Ssilissa was the only other being in the chamber. I watched with growing amazement as she pulled on a heavy leather apron and gauntlets, and lowered smoked glass goggles over her eyes. Then she stooped over

the alembic, and opened the thick access doorway in its top – but what she did there I could not see, for a blinding light filled the wedding chamber and a strange sort of music began. Dark, wavering notes wove together in unearthly harmonies. The deck began to throb and shiver, and the pipes I hid behind started to grow warm. Frightened, I edged backwards, opened the door and slithered back out into the main part of the ship – only to feel a strong hand close on my shoulder.

Jack Havock hauled me to my feet. His dark face had turned a few shades darker, and he said, 'Spying, eh?'

'No, sir!' I protested. 'Please, sir! I was only looking! I have never seen the chemical wedding before . . .'

'Nor have I,' said Jack, relenting a little and letting me go. 'Aboard this ship the wedding chamber is Ssilissa's domain, and the rest of us leave her alone there to do her work. You'd best do likewise.'

'But she's –' I said, 'I mean, she's not –'

'You thought only human beings could perform the chemical wedding, did you?' Jack asked. 'Only British gentlemen, indeed. That is what the Royal College of Alchemists would like us all to think. But it ain't true, as you've just seen. Ssilissa's got a talent for it. Speeding through the aether is as simple as walking to Ssil. Thanks to her we've flown rings around Her Majesty's Navy.'

'But how did she learn the secrets of the craft?' I asked. I knew that real alchemists have great racks of books and tables of logarithms to tell them what quantities of the elements to mix, and to help them steer clear of asteroid reefs and avoid crashing into passing planets, but I had seen no such books in the *Sophronia*'s wedding chamber.

Jack looked sly. 'I've said too much already,' he snapped. 'She *does* know it, that's all that matters. And she guards it as fierce as the College themselves. If I catch you snooping again I'll give you to her, and let you see *how* fierce. She'll cast you into the great alembic and let the dreadful elements bake you to a cinder!'

He pushed me away and strode off along the thrumming, humming deck, shouting, 'Weigh anchor, boys! Mr Munkulus, lay us a course for Mount Ghastly that won't take us within sight of human eyes.' The Ionian touched a knuckle to his knobbly brow by way of salute and went swarming up a ladderway to a high platform where the wheel was mounted. The others heaved the capstan round, and as they heaved, the anchor chains rattled in the cable tiers and the *Sophronia* shuddered and lurched, leaping high into the sky. I felt as though I'd left my stomach behind me on the ground.

I dashed to the nearest porthole, wondering whether I should awaken Myrtle. But she would only have started to drizzle on about the clutter and the peril we were in, and when I saw what lay outside the glass I suddenly did not want to have my first flight filled with her complaints.

It was sublime! The *Sophronia* had unfurled her space wings and was flying very low, so that the Moon's gravity still kept me on the deck. For a moment I could see our deep black shadow racing beside us along the white walls of the mountains, and then the mountains fell astern and we were soaring over flat, broken-up country where mushroom-trees grew in great profusion and herds of wild snails grazed peaceably on lawns of moon moss, their silvery trails stretching away across the plains like shining roads. A river wound down out of the highlands, growing wider and shallower as it snaked out of the twilight country and into the bright light of the Sun, opening at last into a shimmering lunar sea. I watched the slow waves for a while – the water was so shallow that you could see the sea floor quite clearly – and then, wanting to see more, I scurried to the front of the ship, where the kindly Nipper lifted me up so that I could look out of a higher porthole.

'Where are we?' I asked of him. 'What sea is this?'

'T'ain't got no name,' said Nipper, his huffly voice emerging from a slit in his shell, along with a faint smell of fish. Two round, honest eyes blinked at me from inside the slit; two more, on stalks, curved down to study me from above. I wondered what strange world he had come from. Some sea-moon of Jupiter, I guessed, where the natives took all sorts of peculiar forms.

'No earthly name, leastways,' he went on. 'The fungus-folk call it something, no doubt, but nobody knows what. Not many of your kind have ever come to this part of the Moon. Unmapped, it is, and set to stay that way, for there's far worse and stranger things than the old Potter Moth living up in those dusky hills behind us, ready to snatch any explorer who goes snuffling there.'

Ahead of us, above the brightness of the sea, another range of hills appeared, and seemed to rise higher and higher as I watched; tall snowy summits poking up over the curve of the Moon. I recognised their jagged profiles from *A Boy's Atlas of the Solar System*: Mount Ghastly and her neighbours Mount Horrible, Mount Vile and Mount Absolutely Beastly. Captain Frobisher must have been in a sour mood on the day he named them, for as far as I could see they looked no worse than any of the other mountains we had seen here on the Moon.

'The prison colony lies on the far side of that big one,'

said Nipper. 'We'll soon be there.'

'And are you quite sure it's safe for you to fly so close to Port George?' I asked, for I would not have liked our rescuers to risk capture and execution on our account.

'Bless you, young Earth child,' huffled Nipper. 'Captain Jack wouldn't have offered if he didn't think he could fly you in safe. Don't you worry – as soon as we've set you and the young Miss Mumby ashore Ssil will see to it we leave orbit so fast there ain't a revenue cutter on the whole Moon that can catch us. We're as safe as the Bank of Mars.'

At which moment there came a loud 'bang', the entire ship quivered, and I saw a hole the size of Nipper's head appear in the planking above us, and then another, still larger, in the opposite wall, as the cannon ball that had made the first hurtled across the cabin and smashed out through the far side.

CHAPTER SEVEN

HURRAH! A SAILOR'S LIFE FOR ME

ENLIST IN THE ROYAL NAVY

IN WHICH WE ENCOUNTER THE GENTLEMEN OF
HER MAJESTY'S ROYAL NAVY.

Moon wind burst in upon us, flinging ropes and
papers about, tearing at my hair and clothes as
Nipper hastily set me down.

'What was that?' I shouted, but the great crab was
scuttling away. *All* the pirates were scuttling and scurrying,
and once more it was only I who knew not what was
happening, nor what I was supposed to do.

I crept up some iron rungs which had been set in the wall close by, and gingerly poked my head around the ragged, splintered edge of the hole. The wind threw moon dust in my eyes, but my goggles were still around my neck, and when I pulled them up the first thing I saw was another vessel flying alongside. There was gold scrollwork at her bows; a white chequerboard of gunports stretching along

her flank. From a mast upon her upper hull, the Union Jack flew out proud and bright in the lunar sunshine. I could even see sailors running about upon her top deck, manning a gun which went off as I watched with a white smudge of smoke and sent a second cannon ball whirring past *Sophronia*'s bows.

'Huzzah!' I cried, filled with patriotic fervour at the sight of our brave tars. Then I added, 'Oh no!' for I realised that rescue for me and Myrtle would mean certain death for Jack Havock and his crew.

'Stand aside there!' growled Mr Grindle, elbowing me out of the way so that he and the Tentacle Twins could patch the shot-hole with a sheet of oiled tarpaulin. 'And keep your head down,' he added, glancing back at me as he set to work with hammer and tacks. 'There's going to be a fierce old fight!'

I looked behind me. Nipper and the others were hastily loading the *Sophronia*'s fat cannons with anything they could find – stones, coins, cutlery, old fish-paste sandwiches – and preparing to roll them up to the gunports. Up on the steering platform, Munkulus spun the wheel while Captain Jack stared intently into a brass periscope. He looked grim, and after a moment he stepped back and picked up his speaking-trumpet. 'It's no use, lads!' he shouted. 'We can't outrun her. Heave to!'

'Heave to!' bellowed Mr Munkulus, relaying the order to Ssillissa in her wedding chamber. The *Sophronia* slowed, the song of her engines ending with a dying fall. She settled gently into the lunar sea, and above the creaking of her timbers and the lap of water I heard the wing-beats of the other

ship as it swung over our heads. Jack's crew were groaning, cursing and shaking their fists. Squidley and Yarg cooed softly, waving their tentacles in complicated gestures of mourning and despair. Grindle was weeping.

'Rotten bluecoats!' said Nipper bitterly. 'They've followed us all the way from Martian space, and why? Because we took a few trinkets from a couple of Earthbound merchantmen, that's all!'

I ran to check on Myrtle, but she had slept all through

the short chase, and she was sleeping still. As I rose from her side Captain Jack came hurrying down the stairs from his steering platform and passed close by me.

'What are we going to do, Jack?' called Grindle, embroidering his question with several foul curses which I shall not repeat.

'Surrender, of course,' said the young captain, very grim. 'They'll hang me for certain, but maybe if we give up quietly you'll be spared.'

His crew-beings all protested; they'd rather die fighting, they said, than see their captain taken. I felt much the same sentiment myself, even though I had known him but an hour or two, and knew that he was a most terrible pirate. He had saved me and Myrtle from the Potter Moth, after all, and I hated to think of him being dragged in irons to Execution Dock. I cried out, 'Is there anything I can do to help?'

'You?' He glanced at me, incredulous. 'Of course there ain't!' he scoffed. But then his eye fell upon my insensible sister. Myrtle is always at her best when she is unconscious. Her spectacles had fallen off, and she looked almost pretty, lying there all pale and swoonsome. Jack Havock frowned thoughtfully, tugging at the brim of his wideawake hat. 'Or maybe there is,' he said softly.

He issued some orders, too quick and full of spacefaring jargon for me to understand. The next thing I knew, Mr Munkulus had grabbed a hold of me, and Nipper had picked up my sister again, and Jack Havock was leading us back up the twisty ladder to the steering platform, and on again up another, through a circular doorway in the ceiling and out on to the *Sophronia*'s star deck, which is the top part of the ship, open to the sky.

The warship sailed past, wafting us with slow beats of its big, black, bat-like wings. Upon her star deck a group of uniformed officers had gathered, and a round, red-faced young man lifted up a brass speaking-trumpet and bellowed at us across the gap which separated the two ships.

'*Sophronia!*' he cried. 'I am Captain Moonfield of Her Majesty's Spaceship *Indefatigable*. I have orders from the British Admiralty to apprehend the notorious pirate Jack Havock. I advise you to hand him over, or I shall open fire.'

Jack stepped up to the rusty handrail which ran around the *Sophronia*'s star deck. He didn't need a speaking-trumpet. 'I'm Jack Havock!' he bellowed, and you could hear the echoes dancing off for miles across the sluggish sea.

'Stuff and nonsense!' exclaimed Captain Moonfield. 'You're just a boy! Let the real Captain Havock come out at once and talk to us!'

'I'm Havock, all right,' Jack hollered back. 'And these Earth children here are my hostages! What do you think of that?'

I saw telescopes glinting as they swung to point at me and Myrtle. Nipper shook my sister a little, to make it appear that she was struggling; Mr Munkulus used one of his spare hands to give the back of my leg a pinch so that I writhed about.

'We're leaving now,' Jack vowed. 'You try to stop us and this sweet young lady and her brother will both die. Fire on us, and I'll blow the *Sophronia* to kingdom come, and them along with her.'

This caused great consternation aboard *Indefatigable*. All sorts of telescopes and perspective-glasses were trained upon us, and I could see Captain Moonfield talking angrily to his officers, doubtless asking who these hostages were and why he had not been warned of this new complication. I wondered whether he was a kindly sort of captain who would have pity on us, or the sort who would put his orders and the good of the Empire first, and it made me writhe and wriggle even more to think that he might be the latter, and that I might die at any moment in a storm of shot and ray from the *Indefatigable*'s batteries of Armstrong Guns and Rokeby-Pinkerton Phlogiston Agitators.

But Jack, who must have anticipated the confusion his words would cause aboard the other ship, stamped once upon the *Sophronia*'s hull, and somewhere below us Ssilissa heard his signal and coaxed her idling engines to full power. The *Sophronia* shot forwards, the *Indefatigable* and the pale seas of the Moon dropped away beneath us at a dizzying rate, and behind us the thin air filled with the light and noise of the chemical wedding. As Jack opened the hatch and

threw me through it I had a glimpse of the blue eye that was distant Earth whirling across the sky ahead.

I missed the stairs entirely and fell, but it did not matter, for we were free of the Moon's weedy gravity by then and everything not strapped down was floating about in mid-air. I tumbled harmlessly through an airborne Sargasso of clutter, while Jack, Nipper and Munkulus came floating down behind me. Myrtle's legs kicked weakly amid a cloud of petticoats as she drifted free of the great crab's careful claws. She turned upside down, and her skirts fell over her face, which woke her. Struggling her petticoats back into place and holding them down, she glared at us all as though she were the victim of some impudent prank. But even Myrtle could not ignore for long the alarming creaks and complaints that issued from the old ship's timbers, nor the pallid, golden light that streamed in through every porthole, like evening sunlight shining through a mist.

'Where are we?' she gasped.

'On Sir Isaac's Golden Roads,' said Jack, floating past her with a triumphant look. 'Ssilissa has worked her magic in the great alembic, and pushed us almost to the speed of light. No mortal eye can track us now, nor any ship follow us.'

I swam through the littered air to take my sister by the hand. 'It's all right, Myrtle,' I promised. 'There was a small misunderstanding with some gentlemen of the Royal Navy, but all is well now; we are safe, and en route to Mount Ghastly again.'

'I'm afraid you ain't,' said Jack, turning suddenly sombre. 'I can't risk another set-to with that frigate. The fact is, we're wanted men. Why, just last week we boarded and robbed two fat vessels coming home from Mars, all full of rich nabobs and their ladies travelling back to Earth for this famous Exhibition affair. I had thought if we laid low among the mountains of the Moon a while the hue and cry would die away, but it seems the bluecoats are still a-hunting us. We shall have to hide ourselves further afield, at a place I know, far out of harm's way in the darksome deeps of space.'

'But what about us?' wailed Myrtle, starting to sniffle.

Jack Havock gave the gravity-free equivalent of a shrug. 'We'll touch at a port again in a week or so,' he said. 'Till then, you'd better make the most of our spacefaring life, miss. You and your brother are going to be pirates for a while.'

CHAPTER EIGHT

IN WHICH MYRTLE AND I ENJOY BREAKFAST WITH OUR
NEW SHIPMATES.

When I woke next morning, in a swaying hammock strung up between the beams of one of the *Sophronia*'s little narrow side-cabins, it took me a few moments to recall where I was, and what had happened to me. Then, like a douche of cold water, all my terrible memories of the day before came crashing down on me: the white spiders, Father's capture, the Potter

Moth and the battle with the *Indefatigable*.

I pulled aside the thick felt curtain which hung across the porthole near my hammock, and golden light filled up my little cabin. I had seen it often from a distance, that glow of alchemy which surrounds our aether-ships as they speed across the Heavens.* To be wrapped up inside that mystic, protecting veil of light myself was wonderful, and suddenly, despite all the dreadful things that had befallen me, I could not quite suppress a feeling of excitement.

I rolled out of my hammock, drifted to the cubby hole where I had stowed my clothes, and dressed. Enticing smells were seeping between the planks of my cabin door, and when I ventured out into the main part of the ship I saw the crew gathered around a table, tucking into a

*The Royal College of Alchemists call this light the 'Benign Effulgence'. Somehow, as the chemical wedding reaches full pitch, it causes the aether around the ship to slip slightly out of harmony with the rest of Creation, forming a bubble or cradle of Alchemical Space, in which she may travel along at tremendous speeds without being torn asunder, or having her crew smeared across the back wall like dollops of raspberry jam. The luminous bow-wave of alchemically-altered particles which surrounds our ships have led our aethernauts to talk of 'riding upon Sir Isaac (Newton)'s Golden Roads' when they speak of travelling at speed between the worlds.

breakfast of fried Red Whizzer and potato cakes.

I hung back at first, afraid to join them, for they looked more fearsome and outlandish than I'd recalled, but then Ssilissa saw me and bobbed her long, delicate head in my direction, and Nipper turned and drew me down to the table with a friendly claw.

'Where are we?' I enquired, as I watched Grindle (who was ship's cook) fill a pewter dish with food for me and clap a lid quickly over it to stop anything floating away.

'Running fair and true down the Golden Roads,' replied Nipper.

'Out in the darklymost deeps of space we be, far south of Earth,' chuckled Grindle.

'Don't tell him all our business,' said Jack Havock, who lounged in mid-air at the far end of the table, picking his teeth and looking thoughtful.

'But he's one of us, now, Jack!' Nipper protested.

'Is he?' Jack flung his toothpick aside and it floated up into the drift of clutter which hung bobbing beneath the ribbed roof. 'I don't think so. Does he know what it's like to be an object of curiosity, and a fugitive from the law? He's only a kid, so we must feed him and keep him safe, but don't get to thinking he's one of us. He'd sell us out in an instant, if ever he could.'

'Oh, but I wouldn't, I swear . . .' I declared, and I was about to pledge my allegiance to the *Sophronia* and its crew, but Myrtle spoiled things, as usual. She emerged from her own cabin with her hair all tangled and straggling up on end in the no-gravity.

'Why is there no water for me to wash in?' she demanded angrily. 'And, Art, I forbid you to eat anything that creature cooks; his hands are quite black with grime. Indeed, this entire vessel is in a most disagreeable state of filth.'

I blushed with shame; some of the crew-beings laughed, others looked shocked. Jack Havock simply glared at my sister. Then he reached out and snatched one of the pewter globes which served the crew as drinking cups. He unscrewed the two halves, and flicked out a wobbling sphere of water. 'You want water, miss? Here, have some.'

I suspect that Jack and his friends must sometimes have indulged in water fights to while away the boredom of the spacial deeps, for his aim was perfect. Like a great, uncertain balloon the water globe went rolling through the air, and struck my sister full in her angry face, where it burst into a million smaller globes which swam off in every direction. 'Oh!' cried Myrtle, and some other things too, but her words were all drowned out by the coarse, delighted laughter of the crew.

Jack Havock didn't laugh. 'I'm sorry you find our home so dirty,' he said coldly. 'Fact is, we are kept too busy running from your navy to ever take much trouble cleaning her. We don't carry passengers as a rule, neither. Them as ship out aboard *Sophronia* have to work their passage. I didn't think you and your brother looked much good for working, miss, but now you have set a notion in my head. While you sail with us, you'll be our cleaners. You'll scrub and polish and tidy up after us, and see if you cannot get our vessel into a state that *does* please you.'

He pushed himself away from the table and went soaring up towards a high platform. Grindle and Munkulus tumbled about in mid-air, bellowing with laughter, while my poor sister stood wet and furious in the open doorway of her cabin. Tears squeezed out of her eyes and bobbed up to join the spreading halo of water that hung above her.

I wondered if I should go to her aid, for I did feel a little sorry for her, but I was angry too. I had felt that the pirates were beginning to accept me, and now, thanks to her outburst, I was to be nothing but a skivvy aboard their ship. So I turned my attention to my breakfast (it is no easy matter eating Red Whizzer and potato cakes in zero BSG, but years of experience at Larklight had made me pretty good at it) and in the end it was Ssilissa who went quietly over to take Myrtle's hand and lead her to the table. 'There, missss,' said the blue girl, quite kindly, pushing breakfast and a globe of tea towards her. 'We have not always time to wasssh aboard *Ssophronia*, but eat, and I shall find you ssoap and water when you're done.'

Myrtle scowled at the dish before her and said, 'I cannot accept food that has been stolen from poor, murdered people.'

'What people?' asked Nipper innocently, and Grindle cried out, 'A murder? Where?'

Myrtle tilted her chin haughtily at them all. 'Can you deny that your vittles were all stolen from those ships your captain boasts of having boarded and robbed so recently?'

'I caught them fish myself,' cried Grindle angrily, 'up on the star deck with my rod and line.'

'The potatoes were stolen though,' admitted Nipper, looking sheepish.*

'But we have not murdered anyone!' said Ssilissa, her frill of head-fronds bristling with shock at the very suggestion. 'We may be piratess, misss, but we are not murderersss! Why, we only ever aim our cannon at their wingss and exhaust-trumpetss, and when we board them we carry unloaded gunsss.'

'We flourish our swords about a great deal, to be sure,' Nipper admitted.

'And ssometimessss we have to thump some eager aethernaut on the head to stop him harming ussss . . .'

'But we would none of us wish to *kill* anyone.'

'But all the stories in the public press . . .' Myrtle began.

How the pirates laughed at that! 'They are just sstories, misss,' said Ssilissa. 'The newsspapermen exaggerate, and perhaps the crews of the shipsss we rob exaggerate too . . .'

---

*Well, he still looked crabbish really, but I am sure you take my meaning.

'Wouldn't look good for 'em to go home to their owners and say they'd been boarded and stripped bare by a young 'un and a bunch of harmless creatures like ourselves,' chuckled Grindle, and tears of mirth popped from his eyes and orbited his head like a cloud of sequins.

'I've seen it said Jack's ten foot tall, with a great black bushy beard!' giggled Nipper.

'Then what about the Saturn Expedition?' cried my sister. 'The aether-ship *Aeneas* lost along with a hundred men, and *everyone* knows it was Jack Havock and his crew who were to blame!'

'Everyone knowss wrong then, misss,' Ssilissa said.

'Uncharted aether lies between Jupiter and Saturn,' said Nipper, lowering his eye-stalks in respect for the lost expedition. 'Anything could have befallen the *Aeneas* out there, and it was nobody's fault but Dr Ptarmigan's, for being so rash as to go there.'

'Why would we want to attack a scientifical expedition, anyhow?' demanded Grindle.

'They don't carry nothing but instruments, and brainy coves in wigs and frock-coats. Those Company ships from Mars though; they was stuffed with gold and silver . . .'

'Crystal!' said Nipper happily.

'Lovely sssilk gowns,' sighed Ssilissa.

'And all we had to do to get them was fire a few shots across their bows and run aboard whooping and hulooing and waving our empty guns,' said Grindle. 'It was Jack Havock's reputation that did the rest. Those rich Earthlets were falling over themselves to surrender to us and give us their worldy goods. Why, if Jack had let us take all they offered they wouldn't have had air or food enough left to get themselves to London.'

'We ain't murderers though, miss,' said Nipper, seeing my sister flinch as Grindle cackled toothily at his memories of past robberies. 'We're most of us just poor orphans, who were imprisoned till Jack freed us and found a way for us to make a living out here.'

Myrtle looked suspiciously at him. She had not spoken directly to Nipper yet, for I fear she thought it was beneath her dignity to talk to a crustacean, but his words intrigued her enough that she asked, 'Pray, what were you imprisoned for, Mr Nipper?

It was Ssilissa who answered her.
'For being different, misss. You are
mossst of you kind enough, you
earthly people, but there are
some among you who cannot
sssee an unusual creature like
Nipper or Squidley or Yarg or
myself without feeling a need to prod
and poke and quiz and otherwise examine us.
With the exssseption of Grindle and Mr Munkulus, we all
grew up in a place where we were ssstudied and tormented,
and might have died, had it not been for our dear friend
Jack.'

'The Royal Xenological Institute,' said Nipper, and
for once there was no kindness in his voice, just loathing
and a trace of fear.

I stared at Myrtle, hoping to catch her eye and remind
her that it would not be a good idea to let on to these
assorted monsters that our own poor father had been a
corresponding member of the Institute. But Myrtle was
looking up at the helm, where Jack Havock was studiedly
ignoring her.

'Mr Havock seems to have a fondness for orphans,' she

remarked, and blushed red, causing her to clash horribly with Ssilissa, who had come out in purple blotches.

'He is an orphan himself,' confided Nipper. 'His parents were part of the colony on Venus. And you know what happened *there,* miss.'

'Then they are not exactly *dead,*' I said. 'I mean, not *technically* . . .' But Myrtle booted me hard under the table. I think she was afraid that I would hurt Jack Havock's feelings, which seemed pretty ripe, considering it was she who had been calling him a murderer and so forth not five minutes earlier!

'Venus,' she said quietly. 'Oh, how dreadful! And how glad I am that fate never took *me* anywhere near that accursed orb.'

'Oh, but fate's taking you there now, miss!' said Nipper cheerfully.

'At leasst, the *Ssophronia* is,' Ssilissa said.

'What's an orb?' asked Grindle.

Jack Havock rejoined us, drifting down light as any feather to hover at my side. For all his show of ignoring us he had clearly heard every word we spoke, for he said, 'Nothing to fear. It is a good hiding place, that's all. After all, who would go to Venus now?'

CHAPTER NINE

IN WHICH WE MAKE LANDFALL ON THE MORNING STAR.

You will know all about Venus, of course. Everyone knows what befell the colonies there in '39 when the Changeling Trees came into flower.

I thought that Myrtle would faint again when Jack told her we were going there, but she didn't. She just went very quiet and ate her breakfast, and afterwards set to work cleaning the ship. I believe that what she had learned about

Jack had made her change her opinion of him. Before that she had thought him irredeemably wicked, but now she had decided that he was simply a poor sinner who had suffered, and had gone astray, and that by setting the right example she might persuade him to give up his life of crime and piracy.

In the days that we spent travelling to Venus she must have scrubbed and buffed and polished every inch of the *Sophronia*'s great main cabin, and she made me help, I'm sorry to say. It did not look bad when we had finished, and I think the pirates were impressed – or maybe they were just amazed at us; it is hard to tell when you are dealing with crabs and sea squirts and hobgoblins. The hardest part was gathering up all the crumbs and scraps and half-eaten crusts which floated about. Chasing after them with her dustpan and brush, Myrtle declared, 'What you really need, Mr Havock, is a good-sized herd of hoverhogs.'

'Hoverhogs? Not on my ship,' replied Jack Havock sullenly. I believe he knew that she was trying to improve him, and rued the day he had appointed her ship's cleaner. They had what I believe learned coves call a 'Clash of Personalities', my sister and the pirate chief. Often I caught her staring at him when his back was turned, as if

considering other ways to save his soul, and when *her* back was turned Jack Havock stared at *her*, probably thinking how much simpler his life would be if he just opened a hatch and kicked her overboard.

In the breaks between her bouts of tidying, Myrtle would retire into the small cabin that we shared, and there scribble furiously in her diary, doubtless noting down all sorts of details which she hoped might one day be used in evidence against Jack and his crew when they were brought to justice. Meanwhile, I busied myself repairing the chain of her locket, which you will remember she had contrived to

break when we were upon the Moon. I did it pretty well too, but when I offered Myrtle the locket back she said, 'Please keep it safe upon your person for a little longer, Art. I fear that if Jack Havock sees it he will be tempted to rob me.'

I returned the locket to my jacket pocket, though privately I felt certain that Jack and his friends would not have tried to steal it. They were too busy dividing up the mounds of loot which they had stolen from those Martian ships they'd raided. I do not know quite who it was who started the rumour that crime does not pay, but I can assure you they were wrong. It pays very well, and my shipmates' ill-gotten gains included chests of gold and silver, diamond necklaces, crates of fine-quality Martian crystalware, as well as all manner of pocket watches and cufflinks and other trinkets. As for the silk gowns which Ssilissa had stolen, I suspect they made even Myrtle think that piracy on the high aether would not be such a bad way to make a living.

All told, there was so much going on that I almost forgot we were bound for the most notorious world in the Empire. But eventually the dread day came when the engines slowed, the golden glow of our swift progress through the aether faded from the windows, and the cold green light of the Morning Star spilled in upon us.

Nowadays our former colonies on Venus are all fallen into ruin and decay, and the planet is deserted but for a few

mining camps down near the southern pole. So at least we did not need to fear being observed as the *Sophronia* carried us down into that steam bath of an atmosphere and settled upon a stretch of blue grass between the foresty uplands and the edge of the sea. But I feared other things. I glanced nervously towards the forests, which seemed to be exhaling mist. The blue-green foliage of the Changeling Trees stirred softly in currents which had nothing to do with the wind.

Nipper slapped me on the back with a friendly pincer. 'Nothing to fear, young Art. Once every fifty years; that's when the Changelings flower. Jack says they won't be in bloom again until 1889, by which time we'll all be old and rich and far away from here.'

'Of course,' I said, trying to sound brave. *But what if he were wrong? What if some of the trees were blossoming at that very moment, and their invisible pollen was hanging all about us in the steamy air?*

No such gloomy thought seemed to trouble my shipmates. Myrtle is always too busy reading about dresses and things to take an interest in the articles in the *Boy's Own Journal* and other important journals, so perhaps she did not know the details of what had happened to the Venus colonies. (Or maybe she was too proud to let Jack Havock see they worried her. She was certainly giving him a very funny look as we disembarked.) As for the rest, I believe they would all have followed Jack into the gates of Hell if he had asked them to.

Not wanting them to think me funky, I went down the gangplank with them and stepped on to the grass of Venus, which feels thicker and more rubbery than earth grass. The blue blades writhed nervously as we walked on them. On Venus the distinction between the Animal and Vegetable kingdoms is not nearly so definite as it is on other worlds, and there are many species of plant which can move about all by themselves. Indeed, all over the slope where we had landed, small shrubs, unsettled by the *Sophronia*'s descent, were uprooting themselves and stomping off. I even fancied that I could hear some of them grumbling to themselves. I took a deep breath of the hot, misty air, and thought, *Well, Art, if there is Changeling pollen on this breeze you have a lungful of it now, and nothing can save you from the Tree Sickness, so there is no point in fretting.*

Then, like any good tourist, I turned around to have a look at the view.

It was quite a spectacle. To the east and west of us the

wild, wind-sculpted cliffs stretched away, and the white surf nibbled at their feet. Behind us the forests rose in blue-green waves, and ahead a narrow spur of land jutted out to form a rugged promontory on which the tumbled, overgrown remains of buildings stood. Their roofs had long since fallen in, but their walls and chimney stacks still stood among the trees, sad mementoes of Britannia's doomed attempt to gain a foothold on this world.

'What is that place?' my sister asked.

'It was called New Scunthorpe,' said Jack Havock, rather sharply. 'People lived here, till the Changeling Trees flowered. Now it's our hidey-hole.'

We followed him in a line along that windswept promontory, with the waves grumbling below. A thick grove of armour-plated palm tree things had grown across the gateway in the settlement's wall, but when Jack shouted and waved his arms they uprooted themselves and edged aside. Changeling Trees stood like silent sentinels among the empty buildings, rustling their leaves as we passed. Sticky webs, woven by some carnivorous plant, wavered like dirty lace curtains in the blind windows. 'Well,' sniffed Myrtle, 'I hope he will not expect me to clean this place too.'

I paid her no heed. I was too awed by my surroundings. It is one thing to read about the Tree Sickness, quite another to walk among the homes of all the poor colonists whom it had claimed. Truly, this was a terrible place!

But to Jack and his friends it was just a hideaway; a place to stash their stores and loot away from prying eyes. In an old chapel, where planks of green sunlight sloped down through fern-choked rafters high above, they had made a nest of crates and barrels and tarpaulined heaps of plunder. They moved among them laughing, their voices echoing from the mossy walls. Grindle opened a chest of rum, and everyone took a swig except me (I was too young, they said) and Myrtle (who disapproved of strong liquor). Ssilissa, slightly shy, took Myrtle by the hand and led her off to look at something on the far side of the chamber. 'Girl stuff,' said Jack dismissively, as he watched them go. 'Your sister's a bad influence on Ssil.'

I wondered what he meant. I wondered how he had come to find out about this strange place. I wondered – not for the first time – how he came to be here, sailing the aether with his inhuman crew, so young. But for the next few hours there was no time to try and discover any answers to my wonderings. We were all too busy, with barrows and handcarts, transferring stores from the chapel to the *Sophronia*, and loot from the *Sophronia* to the temple.

The months-long Venusian day was nearing its end, and the mists turned lilac and rose as the Sun sank slowly towards the east. We returned to the *Sophronia*, and ate, and Myrtle and I washed the dishes – rather grudgingly in my case, but Myrtle reminded me in a loud voice that 'Cleanliness is next to Godliness.' Then we went to join the others, who had lit a driftwood fire on the grass outside, and were sat around it talking, and singing the peculiar-sounding songs of other spheres.

Now I shouldn't want you to think, because I have not spoken much about the grief I felt for Father, that I had not been thinking of him during our trip to Venus. Quite the contrary, I thought of him often, and dreamed nightly of the last time I had seen him, wrapped up like candyfloss in the grip of that great spider. In my dreams the spider blended with the Potter Moth, and with my memories of lying in the moth's jar, motionless, as if turned to stone by its venom. I began to think a great deal about venom, and about the nasty ways of spiders and other insects. And those webs down among the ruins of New Scunthorpe, in which small, bundled-up insect mummies had hung, now prompted me to speak my thoughts to Myrtle.

'What if Father is not dead?' I asked. 'After all, don't earthly spiders paralyse their prey and wrap it up alive to keep for later, just as the Potter Moth did to us?'

'Oh!' gasped Myrtle, who clearly had not thought of this. 'You mean poor Papa may even now be hanging in some spider's larder, waiting to be ate? Oh, how dreadful! Art!' (Et cetera, et cetera.)

'But those were no ordinary spiders,' I insisted, talking quite loudly to make myself heard above her fussing. 'They were *intelligent*. At least, their leader was. He had a spacecraft and a hat, and spoke quite passable English. What if he were keeping Father for some other purpose? To be a slave, perhaps, or so that he might question him?'

'Art, you read too many cheap novels,' Myrtle declared, pulling out a handkerchief and blowing her nose. 'What would they wish to question Father about? He is not a spy, or an officer of government. He doesn't know anything, except about Aetheric Icthyomorphs, and he will happily talk of those to anyone who will listen; there is no need to wrap him up in cobwebs first!'

Jack Havock, who had been lazing on the far side of the fire, now came across and sat down beside me, ready to back Myrtle up. This was a little embarrassing, for I had not intended him to hear what I was saying. I had hoped him to think me a very swashbuckling, devil-may-care fellow, and it pained me that he should know how I was pining for my father.

'Listen, Art,' he said kindly, 'I know you want to keep your hopes up, but your father's gone, and you must accept it. I know how bitter it feels . . .'

'Oh, fiddlesticks!' said Myrtle, who I suppose thought him very ill-mannered to be poking his nose into our private sorrows so. 'How can you know? You've been an orphan for ever, no doubt. For us the pain is still fresh.'

Jack fell silent, staring at the fire. The others were quiet too, wondering what he would do. At last he stood up, but instead of returning to his former place he held out his hand to me and said, 'Come, Art.'

Myrtle said, 'Where are you taking him? I will not allow it!'

'You can come too, if you wish,' said Jack, without so much as looking at her.

I took his hand and let him help me up. Side by side we set off down the slope towards the shining sea, Myrtle stomping along behind us. The pirates by the fire began to mutter as we left, and then Mr Munkulus set up a cheery song, but the sound of their singing was soon lost as we walked out along that gloomy promontory, between the shadowy ruins. The sea whispered, and between the shush of each wave's breaking and the long sigh as it washed out again I fancied that I could hear the faint, slow heartbeats of the Changeling Trees.

'Where are we going?' demanded Myrtle.

Jack did not reply, but led us inside one of the old houses; a small, square place where weeds grew thickly, rustling and muttering at us as we invaded their home.

'And why have you led us here?' asked Myrtle, hands on hips. Her fear of the gathering darkness and all the Venusian creepy-crawlies which might lurk in it made her speak more loudly than usual, as if she were addressing a deaf person.

'This was my parents' place,' said Jack.

That shut her up. Me too.

'The first sign of the sickness was a dizziness, and a pleasant sort of sleepiness,' said Jack, looking about him at the crumbled-down walls. Out in the streets the Changeling Trees clustered, thick and still. It was easy to imagine they were listening.

Jack said, 'I was only a kid, but I remember how sleepy everybody got, dozing off over their work and suchlike. They said it was just a summer cold at first, but slowly their waking periods got shorter and shorter. They used to stand for hours, just staring at the Sun. Their talk slowed down, till a single word might stretch out to fill an hour, and a sentence take a day to utter. Soon they stopped using words at all. Their skin turned hard and silver-grey. One by one

they went out into their gardens or up into the fields and forests and found a place for themselves and curled their toes down into the soil and never moved again.'

Myrtle said softly, 'But you can't *remember* that. You can't have *been* here. Nobody survived the Tree Sickness!'

'Everyone survived,' said Jack. 'It's just that once the illness had run its course they were not themselves any more. Except one boy. When the rescue parties arrived, in their rubberised tarpaulin suits and goggles and filter masks, they found one little boy. Kept it quiet, of course. Thought he'd been affected by the Changeling Tree pollen in some other, subtler way to all the rest.

Thought maybe he was a carrier of infection. Took him away to a quarantine place on the back of the Moon, and then, after a few months, to the Royal Xenological Institute in Russell Square, London.'

'And that boy was you?' I asked.

'Well, what would be the point of the story if it had been someone else?' snapped Myrtle. 'Really, Art. Do try to keep up.' She sighed, and gazed at our companion with a soulful look upon her face. 'Poor Jack! How terrible it must have been for you here, your father and mother dead . . .'

'Not dead,' said Jack. 'Come and see.'

A band of lemon-coloured light stretched along the horizon, above the sea. It shone on our faces as we walked on along the promontory. Outside the ruinous houses the Changeling Trees stood in little clumps and spinneys, always two or three or four together. Their vegetable hearts pulsed slow and steady. The ground sloped upwards, rising to a low headland.

'My brother Syd was the first to turn in our household,' said Jack. 'I remember well how we brought him out here, Ma and Pa and me, when it came time to settle him. There'd been riots in some of the other settlements, with frightened people burning and hewing the new trees, and we didn't want that for Syd.

'By then Ma was changing too. I remember how her hand felt, holding mine. Hard and scratchy it was, but warm, like bark. And it took ages to walk up here, because she kept stopping and standing still. "Mammy, Mammy," I'd go – I was only four-and-something – but she was already drifting away from us, thinking her tree thoughts. The following week she came up here herself, and stayed, and the week after that it was Pa's turn. And then I was all alone. There was plenty of food to be had – it was high summer, remember, and a bumper harvest in the fruit cages and the market gardens that year. I looked after myself as best I could, and sat up here most of the time, waiting to change. But it never came to me.'

We climbed the last few feet to the top of the headland. The sea lay below us, gleaming like bronze in that strange, slow sunset. On the headland's crown, among weathered rocks and soft blue grass, Jack's father and mother and brother stood as if waiting for us, their leafy branches casting dappled shadows on our upturned faces. They made handsome trees, with their silvery bark and those pale green leaves that showed almost white when the wind rustled through them.

'I kept thinking about this place,' said Jack, 'all the time they had me penned up a prisoner in Russell Square. Came back here as soon as I had the *Sophronia*. That was when I saw it would make a good place to lie low, and make repairs and such.'

'Oh, come,' said Myrtle, following him down into a gentle dell between the three trees. Her heart had been touched by the picture he had painted for us of that lone little boy in the abandoned town, and she wanted a happy ending to the tale. She said (but quite sweetly), 'I am sure you were not *really* a prisoner. Presumably the gentlemen of the Royal Xenological Institute treated you with kindness?'

'Funny sort of kindness,' scoffed Jack. He looked thoughtful for a moment. Then he sat down with his back to a stone, and gestured for us to do so too. And there, in the twilight of the Morning Star, beneath the spreading trees who had been his family, he told us his story.

CHAPTER TEN

A Brief Digression, in the Course of Which We Learn
Certain Facts Concerning the Early Life and
Adventures of Jack Havock.

Imagine London. Imagine the capital of Great Britain;
the Heart of Empire; the largest and the greatest city
in all the worlds of the Sun. Imagine the launching
towers of the aether-ships, rising above the rooftops of
Shoreditch and Wapping like a mighty forest, the masts of
seabound shipping in the Thames another, and in the east

the shaft of Mr Brunel's new space elevator, shining in the sunlight. Imagine the Houses of Parliament, the palaces and villas, the endless bustle in the teeming streets. And now imagine a boy growing up in the heart of such a city, but hidden away, locked up, knowing nothing of the world beyond the dark, echoey building in which he lived, nothing of the outside world at all except for the drear, high-walled garden where he was allowed to play sometimes.

The Institute (as he learned to call the place) smelled of wax polish and formaldehyde and carbolic soap. There was a kitchen in the basement from which stodgy meals emerged at regular intervals, along with an odour of boiled cabbage. The women who worked in the kitchen sounded

cheerful; sometimes Jack was able to press his ear to the door and hear their voices; their muffled laughter. But they were not allowed to talk to him, or come out of their kitchen into the dreary halls.

There were lots of scientific gentlemen in the Institute, and lots of mechanical servants, but the mechanicals could not speak, and the gentlemen spoke only to each other.

There were also other inmates. Other children? Jack was not sure. They were not human beings. He saw them sometimes, walking in the garden, or passing along the corridors in the care of sombre, dark-coated doctors and professors. A pair of things like walking sea anenomes, specimens from Sir Abednego Steam's recent expedition to the ocean-moon of Ganymede. A giant land-crab, known as Nipper, who had been collected on the same trip, and who now served as a sort of general dogsbody* to the Institute. A simple, harmless monster, Nipper was often to be heard humming to himself as he patiently swept the endless stairs and corridors, or black-leaded the grates. Jack liked Nipper. He was always friendly, and sometimes, returning from some errand in the outside world, he would

*Or perhaps I mean *crabs*body.

smuggle in a pastry for Jack, hidden in some nook of his shell. The pastries usually ended up tasting slightly of fish, but Jack was still glad of them, and glad of Nipper's friendship.

He felt less sure about another monster, the slender blue lizard-thing with spines for hair, who smiled at him sometimes, a smile so full of sharp teeth that he thought it must want to eat him. He always felt uneasy when he had to go past the lizard-thing's room, number seventy-six, in the west wing. He heard the lizard-thing crying in there once, and he was afraid it was crying from hunger and might pop out and gobble him up if it heard him passing by.

Jack had a room of his own, high up under the roof, with a window looking down into a courtyard. An iron bed and a wash-stand. Scratchy clothes in dark colours hanging in a cupboard. There was a cupboard full of toys too: colourful blocks and balls, lead soldiers, model aether-ships, a woollen rabbit that Jack loved and would secretly cuddle each night when he went to bed.

Each day, ever since he could remember, began with lessons. He studied History and English and the Scriptures. Also Mathematics, which he was good at. Then there was luncheon, always the same: brown bread and grey soup.

Then a walk in the garden. Then more lessons, except sometimes the doctors would take him into one of the big rooms on the ground floor, where the light came in wanly through tea-coloured blinds. It was a lecture theatre, and stern old faces would stare down at him from the steep-raked banks of mahogany seats, as the gentlemen of the Institute measured him and asked him questions, and made him play odd little games with balls and numbers. Then they would all whisper among themselves, scribbling notes in their big black books.

'Still no sign of infection . . .' Dr Allardyce might say, sounding disappointed.

'He appears to be a normal, healthy child,' Professor Snead might agree, purse-lipped.

'He *is* a normal, healthy child, Snead,' Dr Ptarmigan would hiss. 'When will you admit that and let him out of here?'

Then the others would shake their heads and murmur, 'Too risky, Ptarmigan,' and, 'Can't be sure,' and, 'Much more evidence required,' packing away their papers and pencil cases, leaving the pale, nervous young Dr Ptarmigan to lead Jack back up the spiral stairways to his room.

Dr Ptarmigan was different from the rest. Kinder. More

inclined to see Jack as a person, not a thing. Once or twice, shyly, Dr Ptarmigan brought Jack a gift – a toy from some shop out in the invisible streets beyond the Institute's high walls – a book called *Sea Stories for Boys* which Jack read and read, drinking in tales of pirates and buccaneers and places where the skies were blue, not smoke-coloured.

It was Ptarmigan, of course, to whom Jack turned when he was older and beginning to wonder, W*hy am I here?*

'What is this place, Dr Ptarmigan?' he asked, one ditch-dank November Wednesday.

'This is the Royal Xenological Institute,' the young doctor replied. 'It is where we study anomalous specimens of unearthly life.'

Jack looked at his hands. He knew he was a darker, richer colour than pasty Dr Ptarmigan and the other gentlemen who studied him, but in all other ways he seemed much like them. He said, 'Am I such a specimen?'

'Why no, Jack! You are as human as I. At least . . .'

'What?'

The pale young man looked awkward. His Adam's apple bobbed down to hide behind his high, starched collar and popped back up again. He led Jack into a gallery filled with the bones of fossil Icthyomorphs, deserted except for

Nipper, who was patiently sweeping in a far corner, and there he told him quickly of the fate that had befallen Jack's parents.

'You were immune to the Tree Sickness, Jack,' he whispered. 'We don't know why. I believe it is simple luck, like the luck which allows some people to emerge alive from houses where smallpox or diphtheria has carried off every other soul. But the other Fellows will not see it like that. I swear Dr Allardyce is half expecting you to sprout leaves and branches on your twelfth birthday!'

Jack wanted to know more, of course; what his parents' names had been, why they had been on Venus, everything. But Dr Ptarmigan would say nothing. 'I cannot, Jack,' he explained. 'My career is at a precarious juncture. The Government has finally agreed to let me take an expedition to Saturn. The aether-ship HMS *Aeneas* is being made ready at Farpoo. I shall be among the first Natural Philosophers to visit that lonely sphere, where I believe wonders of great import lie waiting to be discovered. If I were to arouse the displeasure of the Institute now, some other man may take my place. I do apologise, Jack.'

So that was that, thought Jack. But the very next evening he found a key lying on his bedroom floor, just inside the

door.
He guessed at
once who had left it
there, and what room it would open.
That night he lay wide awake, offering up prayers of thanks
for Dr Ptarmigan's kindness, and waiting impatiently for
the sounds of the building to fade into silence.

At last, when there were no more footfalls or voices to
be heard, and even the whoops and jabberings of the
strange animals in the east wing had subsided, he hurried
downstairs. No one was about; only the old night-
watchman, Slapestone, perched in his cubby-hole by the
street door, reading a sporting paper. Jack slipped past him
like a shadow and made his way to the records room.

There were a great many files there, but they were all
arranged neatly in alphabetical order, and it did not take

long for Jack to find the one marked *Specimen 1072: Jonathon Havock.* He pulled it from the shelf and opened it. And there he saw for the first time the names and faces of his parents: Josiah Havock (1809–1839), a surgeon in the Royal Navy, and his wife Maria (1805–1839), a freed slave-woman from the Windward Islands.

He held his flickering stub of candle and turned the pages quietly, reading the neat, impassive copperplate. His father, he learned, had been the youngest son of a fine old Scots family, the Havocks of Stirlingshire. But they had been outraged when Josiah brought his black bride and young baby home, and had cut him off without a penny. Undaunted, Josiah and Maria had answered the call for settlers to go and live in one of the new colonies on the planet Venus. Josiah was a surgeon, and his wife was a lady doctress (they had met, a footnote explained, while tending sailors sick with Yellow Jack in the West Indies.) The colonists were too sorely in need of good doctors to worry about whether Mrs Havock was black, or red, or green; wives of all those colours were quite common in the outer colonies. Soon the couple were set up in a pleasant cottage behind the hospital at New Scunthorpe, Venus, and there, on December 12th, 1838, their second son, Jonathon, was born.

Jack looked at their pictures for a long time, and his flickery, confusing memories of sea and sky and happiness began to make sense. He remembered the trees too; the rescue parties in their rubberised suits, and the men who had brought him to this chilly Institute.

There was a picture of his family; of what had happened to them. Jack stared at it for a long time, remembering the headland, and the shushing of the sea, and how he had waited for the change which never came.

Everyone who was on Venus that spring succumbed to the sickness, the notes said. Even those who were taken off soon after it broke out fell sick and made the change in the cabins and state rooms of the rescue ships. Of twenty thousand settlers, only young Jonathon Havock was spared.

Why? Why had the pollen which infected everyone around him not changed him as well? What was the secret of his immunity? Or had the Tree Sickness simply taken a different course in him; changed him into something not quite human? That was what the learned gentlemen of the Royal Xenological Institute had been striving all these years to find out. But as far as Jack could tell, after scouring through page after page of their notes, they had not yet found an answer.

He tried to ask Dr Ptarmigan about it the next day, and the day after that; but Dr Ptarmigan had suddenly become almost as cool and uncommunicative as the other gentlemen.

Jack kept the key, and from then on he would often creep down to the records room when the rest of the Institute was asleep. On his first few visits he was content to read and re-read his own file, especially the parts about his parents. But it only served to fill his head with more and more questions, to which it held no answers. At last, tiring of it, he began to explore the other files which lined the shelves. He began to learn the names of some of the Institute's other occupants, the strange creatures he had glimpsed sometimes in the corridors and gardens. Until then, with the exception of amiable Nipper, they had been frightening; like hobgoblins or creatures out of nightmares. Once he had put names to them and knew a little of their histories, he began to think more kindly of them.

Specimens 1010a and 1010b, the twins who looked like big walking sea anenomes, were believed to be intelligent beings who communicated with each other by the power of thought. Specimen 1026, the blue lizard, had hatched from an egg found frozen in a comet mine way off in the deeps beyond Jupiter. She had been Christened Millicent, after Dr Allardyce's sister, but the nearest sound her lizardy mouth could make to that name was Ssilissa, and after the first twenty pages or so the record-keepers had taken to calling her that instead. She had, a curious note suggested, an aptitude for Alchemy, which should be investigated. If her unknown race were all as quick as her at calculating courses through the aether and grasping the fundamentals of the chemical wedding, it might spell danger for the Empire . . .

Around the time of Jack's twelfth birthday there were changes at the Institute. Dr Ptarmigan went away to Io, where he was to go aboard the aether-ship *Aeneas* and begin his historic voyage to Saturn. At almost the same time, old Dr Allardyce retired, and in his place a new director was appointed; an outsider with friends in Government. His name was Sir Launcelot Sprigg, and he was a youngish, ginger-haired man with a plump, freckled face and grey eyes as narrow and as cold as razors. When Jack was presented to him, and the other gentlemen explained how and why he had come to the Institute, Dr Sprigg made his eyes go even narrower and said, 'Been here seven years, eh? Seven years of vittles shovelled into this black savage at the taxpayers' expense, and to what end, pray? With what result? Eh? Eh?'

'We have conducted a great many tests, Sir Launcelot,' quavered Professor Snead.

'The results are all on file, Sir Launcelot,' twittered Professor Footlinge. 'He appears to be a normal, human boy.'

'Tests be d——d!' snorted the new director. 'Files be d——d! And as for whether he's human or no, I'll decide that for myself. It's as bad as the way you maunder about with that blue lizard wench; bringing alchemists here to talk to her, humouring her in her wild, improbable claims, as if a subhuman brute such as she could ever understand Sir Isaac's great discoveries. Well, there'll be no more of it! New times, gentlemen, demand new methods. Methods that bring results!'

Jack was stripped, measured and photographed with an experimental camera. The photographer's assistant set off a tray of flash powder which filled the theatre with smelly blue smoke and made everyone sneeze. Sir Launcelot blew his nose on an enormous paisley handkerchief and said, 'Very well, gentlemen. That is all we can learn from the *outside*. Bring the boy tomorrow at . . .' (he consulted a list) '. . . eleven in the forenoon. I shall fit him in after Specimen 1029. Good day to you all.'

What did it mean? Nothing good; of that Jack was

Jack was stripped, measured and photographed with an experimental camera.

certain. The old gentlemen looked at each other and at Jack, and shook their heads and whispered. Doctor Snead said, 'Poor child!', but none of them would speak to Jack directly, for fear that Sir Launcelot should hear of it and dismiss them. They were all quite elderly, and most had been at the Institute their whole careers. They would have been as lost and helpless as Jack himself if they had been forced to try and find a living in the world beyond its walls.

That night, Jack lay on his bed, unsleeping, watching the Moon through the bars of his small window, and trying to make out the seas and cities which he knew were on its surface. He had just spotted a clipper taking off from Port George when there was a knock at his door. He sat up, surprised. The knock came again.

He opened the door, and Nipper came into his room. 'Oh, Jack!' the crab said, his eye-stalks weaving about in great anxiety. 'You have to go! We all must, all of us, tonight!'

'Why, Nipper? What's wrong?' asked the boy, running to the kindly crustacean and stroking his shell.

'I've heard what he's planning!' Nipper whispered. 'Heard them talking, through the door. Saw them making ready in the lecture room. Oh, Heavens! Oh, help!'

'But what's the matter? What's to happen?'

'That new man – that Sir Launcelot; he means to cut you open and look at your insides! Dissection, he calls it. The only certain way to knowledge, he says. Not just you, Jack; Ssillissa and the anemones as well! Oh, help! Oh, Heavens!'

'He wouldn't!' Jack cried.

'He would, Jack! He will! Unless you leave tonight! The others too! I'll help you, Jack, dear. He doesn't like me, that Sprigg. How long before I'm cast out on the street, or dissecticated like the rest of you? We'll flee, Jack – join the circus, maybe, or take off for the gold fields of America or the salt pans of Spoo . . .'

He reached inside his shell and drew out a big iron ring, jangling with scores of keys. 'I took these from Slapestone's cupboard, Jack. Just like that other key I gave you.'

'You gave me the record-room key?' cried Jack, feeling amazed, and also disappointed. For he had always believed that it was Dr Ptarmigan who had given him the means to learn about his past.

Nipper bowed his stalks, which was his way of looking bashful. 'Heard you questioning Doc Ptarmigan about it in the bone hall that day,' he admitted. 'I knew you wouldn't get an answer from him. Too fearful for his position, he was, and his place upon that expedition. So I took a key for you. Slapestone has spares, and he's too drunk usually to notice if they're missing. Like tonight; I left a bottle of gin beside his desk, so he won't stop us from leaving. It'll be scary, Jack, out there in the wide worlds all alone. But as long as I've got you . . .'

Jack patted the big crab's spiny shell. He was very scared, but having Nipper to look after made him feel braver somehow. 'We'll be all right, Nip,' he promised.

Taking the keys, he sped to the rooms where Ssillissa and the anenomes lived and unlocked them. The anemone creatures did not speak English, and only cooed and trilled at him when he explained what was afoot, but their coronae of tentacles flushed blue and red and he believed that they had understood his thoughts, if not his words. As for Ssillissa, she grasped their predicament at once and looked for a moment perfectly terror-struck; she curled up into a ball as if she was wishing herself back inside her egg. Then she seemed to regain her nerve. She smiled at Jack, and this time her pointy grin did not fill him with fear but with new strength, because he knew that here was a friend and ally.

Together, they all five crept downstairs to the hall, where Slapestone was snoring behind his desk, the dregs in the bottom of the gin bottle shining faintly in the glow from his butler's lamp. But Jack was not ready to leave. 'Wait here,' he hissed at his companions, and with Nipper at his heels he ran fleet-foot to the room he had visited so often before; the room of records. Into the pockets of his topcoat he stuffed the contents of his file, his parents' pictures and his father's journal. Then he took the files of Ssilissa and the anenomes as well, reckoning that they would be as glad as he had been to learn their histories.

He was halfway back to the hall when another thought struck him. He and Ssilissa and the anenomes were the only *thinking* beings in the Institute, but what about all those who did not think, or not in ways the Institute could recognise? The east wing was stuffed with unearthly animals and birds sent back by naturalists from the new worlds of space. Must he leave all those poor creatures to be cut up by Sir Launcelot Sprigg?

He could not, of course.

'Can you be fierce?' he asked Nipper.

'I cannot, Jack. It ain't in my nature. But I could pretend, perhaps . . .'

They ran to the east wing. They had no key to that part of the building, but Jack broke the lock and forced the door open. There was a custodian on duty there, a man like Slapestone, but awake and sober. It did not matter. Nipper, growling low, advanced upon the poor man, his pincers clashing. He could not help giggling a little at his own performance, but to the terrified custodian that only made him seem more terrifying. ''Ave mercy!' the poor fellow screeched, backed up against a wall. ''E's gorn mad! Call 'im off!'

'Do as I ask and I won't let him harm you,' Jack

promised. He gagged the man with his own neckerchief, and used his braces to tie him to a chair.

'Was I fierce enough?' asked Nipper, as Jack fished a bundle of keys from the custodian's pocket.

'The fiercest ever, Nip!'

They ran into every room in the east wing, unlocking the tall cages that they found there, upending the glass vivariums. The dim corridors filled with jibberings and squeakings, with croaks and chitterings and howls. Blind polypods and spindly insects, furry snakes and beetles the size of writing desks spilled panicky from their prisons and ran this way and that. An ungrateful Snapping Thistle snapped at Jack, and might have eaten him had Nipper not been there to growl and wave his claws and drive it back. When the last cage was opened, and the east wing was

echoing like a jungle glade to the cries of the freed captives, the great crab took gentle hold of Jack's coat sleeve and tugged him back towards the entrance hall, reminding him of his waiting friends.

They were waiting still; Slapestone was still asleep, a bubble of spit gleaming on his slack mouth. Jelly Birds and Martian Umbrella Bats flapped about, filling the hallway with alarming shadows. Jack ran to the street door, turned the big key in the lock, heaved on the handle, and looked out for the first time into the world beyond the Institute.

He saw iron palings surrounding a dismal garden; gaslight gleaming on wet pavements. Steps led down to the street. He was about to start down them when he heard a clattering sound that grew louder and louder, and around the corner came a gleaming black carriage drawn by two white horses.

Jack stood as if frozen in the open doorway and watched, with his comrades bunched behind him. A Behemoth Beetle whirred past him and flew towards the glow of the nearest gas lamp. The carriage swerved to a halt at the kerbside, horseshoes striking sparks from the cobbles. Sir Launcelot Sprigg leaped out, wearing evening dress and a long black cape which swirled around him as he started up the steps. He brandished a cane in one hand, and in the other something round and black which he shook violently at Jack. Jack and the others all jumped back as the black thing turned into a shiny top hat, which Sir Launcelot set upon his head. 'What is the meaning of this outrage?' he bellowed. 'I was dragged from my box at the opera in the middle of Mrs Paradiso's aria by reports of a disturbance, and now I find . . . Where is Slapestone?'

Another carriage came racing down the street and, halting behind Sir Launcelot's, disgorged a line of constables with truncheons at the ready. Jack looked up, and saw the sky above the Institute swarming with unearthly shapes: Helix Flies and Dragonets, Moth-Kings and Gulpers. A shoal of Icthyomorphs flitted by.

Sir Launcelot, his round face darkening with fury, raised his cane and came heavily up the steps. Ssillissa growled, but Sir Launcelot ignored her; he was used to dealing with unearthly brutes, and believed the best thing was to show no fear. He reached out and grabbed Jack by the collar, lifting the silver knobbed cane high, ready to deal him a blow that might easily have killed him, had Ssilissa not come to his rescue.

Since her hatching, Ssilissa had been made to wear a blue serge dress, very plain and simply cut, whose skirts reached almost to the floor. Because of this, Jack had never realised that she had a tail. In fact, she had a long, muscular, infinitely useful tail, with a bony club at the end far larger than the silver knob of Sir Launcelot's cane. As the angry director readied himself to strike, she struck instead, half turning, her skirts ripping loudly as her tail lashed round. The bony club collapsed Sir Launcelot's opera hat, and thudded against the top of his head. He gave a groan and pitched backwards, rolling down the steps.

''Ere! Stop that!' shouted the constables, waving their truncheons as they ran to Sir Launcelot's aid. 'Leave it out! You're nicked!' Whistles blew. A crowd was beginning to gather, lights showing in windows and doorways on the far side of the square as the Royal Institute's neighbours looked out to see what was causing all this unwonted noise.

And then, just as the constables were closing in, and Jack was urging Ssilissa not to use her fearsome tail on them as well, for fear of making things even worse, then, with a bellow and a trumpeting, a striped, fanged, four-headed monstrosity from the Martian badlands came bursting out of the Institute's front door, bowling over the twin anenomes, knocking Jack halfway down the steps and scattering constables in every direction. It prowled down the stairs, lashing its quills, claws like scythe blades slinking on the stonework, and Jack could hear panic spreading across the square as the onlookers saw it.

He reached back for Ssilissa, found her hand, called for Nipper, and thought hard for the Tentacle Twins (as he had already decided to call them) to follow. Down the steps they ran, scrambling over Sir Launcelot, who lay insensate at the bottom. The Martian beastie roared its defiance at the constables, who had found a net from somewhere and were trying to recapture it. None of them saw Jack and the others cross the road and run to the far corner of the square. From there, Jack took one last look back at the towering, soot-black building which had been his home.

$$\rightarrow\!\!\!\succ\!\!\prec\!\!\!\leftarrow$$

'And then what did you do?' asked Myrtle breathlessly. 'Had you a plan of action?'

'I had not.' Jack looked out at the sea and scowled at his

memories. 'I had no notion what to do at all. But I had to *pretend* I had, for the others were all looking to me to lead them. We scurried along backstreets and byways, and somehow we found our way east into the great space harbour at Wapping. The streets and taverns there were crowded with sailors from other worlds, so Ssil and Nipper and the Tentacle boys did not stick out quite so bad. We found an old shed to hide them in, and Nipper and I went looking for a ship, out among those thickets of mooring towers and fuel stacks. I had no money, of course; not a penny to my name. In the taverns and chop houses all the talk was of the terrible events of yesternight: Sir Launcelot Sprigg in hospital concussed, unearthly fauna being hunted all up and down the capital, a brace of Ionian Skeet Lizards nesting atop St Paul's cathedral. I began to realise how much trouble I was in. I wondered if I should not just make my way to the river and put an end to my miserable existence once and for all . . .'

'But you didn't?'

Jack glanced wearily at me. 'Course I didn't, Art. I'm here, ain't I?'

'Oh, yes,' I said.

→>‹‹←

And so Jack told us how he and Nipper had gone scouting through the harbour, hunting for a ship aboard which he and the other escapees might stow away. Not one of the great elegant clippers at the central berths – their white-suited aethernauts were too alert, their cable tiers and underdecks too clean and clear of clutter. Not one of the military ships, with all their cannon and marines. Not the miners, bound for nowhere good. Farther and farther they went through the warehouse maze of Wapping, past mountains of coal and anthracite and culm, down alleys where the air was thick with alien spices and the colourful curses of dockyard hands and barrow boys, down at long last into the rookeries of Rotherhithe, where the stink of the river filled the foggy air and the space docks started to give way to boatyards and the berths of sea-going ships. And there, dumped on a cobbled dock, they saw the brig *Sophronia*, with the misty sunlight a-glimmer on the funnels and trumpets of her alchemical exhaust.

They walked all round her once, the boy and his land-crab, looking up at her spindly masts and the space barnacles clinging to her planking. There seemed no one about. But when Jack went up and tried a hatch near one of the exhaust funnels a window in the stern gallery popped open and a pair of glum, inhuman faces peered down at him.

'Clear off and be d——d!' shouted one.

'Looking to stow away?' asked the other, more kindly sounding, guessing Jack's intent so accurately that he wondered for a moment if this stocky Ionian could read his thoughts just like the Tentacle boys. But Mr Munkulus (as the Ionian turned out to be called) was not a mind-reader; just an old sailor who'd been long enough upon the aether seas to know what was in the hearts of boys who came nosing round the mooring yards.

'*Sophronia* ain't the ship for you,' he said, sounding sad about it. 'She's only got one voyage left in her.'

'Where's she going?' Jack asked, thinking that anywhere would be better than London.

'Breaker's yard in Aberdeen,' growled Mr Munkulus's goblin shipmate, looking as sad about it as his friend, but angry too. 'Best little ship in the aether, but the company has decided she ain't *eek-o-nomickal* any more. They've had a fleet of flash new clippers built, and won't pay for poor *Sophronia*'s overhaul.'

'Me and Mr Grindle here are the skeleton crew,' sighed Mr Munkulus. 'We'll be taking her up to Aberdeen this forenoon, when the company alchemist comes aboard to fire up her wedding chamber. There she'll be scrapped, and us too – laid off, without a pension or a by-your-leave.' Two big tears trickled down his broad phiz* and dropped off his chin, plopping on Jack's upturned face like salt rain. 'Thirty years I been helmsman of this ship, man and larva. I know her little ways, the way she gripes, how to keep her head up in an aether storm. And it's all been for nothing but the scrapyard.'

Jack felt sorry for the old aethernauts. 'Why don't you just take her?' he asked. 'If the owners don't want her, why not take her for yourselves? Then you could take me and my friends along.'

* phiz = physiognomy, which means face, as any schoolboy knows.

'Take you where?' asked Grindle. 'We can't get off this world without an alchemist, can we? And I don't see the Royal College sending us one of those.'

Jack thought of the file he'd read about Ssilissa. He said, 'I know an alchemist. She's not from the College, but she has an aptitude. She's had all kinds of tests and training.'

'*She?*' said Mr Munkulus.

'I don't believe you, Earthlet,' sneered Mr Grindle, and then, to his friend, 'What's an apti-thing?'

'Even if this lady-friend of yours could get us aetherborne,' sighed Mr Munkulus, 'it wouldn't do no good. We haven't fuel enough to get us more than halfway to the Moon.'

'Then steal some!' cried Jack. He did not know where the notion came from; he was just desperate to escape, and this old ship seemed his only chance. He remembered the book Dr Ptarmigan had given him; those tales of pirates and privateers; Sir Francis Drake singeing the King of Spain's beard. He said, 'Get up in the open aether, south of the Moon, and wait for the next merchant ship to come by. Make them give you fuel and food and . . . stuff.'

'That's flamin' piracy!' said Grindle, shocked.

'We've got no guns,' said Mr Munkulus, but thoughtfully,

as if he were giving Jack's idea some serious consideration.

'Then pretend you have!' said Jack. He looked around. On the far side of the dock, stacked beside a warehouse, a heap of iron gas pipes caught his eye. 'They'd pass for cannon,' he suggested. 'Point one of them at somebody and act like you intended for to use it, and I doubt they'd argue long before they gave you what you wanted.'

'It's still piracy,' said Grindle nervously. 'And you know what becomes of pirates. Hung in chains at Execution Dock . . .'

'But at least we'd have a last cruise in the old *Sophronia* first, eh, Grindle?' said his friend. 'Wouldn't that be something? To take her out among the stars again. Fit her up. Show those penny-pinching company accountants she's got some life left in her?'

He leaned out of the stern-gallery, reaching one of his four big hands down to Jack. 'Bring your alchemical friend here, young fellow, and you'll have yourself a ship. I can fly her for you, and Grindle here can help. But of course the piracy is down to you. Me and Mr Grindle, we don't know nothing about that.'

'Neither do I,' Jack was about to say, but stopped himself in time, for he was already beginning to realise that

Munkulus and Grindle expected him to lead them, just as Ssilissa and the Tentacle Twins had. So he said instead, 'Get her ready to leave,' and went running back to the shed his friends were hidden in, to tell them, 'We have a ship!'

→⋅←

Jack finished his tale. Above our heads the Changeling Trees rustled softly in the breeze. None of us said anything. I was still waiting to hear the exciting bit, about the piracy. Myrtle just looked sad.

Jack seemed sad too. He stood up and rubbed his back and walked away beneath the trees, running his hands over their bark and whispering to them. If I squinted hard, I thought I could just make out the human forms that they had once been, as if Jack's family were still there inside those silvery boles, spellbound perhaps, and dreaming gentle dreams. 'They can't hear me,' he told us. 'I reckon they ain't aware of much beyond the turning of the seasons, the Sun and rain. Thinking tree thoughts.'

'"A green thought in a green shade,"' said Myrtle quietly.*

*This comes from a poem called 'The Garden' by A. Marvell. I looked it up later, and it is awful tosh. My favourite poem is 'How Horatius Held the Bridge', but I suppose that would not have been so appropriate to Jack's family circumstances.

Jack looked round. 'What's that?'

'That is poetry, Mr Havock,' she replied.

Jack put his head on one side, and stared at her, and then he smiled. 'That's pretty,' he said. 'I like that.'

Well, Jack and Myrtle stood there gawping at each other under those trees for so long that I began to feel quite awkward. I was almost relieved when a sudden blurt of noise drew my attention skyward. 'I say!' I cried. 'There is another ship!'

There was, too. It was quite dark now above the hills, so I could not make out what sort it was, but its engine light flared prettily as it swooped in towards the *Sophronia's* mooring place.

'D——!' shouted Jack Havock.

'*Language*, Jack!' wailed Myrtle.

But Jack was not listening. The spell of the peaceful headland was broken, and we all went running back as fast as we could towards the *Sophronia*, Jack in the lead, of course, me hanging back to help Myrtle, who kept tripping over her petticoats and getting her crinoline entangled in the undergrowth. By the time we emerged from the ruins we could see pistol fire flashing around the *Sophronia*, and hear shouts and cries.

'It is the bluecoats!' hollered Jack, and sped off ahead of us, dragging a gun from his belt.

'Oh, Jack!' cried Myrtle, starting after him.

Just then there was a flash of light from up ahead and I saw the newcomers' ship quite clearly. It wasn't HMS *Indefatigable*, nor anything like her, but I knew it all right. It was that same black, spiny, seed-pod looking tub that had been hanging outside Larklight when we left, and I guessed at once that the spiders were not finished with Myrtle and me, and that they had tracked us somehow through the wilds of space.

'Myrtle!' I shouted, running after her as she ran after Jack.

Just then, something big and horrible came out of the dark, all legs and glinting eyes. A great pale limb shot out and grabbed me in its pincered claws.

The spider lifted me up and turned me this way and that, considering me carefully with its big eyes, which glistered like window panes. Myrtle was shrieking and lamenting, the sounds moving away from me, and I realised that there must have been another of the spiders, and that it was making off with her.

'Jack!' I bellowed, top of my lungs.

A pistol crashed, very close, and I felt the shot whisk past me. Some of those window-pane eyes went out, smash! My spider reeled and staggered, dropping me, and I had a nasty view of its many legs all silhouetted against the afterglow. Then the pistol rang out again and it went down twitching and thrashing, and strong hands grabbed me by my shoulders and the belt of my Norfolk jacket and dragged me clear.

'Mr Munkulus!' I gasped, recognising my rescuer.

'All right, Art, lad?' asked the Ionian, throwing his empty pistols aside and drawing out three more. 'There's dozens of the blighters. Came down on us all at once . . .'

'My sister!' I cried.

We ran together towards the *Sophronia*. Again that flash of ghostly light lit up the sky and ground, and this time I saw that it came from the tentacles of Squidley and Yarg.

They were standing close together, and the great pulse of electric current pouring from their crowns sent a spider hurtling backwards in a cloud of choking steam. The campfire was still burning. Ssilissa crouched beside it, tending to Nipper, who had lost an eye-stalk and was bleeding clear, gluey blood.

Jack ran out of the darkness. 'Where's Myrtle?' he shouted.

'I don't know,' I said.

'One of them poxy monsters took her, Jack,' said Grindle.

Another wave of light burst over us, and this time it came not from the Tentacle Twins, but from the engines of the spider-ship. We all turned away or hid our faces as the spiny vessel soared into the sky, the backwash from its wedding chamber setting fire to the grass, which squealed most horridly as it burned, and groaned and grumbled as Mr Munkulus and the others ran around stamping out the flames.

'Myrtle?' people were calling. 'Miss Mumby?'

There was no reply. We fetched out lanterns from the *Sophronia* and wandered to and fro, all the way from the forest's edge to the ruins on the promontory. We found six dead spiders, curled up like clenched, white, bony hands. But of my poor sister there was not a trace.

Jack strode about, tearing down swags of web which the spiders had cast across his ship's hull, as if in the hope of anchoring her to the ground. They had fired some sort of big gun at her as they landed: there were four smouldering craters in the ground where their shots had gone wide, and a horrid hole in *Sophronia*'s side where one had not.

'How did they follow us?' Jack demanded angrily. 'What's so important about Miss Mumby and Art that they'd come across half of space to snatch them? For they'd have had Art too, if we'd not been here to scare them off . . .'

And still he walked about, snatching at the webs, hacking at them with his cutlass. It was as if he *had* to move; there was so much anger in him that it was forcing all his muscles into motion, making his fists clench and his teeth grind and his feet walk and walk about. I was sure it couldn't be my sister's kidnapping that had affected him so, for he had never seemed to like Myrtle any more than she liked him. I supposed it was the way the spiders had invaded his place, and tried to harm his crew.

'They're looking for something, maybe,' said Nipper,

who was sitting up, bandages flapping like a flag from the stump of his broken-off eye-stalk.

'Something they hoped to find in that house of yours, Art,' agreed Mr Munkulus. 'But it wasn't there, and now they think you've taken it with you.'

'But what could they want?' I wept. 'We have nothing of value. We never had anything of value. Only Father's books and samples, and we left all those behind at Larklight. Why must they steal Myrtle away? Where have they taken her?'

Jack shrugged. 'Back to wherever they came from, I suppose. Ssil, you got a good look at these beasties. We seen their like before?'

The lizard-girl shook her head, her eyes fixed on him. We were all watching him, waiting for him to tell us what to do. But for once, Jack seemed not to know.

'What's it matter?' asked Grindle. 'They're no good to us, these Earthlets. If the spiders want them, let 'em take them, that's what I say. Pity they haven't took the boy too.'

'Miss Myrtle was our shipmate!' shouted Jack, to everyone's surprise. 'Anyway, it's bad for business, these creepy-crawlies flying about upsetting things. *We're* meant to be the most fearsome pirates in the aether. I don't want a bunch of old spiders snatching loot that's ours by right.

We need to find out what they are, and where they come from, and what their intentions might be. And we need to learn where they've took Myrtle, for one thing's clear: you don't come all that way to take someone just to eat 'em. They want her for a reason, and they'll be holding her somewhere.'

Mr Munkulus spoke then, in his low, rumbling voice. 'You could ask the Thunderhead. Not much *he* doesn't know. I was thinking how a run back to Io might be needful anyhow. We've got a few repairs to make. Leave the *Sophronia* in a safe shipyard there, and go and ask old Thunderhead about these web-worriers.'

The others looked at each other and back to Jack, waiting for his answer. I said, 'Thunderhead? Isn't he just a story?' (I nearly said, 'a heathen superstition', but I didn't wish to offend Mr Munkulus.)

The Ionian shrugged all four shoulders. 'In the past my people thought he was a god, and some still do, but he's real enough. Not much happens among the worlds but the Thunderhead comes to know of it. If anyone has heard about these spiders, it will be him.'

Jack nodded slowly, then spoke fast. 'Ssil, did the spiders harm our wedding chamber?'

Ssilissa said, 'I don't think they hurt it, Jack. I think if we can jusst cut away all these websss and threadsss they've tied uss down with . . .'

'Jump to it then, Grindle,' Jack ordered. 'Go with him, Art. Mr Munkulus, you'll help me plug that hole. It's a fair way to the Planet of Storms.'

Feeling numb, I began to follow Grindle towards the ship. Jack stopped me as I passed him, and handed me a cutlass. 'For cutting the webs away,' he explained, and then, softer, as if he did not want his crew to hear, 'Don't be afraid, Art. Trust in me. We'll find her.'

And so we set to work. It is a grand remedy for heartache and worry, work. There in the dark of Venus we cleared and cut and tidied and made repairs, and pegged fresh sheets of tarpaulin across the breach in poor *Sophronia*'s hull, while Yarg and Squidley stood guard with their tentacles ablaze to light our labours and to drive off any carnivorous plants which came prowling close.

When we were done, Ssilissa set about her work in the wedding chamber, and we began our journey to the worlds of Jupiter. A long journey it was, and slow, and the vapours of alchemy crept around the edges of the tarpaulin seal and filled the ship with golden haze and our heads with strange, unsettling dreams. But it was not an exciting voyage, by the usual standards of the *Sophronia*, and so, while we are about it, I shall let you know what had befallen Myrtle, and the best way to do that is to let you read a few entries from her diary.

CHAPTER ELEVEN

BEING AN EXCERPT FROM THE JOURNALS OF
MISS MYRTLE MUMBY.

April 23rd

What a very curious day this has been!

I awoke this morning to find myself in a comfortable bed, in this most charming suite of rooms, whose windows look out on to a well-tended garden, with many towering copper beech trees. I knew at once that I was upon the planet Mars, for I recognised the snowy heights of Mount Victoria towering in the distance, just like the painting in the blue drawing-room at Larklight. (How pleasant, incidentally, that the greatest mountain in all Creation should have been conquered by Englishmen, and named after our own dear Queen!)

For a few moments I was quite alarmed, being entirely unsure as to what this place might be, and how I had come here. Also, my mind was filled with memories of a most absurd and alarming dream I had just had, about pirates and spiders and – oh, *dreadful* things – and a person called *Jack Havock* who – (*At this point, several lines have been firmly crossed out – A. M.*)

Presently, a young Martian girl in the uniform of a maid appeared, bringing me a tray of breakfast things, and a most welcome pot of tea. Though only a native, she speaks good English and seems quite civilised, despite her russet skin and purple hair. Her name is Ulla. (She also found me this small notebook, in which I am recording this account of my adventure. How I regret the loss of my own journal, which must have been left behind at Larklight. And poor Mama's locket.)

Ulla tells me that I have been here for several days,

having been carried unconscious from the wreckage of a lifeboat which fell into the desert nearby. It seems that there was a fire at Larklight, though I have no memory of it, only of my peculiar dream. Papa and Art escaped together in the other lifeboat, and are now safe upon the Moon, but for some reason I left alone, and drifted through the aether until I reached Mars. Ulla says that the Governor has been informed of my arrival, and has written to Papa.

It is horrid to think of Larklight burned up, and all our belongings with it. But at least Papa and Art are safe. In my dream – but enough about that foolish dream!

Now to something very extraordinary. This house is none other than The Beeches, country seat of Sir Waverley Rain, the great manufacturing magnate, whose company built the Channel Bridge, and the Martian Railways, and all the auto-servants at Larklight, and is constructing the crystal palace for the Great Exhibition! He is a famous recluse, and sees almost nobody these days, so it is a great honour for me to be a guest in his home.

I wonder if I shall be invited to meet him? I must brush my hair and ask Ulla if anything may be done with my dress, which has somehow become terribly torn and dirty.

Then I shall say my prayers, and thank God for

delivering me from danger and arranging for me to be rescued by such a respectable gentleman.

April 24th

My second day at The Beeches. I have not as yet seen any sign of Sir Waverley. The maid Ulla says that he is a very private gentleman and keeps mostly to his study, when he is not away visiting one or other of his manufactories upon Phobos and Diemos, which are the moons of this world. Last night I saw them glittering in the sky, all wreathed in the smoke of Sir Waverley's mills. What a great man he must be, to have left his mark upon the Heavens like that!

I spent the morning exploring some of the rooms on the ground floor, such as the library, et cetera, which are exceedingly well appointed. My host seems to have a passion for Martian antiquities, and owns many quaint examples of statuary and carvings salvaged from old heathen temples in the upland deserts. Also, many paintings of the famous Martian canals and other curious and picturesque vistas. These were most interesting.

I have always longed to see Mars, the jewel in the crown of Her Majesty's extraterrestrial possessions. I suppose few

Martians could have imagined, in the first years of the eighteenth century, that intelligences far greater and yet as mortal as their own were observing them from across the gulf of space, and slowly and surely laying plans against them. It must have been a very great surprise to them when the Duke of Marlborough landed his army, and brought order and civilisation to their dusty, backward planet!

This afternoon, having taken luncheon alone, I set out to explore Sir Waverley's gardens, which are quite genteel. The Beeches occupies a small island in a lake called Stonemere, the island having been landscaped to resemble an English park, with a small herd of deer and a great many copper beech trees. I confess that the masses of dark red leaves, combining with the reddish sky and the rust-red sands and rocks of the surrounding wastes, lend the spot a rather sombre feel. The lake is also somewhat unsightly, for it is filled not with water, as lakes generally are in England, but with a form of Martian rock which has an unnaturally low melting point. The surface is covered with a stony crust, which is constantly fissuring and splitting into fragments that grind one against another with a most unearthly noise. In the lower depths, I am told, the rock is liquid, sluggishly and incessantly churning. Were I Sir Waverley, I should have the whole thing drained and replaced with a croquet lawn, or perhaps a ha-ha.

Sir Waverley's servants are all most polite, although very few of them are human. The maids and gardeners are all Martians like Ulla – thin, elfin creatures with skins the colour of rust. Apart from Ulla, none of them seems to speak English. There are also some manservants who appear to be a form of sentient cacti; very brutish they look too, with their broad shoulders and flat green hands, and their blind green knobs of heads all studded with spines and prickles. They do not speak at all. They alarm me somewhat, although I am certain that they must be quite well domesticated, or else why would Sir Waverley keep them on?

April 25th

The most exciting news! Ulla has just come to tell me that Sir Waverley Rain has invited me to dine with him this evening! I am beside myself at the thought that at last I shall be entertained in polite society. I pray that I may make a good impression.

Later

Well, what an extraordinarily disagreeable interview! I know that Sir Waverley Rain is a self-made man who has risen to great heights through innate genius and hard work, but however lowly his birth I do not think it excuses quite such eccentricity!

Ulla arrived at my door at a quarter after six o'clock, bringing with her a quite passable dress of sprig muslin, not exactly in the current fashion, but kindly meant, no doubt. For some strange reason, as she helped me dress, I found myself missing the more informal dining arrangements aboard Jack Havock's pirate ship, and had to remind myself sharply that J. H. and his ship had been no more than figments of my silly dream. Why can I not *forget* that strange dream, I wonder? Why *does* it all seem so *real* in my memory?

Just before seven I made my way to the dining-room; a sumptuous room on the ground floor, decorated in the most exquisite taste, though still, I fear, somewhat gloomy. There was a great huge ebony table shining like a pool of oil, with silver centrepieces and cutlery all a-gleam and cactus-manservants standing ready to pull out my chair for me when I had made my curtsey. At the far end of the table sat a tiny, motionless figure whom I took to be Sir Waverley. He does not look the least like a Sir. I had imagined a

rugged, lined, yet handsome face, a leonine mane of greying hair, and an expression of nobility and deep intelligence. Instead, Sir Waverley has a little round greyish face like an aged egg, a little bush of grey hair growing above each ear, and no expression at all. Only his eyes moved, watching me as I entered and following me

as I crossed the room, and closing in a long, slow blink as I sat down in the chair which his servant had pulled out.

'Miss Mumby,' was all that he said.

More servants entered, and set down a shallow dish before me, and another before Sir Waverley. A pleasant smell rose from the dishes; the smell of mock turtle soup, which is my favourite. I waited for Sir Waverley to say grace, or to give some other sign that we might commence our meal, but he only sat there, silent as a stone.

I decided that I should make polite conversation, even if he would not. 'I am deeply sensible of your kindness in bringing me here, and looking after me with such Christian charity,' I began. 'It is like the parable of the Good Samaritan . . .'

Sir Waverley leaned forwards and regarded me with his strange, pale eyes. 'I am glad that you are comfortable,' he said. 'You are among friends here, you know. I hope you feel that I am your friend, Miss Mumby?'

'Why, of course,' I stammered. But he had spoken in such a strange, unfeeling way, not the least friendly!

'Where is it?' he asked, still in the same, lifeless tone. 'Where is the key?'

I had not expected to be addressed in such a manner,

and began to feel quite agitated. 'I do not know what you mean, sir,' I said.

'The key,' hissed Sir Waverley. (Some disagreeable people might argue that it is not possible to hiss 'the key', as it is a phrase which contains no sibilants, but I cannot think of any other way to describe his voice as he asked me this. He most definitely *hissed*.) 'The key. The key to Larklight.'

'I do not have it, sir,' I said truthfully. All Larklight's keys were hanging upon their hook outside the pantry door last time I noticed them, and doubtless they are there still, unless they were quite burned up in the fire. I would have liked to explain this to Sir Waverley, but there was something so cold and uncanny about the way he kept staring at me that I could not bring myself to speak.

Then he seemed to remember his manners. His face changed slowly, until he was smiling at me, though I have never seen a more strained, unnatural smile in all my life; he looked as though invisible pulleys were tugging the corners of his mouth upward. He said, 'I only ask, Miss Mumby, because your father wishes to know.'

'You have spoken with Papa?' I gasped.

'We have corresponded. As soon as I realised who you were I sent word to him by aetheric telegraph. I had a reply this morning. He is overjoyed to learn that you are safe, but most concerned as to the whereabouts of *the key . . .*'

Of course, once I knew that it was for my father's sake I was being questioned I tried even harder to think what key it was, and where it might be, but still all I could think of was that big brass ring with all the cupboard and door keys on. 'All the keys are on the hook outside the pantry,' I said.

The smile fell off Sir Waverley's face like plaster dropping from a damp wall. He looked past me at the cactus-man who stood behind my chair and said, 'She knows nothing. Perhaps that brother of hers is the one. Webster should have taken him too. We must find him. Take her away.'

Before I could protest, the cactus-man's spiny fists clamped around my arms and I was wrenched from my seat and carried off, back through the tasteful, gloomy halls to my room.

It is clear to me now that Sir Waverley is deranged. I do not even know whether he has really informed the authorities of my plight, or whether my presence here in his lonely house is a secret. And what of Father, and poor little Arthur? Are they really safe? And what about my dreams, which seem so real? I cannot forget how they ended, with those dreadful spiders seizing me . . . And was not the leader of their brood called Mr Webster, the very name that Sir Waverley mentioned?

Whatever can it all mean?

To compound my discomfort, Sir Waverley had me dragged from his dinner table before I had taken so much as a mouthful of that mock turtle soup, which means that I am exceeding hungry, and my stomach keeps making the most indelicate noises. I do not see how things could possibly be any worse!

April 26th

Merciful Heaven preserve me! Since my last entry things have become a very great deal worse!

I barely know where to begin. Sir Waverley – the cacti – the worms – it is all quite horrible, like something from one of those sensational novels which Art insists on reading!

I must endeavour to collect my thoughts . . .

Last night, after I had written up the account of my unpleasant meeting with Sir Waverley, I was preparing myself for bed when there came an urgent tapping at my bedroom door. I opened it, and there stood Ulla. She had, until then, always been a very meek and polite creature. I had no sooner opened my door, however, than she barged into my room in a most impertinent manner, declaring, 'You must leave at once!'

'What is the meaning of this?' I cried. I imagined she was there on Sir Waverley's orders, and that this was another instance of his rudeness. 'How am I to leave? It is the middle of the night!'

'And you won't see another day if you stay here,' said the Martian girl. 'I heard Sir Waverley talking with his house guest, and saying how they had no more need of you.'

'But,' I protested, 'but . . .'

Ulla put a hand on my arm, which made me flinch. She said, 'Don't you understand? Everything I have told you is a lie! Except that last bit, of course.'

'What do you mean?' cried I.

'*He* made me lie to you! The story about the lifeboat! No lifeboat fell here. You were brought in an aether-ship, from who knows where. You had been drugged, to dull your memory. It is a spiky, black aether-ship. It often visits. It is moored behind the house even now.'

I gasped. 'The spiders!'

She nodded. 'The white spiders are Sir Waverley's friends. He concocted those lies to put you at your ease so that you would tell him something they badly want to know.'

My mind was reeling. If what I had been told was all untrue, then the things I thought I had dreamed must be real! The Potter Moth, the *Sophronia* and Jack Havock. But where was Art? And Jack himself? Had the spiders destroyed them upon Venus when they captured me?

'We must leave this place,' Ulla vowed. 'I listened at the drawing-room door. Sir Waverley says you do not have the thing they want. He spoke of getting rid of you.'

'I do not believe you!' I whispered.

'You must! Come quickly. I have friends who can help us if we can only get across the lake of stone.'

I could think of no other course but to trust her. After all, Sir Waverley had already proved himself no friend to me. I donned my good old wool serge dress, pulled on my boots, and stuffed this journal into my bodice. Then, offering up a silent prayer, I followed Ulla out of the room and down the staircase. Through the landing windows came the pale light of the Martian moons, casting eerie double shadows which served only to heighten my terror. Ulla pushed me into an alcove to hide as one of the dreadful cactus-servants lumbered past. Then we hurried down to the ground floor. Voices came from behind the closed door of the withdrawing-room. Ulla whispered to me, 'Take a look. See for yourself what company he keeps!'

I have always thought that spying through keyholes is a most ill-bred way to carry on, yet in this case it seemed justified. After all, if Sir Waverley Rain is involved in some criminal enterprise I should learn the facts, so that I may lay them before the authorities when I reach Port-of-Mars. So I kneeled, and put my eye to the big brass keyhole in the drawing-room door, and peeked through.

The first thing I saw was Sir Waverley himself, standing with his back to the fireplace. The sight of his grey, unfeeling face was enough to convince me of Ulla's tale, and then, when I saw to whom he was speaking . . . !

It was one of those spiders, even bigger than the ones in my dreams. It had pulled up all its horrid legs into a knot so that it fitted into one of Sir Waverley's leather wing chairs, and it was wearing a bowler hat.

'We should take her to the rings,' it was saying. 'She might still be useful. For luring the other one, like. They are soft about each other, these apes of Earth.'

'No, Mr Webster,' said Sir Waverly. 'She is of no use, and already she has seen too much of us. We will kill her and drop the body in the lake.'

I am afraid that I could not prevent myself from uttering a little scream. My Martian friend said something most unbecoming, and pulled me away at once, but it was too late. Along the passage from the servants' wing a trio of the spiky cactus-men came hurrying, reaching out towards us with their blunt, thorny hands. And behind us I heard the scramble and scrabble of clawed feet, and the sound of the drawing-room door opening.

I screamed again, but Ulla reached into a pocket of her apron and drew out something that shone faintly in the moonlight. She sprang at the cactus-men and swung the shiny thing to and fro. It was, I believe, a sort of axe, or knife, made in a complicated curvy shape so that it had many points and blades. The greenish sap of the cactus-men sprayed upwards, making a most dreadful mess of Sir Waverley's wallpaper and ceilings. A prickly head trundled across the carpet to my feet. 'Come on!' shouted Ulla.

I looked behind me. The enormous spider was pushing its way out through the drawing-room doorway, which luckily was rather too small for it. The lamps in the room behind it cast nightmarish shadows across the hall. Then Ulla had my hand in hers, and we were running through the darkened servants' quarters, with Ulla shouting at startled Martians to stand out of our way as they emerged blinking from their sleeping cells, and using her axe to cut down any cactus-men who tried to stop us. I believe she hoped to reach the servant's entrance in the west wing, but long before we gained it a whole squad of the lumbering cacti appeared ahead, cutting off our escape, and instead we ran up an iron stairway to the first floor.

We were in Sir Waverley's private quarters, where we fled unhindered through several offices and a library, until we found ourselves in an octagonal chamber where the moonlight slanted in through several well-proportioned windows. I stopped to catch my breath and look around while Ulla attempted to force a window open. On the walls between the windows hung slabs of stone, which I recognised as yet more of Sir Waverley's archaeological treasures. Upon each slab, amid a confusion of other shapes and symbols, were carved the forms of colossal spiders.

A voice from behind me said, 'I see you are admiring my collection, Miss Mumby.'

I turned with a gasp. Sir Waverley stood in the doorway, his pale eyes shining like glass in the moonlight. Behind him I could hear cactus-men lurching through the library, and an unpleasant *tick*, *tick*, *tick* which I feared must be the footsteps of that ungodly spider.

I closed my eyes and waited to faint. In novels, when well-bred young ladies are cruelly put upon, they generally swoon and recover to find that they have been rescued and are safe in the arms of their hero. However, no fainting fit descended upon me, and perhaps that was a good thing, for strangely enough the only hero I could imagine was Jack Havock, whose arms would be most unsuitable. I therefore opened my eyes again, just in time to see Ulla's axe go whirling past me in a sharp-edged blaze of moonbeams. She had flung it at Sir Waverley, and her aim was true; it struck him in the middle of his shirt-front.

I screamed, for I had never seen a man struck dead in cold blood before. And then I screamed again, for there was no blood, and Sir Waverley was not dead. He glanced down with interest at the axe, which stuck quivering from his breast, and then looked up again at Ulla and said, 'You simply can't find the staff nowadays.'

Ulla was not disheartened. She removed her mob cap and withdrew from the coils of her purple hair a suspiciously long and pointy hairpin, which she flourished like a dagger. 'Have a care, sir,' she declared. 'I must inform you that I am an agent of the British Secret Service!'

'Oh, goodie!' I exclaimed, for this surprising piece of news cheered me no end.

Sir Waverley, however, seemed unimpressed. He smiled the strange, false smile which I had seen at dinner. 'I serve an older and a greater empire than yours,' he said. He stepped into the room, and gestured to the stone plaques or tablets on the walls. 'Do you see that one? It was unearthed in one of the ruined cities of your people. The one beside it comes from the moon Callisto, from a temple which fell into ruin long before human beings walked upon the Earth. That one was excavated from the sands of dead Mercury. The fourth comes from the Earth, where it was dug up by workmen laying the foundations for the new Houses of Parliament. It was said to be part of a Druid temple, but of course it is far older. It comes from a time when people still recalled the dominion of the First Ones.'

Ulla and I both stood and watched him as he spoke, and as we watched we became aware of the huge shape of Mr Webster filling the doorway. The enormous spider moved sluggishly, and his breath came in gasps, as if it were a strain for him to creep about in Mars's gravity, which I found agreeably gentle. He was still monstrous and appalling though, and his cluster of eyes glittered with a terrible intelligence as he peered in at us.

'And now,' said Sir Waverley, turning to us again, 'you are of no more use. You may die knowing that both your races will soon be as dead as you. Soon the First Ones will rule again.'

Ulla raised her hairpin, grasping it like an assassin's stiletto. Sir Waverley lifted his empty hand and reached towards her, and quite suddenly his arm seemed to extend like a telescope. His hand shot across the room on the end of a shining tube of metal segments, and closed upon poor Ulla's throat. She dropped the hairpin and struggled to prise his fingers away, her face turning dark as he began choking the life out of her.

'No!' I begged. 'Please spare her!' But the ruthless villain only tightened his grip, and his other hand shot out towards me, propelled upon a similar device. I ducked, and the white glove clutched at empty air, making a sound like snapping scissors. Yet even then I did not swoon. Does this mean I have not been properly brought up? I am quite sure it would have been the ladylike thing to do.

If only Jack Havock were here! I thought, and wondered what he would do were he to be faced with such a predicament. The answer, I decided, was that he would *act*. And so I hurled myself at Sir Waverley. I had no plan in mind, but I succeeded in throwing him off balance. He pitched backwards, his flailing arm clutched me as we fell, and glass shattered as the window gave way beneath our combined weight.

We fell perhaps thirty feet on to a terrace overlooking the lawns and the dismal levels of Stonemere. Sir Waverley fell first, with the full weight of myself and Ulla coming down on top of him. I felt a horrid crunch; a sound of ribs giving way beneath me, as if I had landed on a wicker laundry hamper. I was unhurt, but all at once I found myself enveloped in clouds of acrid, greenish vapour. I scrambled backwards, tearing away Sir Waverley's hand, which felt limp and lifeless now, flip-flopping at the end of its telescopic arm. Coughing at the noxious vapours, I dragged poor Ulla aside, and was glad to feel her stir slightly, and to realise that the Good Lord had preserved her from Sir Waverley's murderous attack.

Sir Waverley lay quite lifeless. I remember thinking, *I have killed the richest man in the Solar System, and I shall most certainly hang*. But as I stared down at his mangled corpse, thinking how terrible it was that I should have been brought to this, and wondering whether Papa and Arthur would come to visit me in prison, I began to understand that Sir Waverley Rain had not been a man at all. For the clouds of green vapour were thinning now, and through the rents and gashes in his broken body I could see the gleam of wires and tubes and gutta-percha air hoses and other things I

cannot name but which were
quite unmistakably the work
of a mortal designer.

'Why!' I declared. 'He is
nothing but an automaton!'

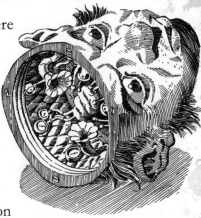

At which moment, rather
horribly, the top of his head
unscrewed like the lid of a jar
and dropped with a thump upon
the flagstones. Out from inside his skull came creeping a
white, fat-bodied spider, coughing just as much as me at the
green smoke. It wore goggles, and as it scuttled clear I
glimpsed the upholstered saddle inside his lordship's head,
and the bank of wheels and steering levers with which the
unspeakable creature must have controlled that mechanical
body.

Then, like a crashed aether-ship in a melodrama, the
body exploded, showering little cogwheels and fragments
across the terrace and knocking the spider-
helmsman off its feet.

The spider cried out in a shrill
scratchy voice, 'Mr Webster!'

I had forgot the other brute, and all his

lordship's cactus-servants. I could only stare upwards in horror as the giant white spider let itself down on a rope of thread from the shattered window and began to creep towards me. Fortunately, my Martian companion had recovered enough to see the danger. She took my hand again and we ran together across the lawn and into the shadow of the copper beeches. There we paused to catch our breath and gather our scattered wits. Oh, how my heart pounded! How I shook! And how I wished that J. H. were there with his elephant gun to save me!

I believe I really might have swooned then, had not Ulla distracted me by suddenly putting both hands to the waistband of her dress and *ripping off her skirts!* 'It will be easier to run like this,' she explained, stepping out of both skirts and petticoat and standing there quite shamelessly in nothing but a pair of frilly white drawers so skimpy that they ended halfway down her shins, leaving her ankles exposed! She looked expectantly at me, and I believe she seriously intended that I should take the same step! Naturally, I pretended not to understand her. I was quite relieved when we heard the heavy footfalls of cactus-men approaching our hiding place. Forgetting her strange notions about rational dress, Ulla grabbed my hand and began to hurry me away down the long slope of the lawn towards the lake.

We were on the wrong side of the island to make use of the bridge, and anyway it would doubtless have been guarded by more of Sir Waverley's fearsome cacti. 'We must go across Stonemere!' whispered Ulla.

I hesitated, for there was a notice near the lawn's edge which read quite plainly **KEEP OFF THE LAKE**, and a well-brought-up young lady does not stoop to trespass. However, I decided that desperate times require desperate measures, and hitching up my skirts, I set out after my Martian friend across the stony surface of the mere. The plates and crumbs of rock that formed its crust ground one against another with the most dolorous noises, and sometimes one would tilt sharply, threatening to plunge us to a ghastly fate in the morass of liquid stone which lay beneath. But when I glanced back at the shore we had left I saw the monstrous white spider creeping to and fro, as if uncertain whether the surface would support his weight, and I knew that we must not turn back.

Then I glanced ahead, towards the farther shore, and saw that we could not go on either, for from among the rocks and tangles of Martian knotweed which fringed the lake's edge yet more cactus-men were rising. They seemed to be growing there, sprouting arms and heads as we watched, and when each one reached man height it would tug itself free of the ground and start lurching down on to the lake. Some slipped clumsily between two plates of stone-crust and were lost in the molten stuff beneath, their struggles made more terrible by the fact that they were entirely silent. Yet there were always others growing to take the place of those who perished, and soon an army of the spiky monsters was creeping towards us.

I looked at Ulla, hoping that she would produce another sword or halberd and prune these vicious vegetables just as she had their comrades inside the house. But the Martian was weaponless, and still weak from her travails. She clutched her bruised throat, and her every breath rasped painfully. The cactus-men were almost upon us, and the slab of crust we were balanced on was far from stable. I realised that I could do nothing but consign myself into the safe keeping of the Good Lord, who watches over all of us. Kneeling, and taking the hand of my startled Martian sister, I began to sing. '*He who would valiant be . . .*'

Ulla tugged urgently at my hand. I thought she was objecting to my hymn. Then I saw what she was trying to show me. At the first sound of my voice the approaching cacti had paused in their advance. They came on again when I paused, but as soon as I sang the next line they hung back again, raising their prickly paws towards their heads as if in pain.

'They cannot stand the noise!' said my companion. 'Keep making the noise!'

'It is not noise, it is one of our fine old English hymns,' I protested, but as soon as I stopped singing the cactus creatures surged forwards again, so I hastily added, '*Let him in constancy/Follow the master,*' et cetera. Truly, John Bunyan would have been proud to see the way that his words drove back the devilish brood who had been crowding so close to us! When Ulla joined in, singing weakly along with me as I arrived at that wonderful phrase, '*There's no discouragement/Shall make him once relent/His first avow'd intent/To be a pilgrim*' several of the thorny thugs actually hurled themselves into the depths rather than listen to us any more!

Hand in hand, still singing lustily, we walked swiftly across the remainder of the lake and reached the shore without further upset.

(Note to self: in retrospect, it occurs to me that – strange though this may seem – it may not have been the rousing

Christian sentiments of the hymn that distressed our attackers so much as *the sound of my voice*. I must ensure that Art never comes to hear of this, for he would be sure to tease me about it in his usual childish manner.)

We stumbled up the shore, leaving Stonemere and its gloomy grange behind us, and as we went I sang 'Jerusalem' and 'Rule Britannia' and then started all over again on 'To Be a Pilgrim'. But in the dry air my voice quickly faltered, and poor Ulla's had never been much more than a whisper to start with. The cacti, who had been following us at a distance, began to gather their courage and close in, waiting for the moment when my voice failed altogether.

I managed another two verses before I broke down, coughing. One of the cacti, a great tall fellow with white flowers sprouting all over his head, came loping forwards, stretching out his sharp paws to snatch me. But just before he reached me something huge and dark rose up behind him in the moonlight, there was a flash of metal, and he came in half, drenching me with gouts of sticky green sap and quite spoiling my dress. 'Oh!' I cried indignantly, and, 'Whatever now?'

A great deal of dust was being kicked up as the panicking cacti turned this way and that. As if through a veil I saw great, dim shapes circling us – blunt heads and segmented bodies, plump and leathery as antique armchairs. I knew what they were, of course; I am not entirely ignorant, whatever Art may say. We were surrounded by a herd of Martian worms.* High on their backs in paper

*Your Martian worm is a maggoty looking fellow about the size of a first-class railway carriage. Apparently the Martians who ride them can tell one end from the other, but I doubt anyone else can. They have a great number of small legs underneath, like a caterpillar, and like caterpillars they are the larval stage of a quite different creature. After living about one hundred years they dig themselves a burrow in the sand, wrap a silk cocoon about themselves, and emerge six months later as dull brown moths no bigger than pocket handkerchiefs, which flap about for a single day, then drop down dead. Isn't Nature wonderful? – A. M.

howdahs naked Martians rode, hurling down half-moon-shaped blades which whirred and sliced, cutting through cactus flesh like butter. Within a minute all the cactus-men had been hacked down, and their severed bits and pieces lay about on the sand, twitching and fidgeting and putting down roots.

'Don't worry!' called a friendly, English voice, and I jumped back as one of the towering worms slithered to a halt beside me. 'It will take many hours before they grow again.'

'Richard!' gasped Ulla, raising a hand in greeting, and the worm's rider jumped down, grinning broadly at us. Behind him, others of his band were leaping from their mounts and hurrying to our aid. They were young gentleman Martians, for the most part, and I ashamed to say that apart from a few barbaric necklaces of metal scales they were all stark naked.

At the sight of them, my delicate girlish constitution overcame me at last, and finally, thankfully, I fainted.

CHAPTER TWELVE

LEAVING MYRTLE UNCONSCIOUS UPON THE RED PLANET,
WE RETURN TO THE NARRATIVE OF HER HEROIC YOUNGER
BROTHER, IN THE COURSE OF WHICH THE FREE-PORT OF
PH'ARHPUU'XXTPLLSPRNGG IS DESCRIBED, AND
JACK HAVOCK AND I MAKE OUR DESCENT INTO
THE WIND-RACE.

P h'Ahrpuu'xxtpllsprngg, or 'Farpoo' as our jolly
British aethernauts prefer to call it, is the capital of
Io, and has been a harbour town for ten thousand
years. Back in the days when Pharaoh was being so beastly

to the Israelites the old city was welcoming the trade ships of the lost Martian empire, and now they welcome ours. In the centuries between, the Ionians quietly minded their own business, trading with their neighbours. For the moons of Jupiter form a little model planetary system of their own, with Jupiter as their sun, as if God tried out his craftsmanship here in miniature before he set to work on the rest of our solar realm. On all those little worlds there is life and intelligence of some kind, and the people who live there have been so content to deal with one another that they never bothered trying to buy or build an engine which would carry their little brass saucer-ships across the wilds of space to trade with Earth and the other great planets.

Farpoo is the crossroads and marketplace for traders from all these moons, and over the centuries it has grown and grown, sprawling outwards until it now covers almost the whole of Io's surface. A single city wrapped around a world! Its lamps glint and shimmer in the darkness off the shoulder of Jupiter, and for thousands of miles around it the aether is filled with the lights of ships coming and going, or waiting off one of its thousand harbours for a berth. Most are system ships: small trading vessels from Jupiter's other moons, bringing in cargoes to sell in one of Farpoo's vast and busy marketplaces.*

They are peaceable worlds, these satellites of Jupiter, but it was not always so. Back in old Pharaoh's time the peoples of the various moons and moonlets fought fierce wars against each other, and statues of generals and captains in elaborate uniforms still speckle the streets of Farpoo, looking like overdressed shoppers who have turned to stone while waiting for an omnibus. But the Jovian's fighting all came to an end with the Spore Wars (circa 5000 BC). Certain plants in the Jovian regions produce *ideospores* which can affect the minds of thinking creatures, persuading them to grow more of said plant, or not to eat it. Clever Jovian weapons botanists learned how to breed ideospores which would infect anyone who breathed them in with a particular notion. So an Ionian general might bombard the armies of Europa with the idea that they should all throw down their weapons and start doing folk dances, or a Pogglite chief fill

---

*These are the lights which so perplexed Signor Galileo when he turned his telescope on Jupiter's moons, and led him to develop his theory that the worlds beyond Earth were full of life. This got him into terrible hot water with the Pope, as every schoolboy knows.

the heads of the Callistan snail cavalry with
the sudden compulsion to ride over the
nearest cliff.

Then the King of Chumbley,
a small and rather unregarded
moon, developed a spore
which was meant to make all
the other moons lose
interest in the whole
concept of war, so that his
tiny space armada could
conquer them all. It worked like
a charm, but unhappily for the
Chumbleyites their spores blew
back to fill their own heads with the same peaceful ideas,
and so the art of war was lost for ever among the moons of
Jupiter. (That, of course, made things nice and simple for
Sir Arthur Welseley when he breezed in with a fleet of
aether-ships in 1806 and declared the entire Jovian system a
British Protectorate. Huzzah!)

The dread spore-cannon still exist on Io, but these days
they are mainly used by commercial gentlemen to advertise
their wares. Several spore-balls burst softly against the

Sophronia's planking as we swept low over the roofs of Farpoo, and by the time we touched down our heads were filled with the ideas that we should not WALK but *RUN* to **PHENUGREEK'S GAS-TEA EMPORIUM**, try a bowl of sizzling Sprune at the **CAFÉ JUPE**, holiday on the leisure-rafts of **EXOTIC GANYMEDE** and be sure not to miss the latest instalment of Mr Dickens' new story in *HOUSEHOLD WORDS*. But luckily the Jovian spores do not affect the human brain very strongly, and the sights, sounds and smells of the huge city soon drove all these curious notions from my head.*

We set the *Sophronia* down at an out-of-the-way shipyard run by a Scotsman named McCallum, who seemed well used to dealing with pirates, smugglers and other ne'er-do-wells. He did not ask our business, simply pocketed the bag of gold Jack passed him and gave us a sly wink, tapping one grimy finger against the side of his nose. Then, as his crew set to work mending the *Sophronia*'s poor battered hull, we

---

*Some natural philosophers, however, have claimed that it is spores from the Jovian moons, drifting across the aether, which are responsible for the peculiar fads and crazes which sweep our own world from time to time. And indeed what other rational explanation can there be for the popularity of check trousers, or ballet?

gathered up our things and prepared to set off into the city.

Ssilissa surprised us all by stepping ashore dressed in one of the pretty crinolines she had stolen. I suppose when she drew Myrtle aside back in New Scunthorpe she had been asking her advice on how such a garment should be worn. Nor did her transformation end with the dress. She had drawn back the spines on her head into a sort of bun and fastened them with a silver clasp. I even thought she had put on rouge, until I realised that the deep mauve blotches on her face were blushes. They grew deeper still as her shipmates turned to goggle and laugh at her.

'Heavens, Ssill,' said Jack. 'What spore got into your head to make you put *those* on?'

'Good thing we didn't a get a dose of it,' chuckled

Nipper, whose laughter sounded like some thick liquid simmering in a tub. He had regrown his severed eye-stalk during our journey from Venus, and the new eye shone with mirth along with all the rest as he contemplated Ssil's unlikely get-up. 'That fashion wouldn't suit me one bit!'

No more did it suit Ssil, poor thing. I had never noticed quite how strange her long, blue body was until I saw it crammed into human clothes. Being a type of lizard she had no bosom at all, and her tail made the back of her skirts stick out in a most undignified way. But she tilted her head and swept past us with a haughty look, doing her best to ignore the laughter.

We followed her out of the dock, pursued by the heartening sounds of hammers and wood saws as Mr McCallum's shipwrights set to work upon *Sophronia*. I had been missing Myrtle quite desperately until then – which is ironical, when you consider how often I had wished she would disappear – but the great joke of Ssilissa's outfit had lightened Jack's dark mood, and made the others happy, and I soon started to feel happy too. Anyway, Farpoo was not Myrtle's sort of place at all.

In the street outside the shipyard we all stopped and

stood and craned our necks, looking up at the sky where we would soon be travelling. The sky above Farpoo is striped like a stocking, with vast bands of orange and ochre and Indian red and puce and curdled cream, and it has a curious, curving-away-at-the-edges look about it, which makes you realise, when you have gawped at it a while, that it is not really sky at all, just the mighty face of Jupiter, which hangs in space so close to Io that it blots out all else.

'There's old Thunderhead,' said Mr Munkulus, pointing with a couple of his hands to an oval of muddy red that seemed to stare down at us out of the cloud bands like an angry eye. I could see it spinning, trailing flags and scarfs of paler cloud, and little stormlets budding off its outer edges to fall behind, spinning and shimmying in its wake. They looked small from this distance, but of course I knew that even those hatchling storms are as large as the whole Earth, and Thunderhead is bigger yet; the greatest of all the eddies which swirl in the wind-race of Jupiter; the storm which has blown for ten thousand years.

'How do we reach him?' I asked.

'Pressure-ship,' said Jack, quite nonchalantly. 'I know of a man.'

We set off through the hum and bustle of the city, all in

a line, and you may be sure I never let the others out of my sight, for fear I might lose them for ever in the crowds. We wound our way through a labyrinth of crooked alleys, past the paper cottages of Martians and the mudbrick towers of Ionian breeding clans, the nest shops of Woopsies and the spice-scented warehouses of Dutch and Chinese merchants. We were spattered with bluish mud by passing carriages and rickshaws, and jostled by passers-by of every race, each intent upon his own business and not one sparing us a glance. We craned our necks and eye-stalks to peer up at teetering, ramshackle buildings, so tall that the streets between them lay in perpetual shadow and had to be lit by crystal globes filled with phosphorescent glow-fish. Hibernating billipedes had stretched themselves across the gaps between the houses, and the householders had pegged out their wet linen on them

I was lost within a minute, and by the time we had gone three hundred yards I would not have been able to find my way back to McCallum's yard if you had paid me. But Jack knew where he was going. He led us to the bank of a slow-flowing river, whose surface shone like liquid lead in the dun light from Jupiter, and we crossed it in a ferry pulled by a huge sea monster called a Bluurg. Nipper told me that these amiable creatures come from his own home oceans on Ganymede, but that they love company, and may be found acting as boatmen on all the worlds of Jove. By way of payment, they ask only for their passengers to scratch their hide with long wooden back-scratchers.

Reaching the far shore, we turned along a narrow street where raucous drinking songs echoed from the mouths of a line of taverns made from enormous, hollowed-out gourds. Jack led us to one called the Grudge and Gastropod. Never having been inside such an establishment before, I stared about me with great interest at the drunks of various species propped against the bar, the shady-looking gents playing poker and pharo, the small crowd gathered about the jangling piano and the six-armed serving girls who darted about among it all delivering jugs of foaming Ionian spit-beer to each busy, greasy table. Jack had a word with one of them, and she smiled at him and used her antennae to point him towards a distant, deeply shadowed corner. There, in a little cubicle filled with fug and smoke, we met the man whom Jack hoped would carry us into the dreadful winds of Jupiter's upper sky, where no ordinary ship can hope to fly.

His name was Captain Snifter Gruel. In his youth he'd

been a harpoonist aboard some of the first whalers to venture down into Jupiter's wind-race, and he had left all sorts of bits of himself behind aboard splintered boats and in the guts of wind-whales. He had one button-bright eye (the other was covered with a patch), one hand (a hook took the place of its twin) and one leg (the missing one having been replaced with an iron peg). 'I'm only half the man I used to be!' he said cheerfully. But he seemed active and vital despite these injuries, and his mind was whole; a shrewd, quick, nimble mind that could steer a pressure-ship through all the rapids and lightning reefs of the Jovian sky, and name a good price for doing it.

'A hundred pound,' he said, when Jack told him we were hoping to pay a call on Thunderhead. 'That'll get you there, but I can't promise he'll talk to you. He's a strange old cove. There's them as he likes, and them as he don't, and if he don't then you might as well talk to the wind.'

Grindle grumbled at the asking price, but Jack hushed him with a stern look. Mr Munkulus leaned in close to mutter, 'You sure about this, Jack? I know this Gruel by reputation. You're letting your heart do the thinking –'

Jack cut him short. 'I don't pay no heed to rumours, Munk, and nor should you,' he said, and lobbed a bag of gold across the table. 'I believe Captain Gruel's honest as the day is long.'

None of us liked to remind him the days on Io are not very long at all.

We settled our arrangements with the captain, then went back outside into the blue mud and the curious, seaweedy smell of the Ionian air. We stopped to eat at a pavement café, and then Jack sent everyone but me back to the *Sophronia*. Before they went he threw a few silver coins to Mr Munkulus and said, 'Pick up a flock of hoverhogs at the market behind McCallum's place.'

'Hoverhogs, Captain?' asked Mr Munkulus, his broad face creasing in a frown as he tried to divine Jack's purpose. 'We never bothered with hoverhogs aboard *Sophronia* before.'

'That's why she looks like a sty,' Jack shot back. 'I mean to keep her good and tidy from now on. Art and me are going to ask old Thunderhead about these spiders, and if he can tell us which world they hail from we'll be flying there to fetch Miss Mumby. I want the *Sophronia* looking clean and shipshape for her when she comes back aboard.'

The crew just stood and gaped at him. They probably thought he had inhaled some advertising spores, but I guessed that he was simply plotting to annoy my sister by showing her that he could be just as neat as she. It was encouraging to see that he was so confident of finding her again.

Ssilissa seemed worried about his plan of entering the wind-race with none but me for company. 'I should come with you, Jack,' she said. 'I don't trusss that Gruel fellow. If sssomething goes wrong down in those cloudsss there will be nothing we can do to help.'

Jack shook his head. 'I'll need you here, Ssil,' he said. 'If we don't come back it'll be up to you to get the *Sophronia* safe away, and look out for the others. But we will come back, of course,' he went on hastily, glancing at me as if he was afraid he had alarmed me (which he had). 'Back by nightfall, with word of those spiders. So the rest of you head home to the ship, and make sure McCallum's people aren't stealing all her fittings.'

Our friends wished us fare-thee-well and turned back towards McCallum's yard, quite happy that Jack was not asking them to risk their necks in the wind-race. I think Grindle and Mr Munkulus were planning to stop off at a few taverns on their way, as well. But Ssilissa stood watching us as we walked towards Gruel's pressure-ship projector. She was still watching as we turned the corner and the long paper porch of a Martian boarding house hid her from view. I suddenly realised that she was in love with Jack, and it made me feel so sad I could have blubbed. It must be quite lonely enough to have hatched from a mysterious space egg and be the only creature of your kind in the known aether; how much lonelier to love someone of a different species, to whom you are just a blue lizard. I thought I understood why Ssil had dressed herself up so outlandishly. It was not the influence of some passing spore, simply an attempt to make Jack notice her.

I resolved to be very kind to poor Ssil, if I lived to return to the *Sophronia*.

→ ·←

There was no mistaking Captain Gruel's ship. The entrance to its projector tower was hung about with colourful signboards declaring **THE CELEBRATED PRESSURE-SHIP** *UNCRUSHABLE* **– SAFEST ON IO – PLEASURE TRIPS INTO THE WIND-RACE – SEE FOR YOURSELF THE INFAMOUS PLANET OF STORMS! NEVER YET SQUASHED!** There were pictures too, of the vast wind-whales and sky-squid and other quaint airborne creatures which inhabit the outward fringes of Jupiter's deep sky.

We announced ourselves to the Ionian on duty at the gate, and he rumbled that Captain Gruel was expecting us and waved us through the creaky turnstile. I followed Jack up perhaps a thousand ringing iron steps, until we could see the gambrel roofs and chimney stacks of Farpoo covering the whole world beneath us and curving away over the horizon, black against the amber face of Jupiter. Inside the tower of scaffolding and girders the *Uncrushable* hung, suspended from thick chains above the muzzle of her launching gun. Like all the best pressure-ships she had been made of stone, from a captured meteor hollowed out and fitted with alchemical rocket engines and thick portholes. We crossed a swaying bridge to go aboard.

Captain Gruel met us at the hatchway and welcomed us inside. He was keen to show off his little ship. He banged

Inside the tower of scaffolding and girders the Uncrushable *hung, suspended from thick chains above the muzzle of her launching gun.*

his iron hook against the inside of her stony hull and said, 'Six yards thick! She'll drop deeper into old Jove's atmosphere than any other boat in Farpoo.' He rapped his knuckles against the porthole glass. 'Six yards thick! Top quality crystal, grown specially in the Martian window farms.'

I put my face to the glass and looked out, and it was like looking through nothing; the skies of Farpoo lay outside, busy with carrier-pterosaurs and air-phaetons, and there was not so much as a single flaw or ripple to tell me that I was watching them through eighteen foot of crystal.

'She's a good ship,' admitted Jack.

'Best ship, best crew,' said Gruel smugly. 'You won't regret shipping out with us, young Captain Jack.'

We strapped ourselves into the big, thickly upholstered seats in the centre of the cabin, while Captain Gruel stomped about shouting orders to his crew. They weren't humans, but things called Dweebs, who came from some moonlet I'd not heard of. They were balls of matted ginger hair from which muscular blue-grey arms would suddenly shoot out to pull a lever or slam a bulkhead door. As the *Uncrushable* was lowered slowly down the throat of her great launching cannon, I amused myself by trying to calculate how many of these arms they each had, but I lost count at seventeen.

The pressure-ship thrummed and clanged, settling itself on to the great gunpowder charge which would soon send it hurtling like an artillery shell into the sky. I began to wonder if there was time to change our minds, and whether, if we did, Captain Gruel would give Jack a partial refund on our fare. Jack sensed my qualms and smiled at me. 'It will be all right, Art. And old Thunderhead will know something of those spiders, I'm sure. We'll soon have your sister back.'

I was about to tell him that it was myself I was worried about, not poor Myrtle, but at that instant the launching cannon went off, and I was unable to say anything, or speak, or move for several minutes thereafter.

I wonder if you have ever been fired out of a giant howitzer in a hollowed-out rock? The feeling is somewhat akin to being sat upon by an elephant, while travelling downhill at speed in a tin dustbin. There is a terrible crushing sensation, which is combined with a degree of juddering and shuddering and rolling and tipping and tumbling. Happily, Captain Gruel had a flock of hoverhogs aboard to clean up all the sick.

By the time the worst sensations had abated (or we had grown used to them enough to think and speak again) the sulphurous orange light of Jupiter was shining in brightly through the portholes, and I realised that we had ripped our way out of Io's atmosphere and were crossing the sea of space which separates her from her mother-planet. Captain Gruel anchored himself to the deck with a cunning magnet built into the end of his peg-leg, and bellowed orders at his hairy crew in pidgin Dweeb. They fired the *Uncrushable*'s rockets, and the pressure-ship tore onwards, scattering vast shoals of Icthyomorphs and tearing through drifts of aether-weed, for the heavens around Jupiter teem with life.

Within a few hours we were plunging into the thin outer clouds of the storm-planet itself.

Jupiter's sky is a million miles deep, and what lies beneath it no mortal knows. Some people say that there is rock down there; some reckon the pressure is so great that the clouds themselves are squeezed into a hot, hard world. Mrs Abishag Chough, Deaconess of the Church of the Lunar Revelations, claimed that Heaven itself lies at the heart of the great world's cloud mass, and jumped out of the pressure-ship *Ganges* in 1836 to try and prove it, but she was never seen again. Since no ship has ever gone deeper than ten thousand miles without being squashed as flat as a lead soldier, nobody can say whose theory is correct.

Luckily for us, Thunderhead keeps to the outer levels, zooming along in the high-level winds. Once we had entered the right wind band Captain Gruel began firing more rockets, steering us into the huge storm's path, while one of the Dweebs popped a set of headphones over what I suppose must have been his head and commenced tapping out a message on the *Uncrushable*'s telegraph machine.

'What is he doing?' I asked. 'Surely Thunderhead cannot have a telegraph receiver? The cables would never withstand all this jostling and ballyhoo . . . '

Captain Gruel chuckled, and translated the innocent question for his shipmates, who all laughed too. 'Bless you, lad,' he said, wiping tears of mirth away with the tip of his hook. 'We don't use cables in the wind-race. Pulses of electro-magnetical fluid carry our messages about. And old Thunderhead needs no receiver to pick 'em up, neither. Why, he is made of electro-magnetical pulsations himself, or at least the *thinking* part of him is.'

He paused, listening, as his crew-thing turned to twitter at him. 'Aha! We've caught him in a biddable mood, lads! He's prepared to talk to you. Come, come, and you may have a look at him while the lads take us in.'

He rolled back the carpet and opened a trapdoor in the metal floor, showing us down a ladder into a little compartment where one wall was made up almost entirely of a huge lens of the thick Martian crystal. Through this window Jack and I could see the sky ahead of the ship, and we both cried out in terror, for it was filled with one vast, slowly turning wheel of cloud: red and orange and brown and bruised purple, flashing and fluttering with busy lightnings.

'Handsome brute, ain't he?' said Captain Gruel, with a

proprietorial air. 'Sorry about the paint on the floor down here, by the way. I had an artist chap as passenger a few seasons back. A Mr Turner by name. He would keep splashing and daubing and dashing away, no matter how rough the weather grew. Didn't care much for his pictures myself. A child could have done better.'

Neither Jack nor I paid the least heed to his babbling. We were intent upon Thunderhead. The approaching storm was like a world in its own right, complete with continents and chasms and towering mountain ranges all of cloud, and the lightning pouring in rivers between them. Far off, a pair of sky-squid circled, looking out for prey, ooshing themselves through the atmosphere with pulses of their mile-long tentacles. They looked smaller than fleas against the bulk of Thunderhead.

'B—— H—!' murmured Jack, and although I know that it is very wicked to curse I could not help but agree with him, for before our astonished eyes a great tentacle of vapour was reaching up towards us from the storm's heart. It was a tornado, and a hole the size of the Americas yawned open at its tip, swallowing our tiny ship into a tunnel whose walls were whorls of whirling, roiling cloud.

CHAPTER THIRTEEN

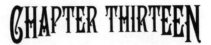

INTERESTING FLORA & FAUNA

Jovian Wind-Whales

№ 7

In Which I Make Conversation with the Great Storm.

Shuddering and groaning, with rivets popping from her moaning metal decks, the *Uncrushable* went whirling down that cloudy throat into the heart of the ancient storm. Hailstones hummed past, even the smallest of them much larger than the ship, but none struck us. Was Thunderhead controlling their flight just as he was guiding ours, making minute adjustments to his internal pressure fronts and wind speeds to ensure we were not wrecked? I hoped so, but I could not put my hope into words; I just clung to Jack and went, 'Oh! Oh! Oh! Oh!'

And then, all of a sudden, the noise and shaking ceased. The *Uncrushable* had flown out into what was, I suppose, the eye of the storm: a worlds-wide cavern of calmer air, where the clouds turned in a slow and stately dance quite different to the violent revolutions we had just been flung through. There appeared to be structures here: arches and pillars of vapour braided into a form of net, all veined with crawling lightnings, blue and white. We were far from the light of sun or star by then, and these electric fires were the sole source of illumination, a crackly, gothick glare that made Jack and I look like phantoms.

A pillar of cloud, boiling up from the depths, formed itself into a flat, white plateau ahead of the ship, and drifting balls of fire as big as moons ignited in the air above it. The *Uncrushable* steered towards it, and we all stumbled as she set down.

'We have landed!' cried Jack. 'But how can we land upon a cloud?'

'Old Thunderhead has ways and means,' said Captain Gruel. 'He can alter the pressure in here, change the make-up of the air, do what he pleases. This is what we call the trading floor. Merchants come from the outer world to buy samples of the strange gases he brews up down inside himself, and in return he likes them to talk to him, tell him things. Care to step out and have a word?'

I had thought till then that we would have to converse with Thunderhead the same way Captain Gruel's crewman had, by tapping out messages upon the telegraph machine. It seemed I was wrong. I was very, very glad that Jack was with me, but even he looked apprehensive as the *Uncrushable*'s gangplank was run out and we walked down it into a sculpted fairyland of cloud which Thunderhead had prepared for us.

It was beautiful. Snow was falling all about us, but none of it settled upon us. All around the careful winds shaped strands of vapour into fluted columns and archways and pillars, but no wind stirred our hair. Above our heads the fire-moons drifted, crackling faintly and washing us in their white light until we each walked at the centre of a star of a dozen shadows, but no fire touched us. And beneath our feet the solid cloud was soft and gently yielding, like a raft of cotton wool a-swim upon a lake of soup.

Out of the lightning-scribbled dark, high, high, high above, the sound of thunder rolled and rumbled, forming into words.

'*Small beings,*' it said. '*Why have you come?*'

Why *had* we come? I was so filled up with awe that I had almost forgot, but Jack still had his wits about him. He said, 'If you please, sir, we'd like to know about the white spiders. 'Bout where they've taken Myrtle Mumby. She's Art's sister, you see, and my . . . well, my . . .'

'They took my father too,' I said, finding my voice at last.

The thunder crashed, the lightning crackled all around us, forming into the shapes of dancing spiders. '*I am old,*' boomed the storm. '*I have blown for many of your lifetimes. I cannot leave my sky, but travellers come to me from beyond it, and tell me tales, and I remember them . . .*' Deep among the folded clouds tall flares of lightning ignited one by one, like memories sparking. '*It is a long time since anyone has come to me with stories of the white spiders.*'

'Then you have heard of them?' cried Jack and I together.

The thunder said, '*I am old. But they are older still. Older than all the worlds of the Sun. Once all this was theirs. Now they live in only one place, weaving their webs among the rings of stone and ice. They have lain quiet for a long time. Now you small beings have roused them again.*'

A branch of lightning reached down and touched my

chest. It did not hurt, but made me yelp with fear. I looked at Jack, wondering if the lightning would touch him too, but he was just staring at me. I felt electricity scrambling up and down the ladders of my nerves, probing the crannies of my brain. After a moment it withdrew, leaving me gasping, my heart hammering, and a taste of metal in my mouth.

'*You are Shaper kin,*' the storm said.

'No,' said I. 'I'm Arthur Mumby. M-U-M-B-Y.'

'*I knew your mother,*' said the storm.

'I beg your pardon?' I asked weakly.

'*I have spoken often with her, in the time-that-is-past. I hope that we shall speak again in the time-that-is-to-come. She was a wise and kind small being, and she told me many interesting things.*'

I looked at Jack, helpless. 'There has been a mistake, your worship,' I explained. 'My mother was Mrs Amelia Mumby of Larklight. She –'

'*Larklight!*' the storm thundered, as if that name reminded it of something. I had the impression that it was not the least bit interested in anything else I might have to say. '*You must keep the key safe. The spiders desire the Lamp of Dawn for themselves, but they must not have it.*'

'The lamp of *what*?' I said. 'What key?'

'And Myrtle?' asked Jack. 'Have you heard anything of

Myrtle? Art's sister, taken by the spiders . . .'

Lightning flicked and juddered, throwing our stuttering shadows across the cloud. The clouds above us seemed to convulse, as if in pain. Thunder drummed, but it was only thunder now. I looked to Jack for comfort, as usual, but he appeared as dumbstruck as I by these new developments. We both clamped our hands over our ears as they began to pop and ache with sudden changes of pressure, and my stomach writhed; I felt suddenly aware again that we were standing on a cloud, at the heart of a great vault of cloud. Apart from the *Uncrushable*, which rested twenty yards away like a speck of grit upon a large meringue, there was nothing solid for thousands of miles around.

Suddenly the thunder formed words again. '*Leave now, small beings. There is . . .*' And then just a long, bumbling crash that might have been, '*Danger!*'

We turned, Jack Havock and I, and began to race back towards the safety of the pressure-ship. The cloud country was starting to come apart as fierce gales tugged at the arches and pillars, tearing them down as easily as you or I might tear off handfuls of candyfloss or tufts of thistledown. Snow whirled giddily about us, and freezing rain stung our faces. I looked up, and wished I hadn't, for it gave me a nauseous, falling feeling, as if I had looked into an abyss. A chasm had opened in the vaults of cloud above our heads, and far, far up something black moved; too big to be a ship or an animal; so big that it could only be another of Jupiter's great storms. Flashes of lightning burst from it, and were met by other flashes which leaped from the clouds of Thunderhead, so that for a moment I was reminded of two antique men-o'-war hammering each other with broadsides of cannon fire.

On the *Uncrushable*'s gangplank Captain Gruel stood waiting, one hand outstretched towards us. I remember thinking what a loyal friend he was to linger in that awful place until we could climb aboard. Then Jack Havock shouted a curse and slithered to a halt in the cloud-tops just ahead of me, and I realised that in the captain's hand there was a pistol.

'Give me the key!' he shouted, over the howling of the wind. 'I heard what the old storm said! You've got a key and the spiders want it. Give it me!'

'But I haven't any key!' I said. 'The storm has it wrong!'

'Thunderhead's never wrong,' growled Gruel, advancing towards us with his pistol wavering from my face to Jack's and back again. 'I've heard whisperings about these spiders. They're strong, and growing stronger. Reckon they'd look kindly on me if I gave them this key they want.'

'But there *isn't* any key!' I wailed.

The pistol swung towards Jack again. 'What if I put a bullet in your friend here? Reckon that might jog your memory, little boy?'

A mint-green zigzag of lightning came down on him. The electric crackling muffled his shriek, and the flash of his exploding pistol was lost in the dazzle. Jack and I stumbled aside, rubbing our eyes till we could see again. By then, though, there was nothing left to see of Captain Gruel except a cloud of greasy smoke that thinned swiftly in the urgent wind.

'*Many small storm systems are attacking me,*' boomed Thunderhead. '*They are pups; young stormlets, only a few thousand years old. I believe they are acting on behalf of –*'

'The spiders!' cried Jack. He snatched my hand and we started to blunder towards the waiting pressure-ship, but the hairy Dweebs had seen their captain vaporised, and were in no mood to wait for us. The rocket engines roared, ripping steam out of the clouds ahead, and the *Uncrushable* jumped into the air and plunged upwards through a dark wing of cloud that was descending fast from overhead. Jack shook his fist after her, and shouted things that would have made Myrtle turn very red indeed had she been there to hear them. I was glad that she was not, for I was already considering our situation, and it seemed to me that, whatever my poor sister might be enduring at the hands of her spidery captors, it could not be half as bad as the fate which now awaited Jack and I.

The black wing tore. A shaft of dim, Jovian sunlight reached down into Thunderhead's heart, and dark specks showed in it like dust motes. A herd of panic-stricken wind-whales had been sucked inside the storm by the sudden pressure changes. Jack clutched at my arm and pointed. 'Look, Art! They're our way out!'

'They're miles away!' I protested. But although I did not see what help those far-off behemoths could be to us, neither could I see any *other* way out of our predicament. Poor Thunderhead was clearly hard-pressed, and could no longer sustain the pillar of solidified vapour upon which Jack and I were standing. Even the atmosphere was growing sulphurous, as hot air from the depths was sucked upwards past us. I held tightly to Jack's hand as the last island of firm cloud was whisked out from beneath us, leaving us to tumble free in that savage sky.

Down and down and down we fell, and up as well, and sideways, hurled this way and that by the hot gales that came battering at us out of chimneys of cloud. My hair was blown across my face, and one of my boots was torn off – if Myrtle had not been kidnapped by those spiders she would have made me double-knot the laces, and I should have it still. Naturally we shouted and wailed and flailed about, although we knew full well that there were no handholds we could hope to grab and cling to.

But gradually I came to understand that Thunderhead had not entirely forgotten us. He was too embattled to conjure up any more castles in the air for us to perch upon, but these whirling winds all had a purpose; he was wafting us towards that school of whales which we had glimpsed earlier.

I do not know how far we hurtled through that mad gavotte of clouds and lightning. It is difficult to judge scale or distance in a place where nothing is familiar, and everything is gigantic. Sometimes it seemed that the whales were close, and then they would be hidden momentarily behind some passing Matterhorn of cloud, and we would realise that they were much larger and much farther off than we had thought. But at last we began to hear their mooing songs blowing towards us on the wind. Soon we were close enough to smell them, and to spy the details of those gigantic, mottled bodies.

They aren't *very* like whales, those wind-whales of Jupiter. More like big, gas-filled jellyfish, but without so many tentacles. There were twelve in the school which we found ourselves plummeting towards: six calves, five cows and an old bull male, from whose scarred hide poked a veritable forest of broken harpoons. His broad mouth gaped at us like a railway tunnel, and for a moment I thought that Jack and I were to be swallowed whole like a couple of airborne Jonahs, but the winds whirled us past. The huge, dim windows of the whale's eye-cluster regarded us dolefully as we went by. Then we struck against his curved flank, bouncing and slithering over the rough, leathery hide. I lost my grip on Jack's hand, and grabbed at his leg instead, and Jack snatched hold of one of those rusting harpoons and brought us to a stop.

The wind wailed, and the wind-whales mooed, and the

thunder crashed. Sometimes it seemed to be forming words, but the gale carried them away before I could glean their meaning. I stared about me at the plain of mustard-coloured flesh which curved away in all directions, harpoons jutting out here and there like the stumps of blasted trees. 'Well, we cannot stay here,' I said.

Jack looked grim. 'I can think of no better place for the moment,' he confessed. 'If we fall too far we'll drop into the pressure-deep and be squashed like beetles. Our best hope is to stick with this beastie and hope we're sighted by another ship.'

Light broke over us. It was not lightning, but the thin Jovian

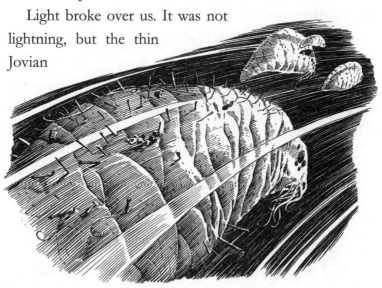

sunlight. Our whale had been flung out of Thunderhead's towering flank into clear sky, its lowing family tumbling and rolling in its wake. The wind blew us swiftly away from the great storm. Looking back, I saw clearly the smaller storms whirling at its edges, while lightning of every colour fizzed and crawled. I suppose they did not know that Jack and I were no longer within Thunderhead's cloudy halls, and even if they did perhaps there was no way for them to break off their attack. But I had no fear for Thunderhead, for he was so much greater than those little storms, and as I watched he tore one into whirling scraps of cloud which were absorbed into his own churning flank, and sent another spinning helplessly into a neighbouring airstream, where it was ripped quickly asunder by powerful winds.

Then an updraft lifted the whales into calmer air, and a pale yellow fog wrapped us round, veiling the remainder of the battle. Warm raindrops the size of hens' eggs bespattered Jack and me.

Creeping gingerly from one harpoon to the next we made our way down the wind-whale's back in search of shelter. After perhaps half an hour we saw ahead of us an ancient, rusting whaleboat which had become entangled in the lines of its own harpoons and caught fast. The hatches were open, so presumably the crew had escaped and we did not have to worry about any lingering ghosts as we heaved ourselves inside. We sat on the rusty thwarts and wondered what the future held, while the old boat shifted uneasily, tipping from side to side as the whale rode the wind-race. With each movement an empty rum bottle rolled to and fro across the bottom boards, reminding us that it was the most awfully long time since either one of us had drunk anything.

'Poor old Thunderhead,' I said, thinking of that sensible storm and wondering how it was faring down in the cloud wrack beneath us. 'Do you think it is because of us he was attacked?'

'A bit of a coincidence if it weren't,' said Jack. 'Those other storms showing up so soon after we did. I reckon those spiders of yours had a hand in it.'

'You mean a leg. They don't have hands. They're spiders.'

'I wonder what they promised those stormlets to make 'em attack old Thunderhead?' Jack mused, ignoring me. 'Stories, I suppose. Information. If the spiders are as old as Thunderhead reckons, they must have seen a deal of history go by and have a great store of stories to share. But how did they even know we were talking to Thunderhead? And how did they get down into the wind-race to make deals with those other storms? Oh, but they're clever bugs!'

'And we still don't know where they come from,' I said. '"The rings of ice and stone." Where's that?'

Jack looked oddly at me. 'What did the storm mean about the key to Larklight? Have you got that?'

I shook my head. 'I can only think Thunderhead mistook me for someone else,' I explained. 'He said he knew my mother, yet I am sure my mother never came to Jupiter . . .'

Yet *was* I sure of that? For now that I happened to think of it, I found that I knew almost nothing of my mother's past, her family, or anything that she had done before she married my father in Cambridge, the year before Myrtle was born. With a heartfelt sigh I leaned against the bulkhead behind me, missing poor Mother dreadfully. Remembering Myrtle's locket, I reached into my pocket and drew it out. (I was terribly relieved to find it still safe. For a horrid moment it had occurred to me that it might have fallen out during our rumble-tumble progress through the sky.) I opened it, and tears came into my eyes as I looked at her kind face. But I consoled myself with the thought that she was in a Better Place, that Father and Myrtle might already be there with her, and that I would probably be going to join them quite shortly.

'What is that?' asked Jack.

'Myrtle's locket,' I said. 'It has our mother's picture in it.' On a sudden impulse I held it out to him. Although he had never known my mother, I felt that he might be comforted as I had been by her kind smile. But all he said as he took it was, 'You have carried this all the way from the Moon?'

'I thought to give it back to Myrtle when we were aboard the *Sophronia*,' I admitted. 'but she asked me to keep hold of it. She was afraid you might search her cabin and steal it.'

Jack looked hurt. 'I would not rob her!' he said. Then he took out his trusty pocket knife, and applied the tip of the blade to the locket casing.

'Oh!' I cried. 'Oh, stop! What are you thinking of!'

'I think there is more to your mother than meets the eye,' he replied.

'It doesn't open!' I warned, reaching for the locket, while Jack patiently worked his knife in the tiny crack between the portrait and its gold casing.

But it *did* open. Mother's picture lifted like a book cover, and beneath it, packed into the tiny space by some craftsman of supernatural skill, minute devices glittered and gleamed. Cogs and wires and coils and ratchets and unearthly things I had no words for shone in the dim light: a whole world of intricate machinery in perfect miniature.

I snatched the locket, and as my hand closed on it the strange machinery took on a faint, blue glow.

'This is what the spiders are after!' cried Jack. 'It has to be! This is what they came to Larklight for, and why they have been following you ever since! They kidnapped poor Myrtle for to get it, and when they found she didn't have it, they trailed us here and came to capture you!'

The whaleboat rocked. The beast we were riding gave a sudden sideways lurch, and its outraged bellowing rang in our ears. I snapped the locket shut and stuffed it back into my pocket, wedging it down carefully beneath my handkerchief. Jack was already in the hatchway, staring out. 'Oh, what's this?' I heard him say.

I hastened to his side. The wind-whale had brought us very high, into the thin clouds of Jupiter's uppermost atmosphere, what our whalers call 'the High Tops'. Clumps of airborne bladder bushes were drifting all around us, staining the sunlight green as it poured through their semi-transparent leaves and gas-sacs. Herds of wild hoverhogs, which had been nibbling peacefully at the vegetation, were fleeing now, along with the whale calves and the females. I could hardly blame them. Bearing down on us out of the eye of the wind was a thousand-armed horror, an octopus of the heights, supported by a colossal, finned balloon of reddish hide. It must already have struck once at our whale – we could feel the poor creature shuddering and starting to list – and now it was coming back to make a second pass. It unrolled its mile-long legs, each armed with dozens of vicious thorns. I guessed at once what its intention was; to puncture our whale's internal gas bladder so that it could no longer stay aloft.

'Oh, will this never end?' I cried. I recalled the squid I had glimpsed as we first approached Thunderhead. I had thought at the time that they were looking out for prey, but now I guessed that it was us they had been watching. The spiders controlled them as they had the stormlets. They had used them to spy on us while we were inside the great storm, and now that we were helpless in the sky they had sent one to capture us. I shouted, 'Will they never stop pursuing us?'

Jack said, 'I don't reckon this to be the spiders' doing, Art. Sky-squid are mindless brutes, just like the whales. It's food he's after, not you and me . . .'

'Then how do you explain *that*?' I cried, and pointed as the creature swept past. For there on its knobbly brainpan, between the great discs of its eyes, a white spider was clinging, riding the sky-squid like some unholy jockey. And even as I spoke the spider must have seen us, for it began tugging viciously at the whip-like cilia which grew from the squid's hide. The squid started to turn, its long arms lashing towards us where we cowered inside the ruined whaleboat. A clawed red tentacle wrapped itself around and around our little shelter, and with a jerk the boat was wrenched free of the old whale's hide.

Jack flung himself at me, groping for the locket. 'That's what they're after,' he shouted. 'Let's give 'em what they want!'

'No!' I cried. 'Thunderhead said we must keep it safe!'

'I'd rather keep you and me safe, and Myrtle. If we give them the locket p'r'aps they'll tell us where to find Myrtle . . .'

A hellish stench broke over us. The squid's tentacle was curling, lifting our poor raggedy boat towards the vast cave of its mouth. I could see the spider on its back struggling to control it and stop it eating us, but I was not sure it would succeed. Compared to the squid the spider looked nothing; a white mite. Could it really hope to curb this giant's instinctive urge to eat? The squid's breath enveloped us, stinking of marsh gas.

An idea came to me, from whence I know not. I shook myself free of Jack. If I could just break the sky-squid's hold we might tumble free in the High Tops for an hour or so, and there was a chance a whaler or another pressure-ship might happen on us before we sank into the Deeps. And even if no help came, and we perished in the wind-race, at least I should have *tried* to fight the spiders who had stolen away my home and family.

The old rum bottle was still trundling to and fro across the bottom boards. I picked it up and felt in my pockets for something that might burn. Not my handkerchief; I needed that to hold the locket safe. My hand found something soft and raggedy, and I pulled out the triangle of web I had cut from Myrtle's bedroom window at Larklight. It had gone dry and crisp. I did not know if spider web was flammable, but I stuffed it into the bottle's neck, then drew out my box of lucifers and struck one. It flared up brightly in the methane-rich air, and I used it to set alight a corner of the web, which, to my joy, blazed instantly with a fierce, yellowish, roaring flame. Before Jack could ask what I was about I shoved past him to the open hatchway and flung the bottle with its little flag of fire towards the squid's gaping maw.

'It is full of methane, you see,' I explained, turning back to Jack, who was staring at me as if he thought I had gone mad. 'I read it in a book. It is the methane inside these creatures that keeps them afloat.'

Jack said, 'So what?'

A wall of yellow flame belched from the squid's mouth. It's tentacles convulsed, and as the whaleboat hurtled free I had just time to glimpse the white spider scrambling frantically to escape as the dying squid began to fall. Then,

with a sound like a Titan breaking wind, the squid exploded,
filling the sky with flame and blazing gas. The blast knocked
our tumbling boat end over end, and I dropped out of the
hatchway. I might have been lost for ever, but luckily I had
the presence of mind to snatch at one of the harpoon
cables which still trailed from the boat. Chunks of
squid skin and singed internal organs whirled past
me. I imagined the spider plunging to its death in
the depths of the sky, and felt like St George
when he killed his dragon.

But it is difficult to feel pleased with oneself
for long when one is clinging to a lashing rope
behind a wrecked and unskyworthy whaleboat
and falling as fast as one's foe. I could see Jack
staring out at me from the hatch, his hands
gripping the other end of the rope as he tried
manfully to haul me back aboard, but the wind
was dragging me away from him, in a tug-of-war he
could not hope to win. I felt my hands start to slip on
the rope. Jack was shouting something. For some reason
he seemed to be laughing, though I could not for the life of
me see why.

Then the clouds above me parted. A huge, dark body

loomed through the vapours. 'Oh no,' I thought, 'not another devilish predator!' And I squeezed my eyes shut, praying that the end might be swift and fairly painless.

'It's the ship!' Jack was shouting. 'It's *Sophronia*! Good old Ssil! Good old Munkulus!'

I looked again, and had just long enough to recognise the *Sophronia*'s figurehead before I hit it.

There was a bang, a flash of blueish stars, and that was the last I knew till I woke up, floating in zero BSG in the *Sophronia*'s main cabin with Nipper wiping a wet cloth over my face. Above him, a herd of young hoverhogs snuffled to and fro, exploring their new home. Turning my head, I saw the amber curve of Jupiter in a nearby porthole, and realised that our ordeal was over and that we were pulling away from the planet of storms.

'How did you find us?' I asked.

'Ssil didn't trust that Gruel fellow,' said the land-crab. 'And then Mr Munkulus heard some stories at the hog market of white spiders being seen on Io and Callisto and a few of the other moons, and a pressure-ship called the *Oenone* gone missing on its way back from Jupiter.'

'The spiders must have taken it so they could follow us into the wind-race,' guessed Jack.

'So we hurried the repairs and went to stand off Jupiter, waiting for a sign of you,' explained Nipper. 'And bless my carapace, it weren't long before Grindle (who was on watch above) sighted Gruel's pressure-ship –'

'The *Uncrushable*,' growled Grindle, who was standing nearby.

'– a-bursting out of the cloud-tops,' Nipper concluded.

'All beat up and ssssscorched, it looked,' said Ssillissa, gazing soulfully at Jack, who was sitting on the deck, getting his breath back after his adventures in the High Tops. 'We went in clossse, to see if they needed help, and they fled from usss.'

'So we boarded them,' grinned Grindle, 'and trained our guns upon those hairy Flummocks.'

'They were Dweebs,' said Mr Munkulus. 'Flummocks are entirely different. They have antennae, and no sense of humour.'

'Flummocks or Dweebs, they told us how Gruel had

tried to double-cross you, and how old Thunderbonce had dealt with him,' chuckled Grindle. 'Flash! Crash! Ha, ha!'

The others all laughed, but I did not join in. I could still remember the smell of scorched meat that had wafted past me after Captain Gruel was struck down.*

'We thought you were both dead,' said Ssil, very softly.

---

*Later we learned that Snifter Gruel had survived. Charred and unconscious he was flung around in the Jovian atmosphere for several days, but Thunderhead made sure the villain never fell deep enough to be crushed, and when he had fought off those other storms he wafted him towards a passing whaler, which took him home to Io. There, Mr Gruel soon recovered from his burns. The only lasting effect of the lightning strike was that he had become magnetic. Pots, pans, cutlery and wood nails all stuck fast to his body, just as they do to a real magnet. Mr Gruel found this irritating at first, and it ended his career as a pressure-ship captain, for all the *Uncrushable*'s instruments went wild when he came near them. But he soon found another way to make his living. He became quite a success at fairs and circuses under the name of 'Attracto, the Astounding Human Magnet', and later wrote a book in which he claimed to have fallen right into the heart of Jupiter and met there with Mrs Abishag Chough and a number of Higher Beings, who had given him his strange magnetic powers and sent him home bearing a message of great importance to all mankind. I don't recall what the message was, but it had something to do with peace, brotherhood and donating lots of money to Snifter Gruel.

'Even if you lived, we could not have reached you without crussshing the *Sssophronia* to sssplinterings . . .'

'That didn't stop missy here making us cruise us back and forth across the cloud-tops hour after bloomin' hour!' said Grindle. '"Oh, Jack!"' he mimicked. '"Oh, poor Jack! What sssshall we do without him?" It was better than a play.'

Ssillissa belted him with her tail-club and said kindly, 'It was a good idea of yours, Art, to set that squid ablaze. The flash lit up the clouds for miles around. Something told me it was not just a lightning bolt. I turned the ship towards the place where the light had been –'

'There was a black stain on the clouds,' interjected Mr Munkulus helpfully.

'– and we found you,' Ssil concluded, smiling her broadest, scariest smile.

'*They* found *us*,' Grindle corrected her.

'Art found us with his head!' said Nipper, laughing his deep, bubbling laugh, and the Tentacle Twins laughed too, which they did by hopping up and down and shaking their tentacles like multicoloured mops.

'You've all done well,' said Jack, standing up, but he sounded impatient. 'Now we must be leaving. Have we fuel aplenty? Provisions enough for a long journey?'

'We're well stocked,' said Mr Munkulus. 'Not too well, but this is the Jovian aether, Captain; plenty of ships and plenty of worlds to go a-raiding and a-trading in . . .'

'We're not staying,' said Jack. He sounded almost angry.

'Where are we bound, Jack?' asked Ssil loyally, ignoring the groans and twitterings of the others, who had been looking forward to a cruise among the moons of Jove.

'We're off to find those spiders,' Jack said. 'Thunderhead told us where they hide, more or less. Among the rings of ice and stone. There's only one world I've ever heard of that has rings of ice and stone.'

Ssillissa turned very pale. I probably turned very pale as well, although I hadn't a looking-glass and so cannot say for sure. We all knew that Jack meant we should go to Saturn, but *nobody* goes to Saturn. It is beyond the borders of the known aether, explored by no one but astronomers. None of the ships which have tried to reach it has ever returned.

Jack touched Ssil's shoulder. 'Can you calculate a course to Saturn, Ssilissa?'

She gulped, and blinked her sideways-lidded eyes a couple of times. 'Reckon I can, Jack,' she said. 'But why? What about the ssspidersss?'

'Don't worry about the spiders,' said Jack. 'When they see what I've got for them, I reckon they'll be ready to trade nice and polite.'

He took something from his pocket as he spoke, tossed it up shining into the lamplight, and plucked it from the air again. A long chain of golden links twirled from his closed fist. I gasped, and checked my own pocket, where I had stowed Myrtle's locket. It was gone. 'You picked my pocket!' I cried angrily, and burst into angry tears.

Jack would not look at me. 'I'm a pirate,' he said, pushing past me and floating up towards the helm, where Mr Munkulus was making ready for our voyage to the spiders' world. 'I steal things, Art. I do deals with folk who no one else will deal with. That's what I am.'

CHAPTER FOURTEEN

ANOTHER DIP INTO MY SISTER'S DIARIES, WHICH MAY BE
WELCOMED BY READERS OF A SENSITIVE DISPOSITION AS A
SORT OF BREAK OR BREATHING SPACE FROM MY OWN
ALMOST UNBEARABLY EXCITING ADVENTURES.

April 26th (continued)

When I awakened this morning I felt, for a short
time, quite content. I was laid upon a soft bed
in some sort of papery tent, whose walls and
roof glowed with sunshine. There was a gentle sense of

movement, most restful after the alarums of the night past. And then I recalled all that I had seen: how my host Sir Waverley had been unmasked as nothing more than an automaton or clockwork man, and how I had escaped with Ulla, and been rescued by those improperly clad worm-riders.

Quailing inwardly, yet determined not to let my captors see that I was afraid of them, I sat up and found that I was (thank God) still fully dressed beneath the coarse linen sheets which some kind hand had cast over me as I lay insensate. I saw that the cactus creatures' spilled sap had dried upon my skirts and bodice in stiff, shiny patches like Gum Arabic, and wondered whether there was any place upon this savage world where I might find a new dress, or at least a laundry.

When I crawled out through the low entry tunnel of the papery tent, I found that I was upon a sort of boat or barge, made entirely from thick sheets of oiled and folded paper,

in the native style. Several Martians were standing at what I believe J. H. would call the *stern*. They were propelling the vessel with poles along a seemingly endless, ruler-straight canal, whose waters shone and danced, swirling slowly under the pale Martian sun. I was very relieved to see that the bargemen were, at least, properly clothed in loincloths and long paper tunics. (I have since learned that it is only when they ride into battle that the Martians go naked, believing in their savage way that it is cowardly to wear armour or anything else that might deflect a blow.)

'Miss Mumby!' called a voice, and I turned to discover that I was being observed by a person who sat on a heap of cushions at the pointy end of the boat. I approached him somewhat apprehensively, recognising the leader of the war party which had destroyed the cactus-men. He was attired like the other Martians, but had a thin, hawk-like face and a peculiar beard. Upon his head he wore a broad raffia hat to keep off the sun. His paper tunic was, I am sorry to relate, hanging open. He wore no shirt beneath, and across his bare chest hung a barbaric necklace of bronze tiles or scales. Yet as I drew close, and he sprang up to greet me, I saw to my astonishment that he was not a Martian at all, but an Englishman, tho' one tanned quite brown by the desert sun.

'I am most pleased to meet you, Miss Mumby,' he said. His eyes, I must say, were most arresting: large and dark and filled with light. He regarded me with an intense gaze which aroused in me the most peculiar sensations. I was quite relieved when Ulla stepped forwards to hug me and said, 'Myrtle, this is my husband, Richard Burton of the Secret Service.'

Well, I declare I was most discomfited to learn that Richard Burton, the great British explorer and secret agent, should have taken a Martian native as his wife. I must have gone quite pale, for Ulla at once asked if I was all right, and Mr Burton advised me to sit down. 'The air of Mars is thinner than that of Earth,' he reminded me, 'and newcomers to our planet sometimes take a little time to grow accustomed to it. When I first came here with the Army I was laid up for several days.'

While Ulla went into the paper cabin to fetch food and

water for me, I tried to recall all that I knew of R. B. (I wish now that I had paid a little more attention when Art was droning about famous explorers, back at Larklight!) But I do recall that he began his career as an officer of the British Mars Survey and was quite celebrated as an explorer, having disguised himself as a native and travelled deep into the deserts, and led the Martian tribes there in their battles to overthrow the dreadful mole-people who were oppressing them. For this reason the natives, who have never shown Britain the gratitude she deserves for bringing civilisation to their dusty world, have taken a great liking to Mr Burton, and have given him the title 'Warlord of Mars'.

Ulla returned, bringing water, and a palatable breakfast of baked root vegetables called *sprune*. While I ate, I watched my host and hostess, and saw many signs of tenderness and regard pass between them. I recalled Jack Havock's tale of how his family's prejudice had driven his mother and father to their strange fate on Venus, and wondered if it were love for his rusty-coloured bride which had persuaded R. B. to turn his back on the comforts of his own home and seek adventure here upon the high frontier. In my weakened state this seemed to me, for a moment, quite romantic and even admirable.

When I had eaten, R. B. said, 'Please tell me all that you know about the spiders.'

I had to think for a moment. While I was at The Beeches I had grown used to telling myself that my memories of the white spiders were just dreams. Amid the horror of last night I had not had the time to stop and think, and come to terms with the prospect that not only were the spiders real, but all my memories too. I began to weep a little as I told R. B. of Larklight, and what had befallen poor Papa. I told him of Jack Havock too, afraid at first that he would think ill of me for associating with such a character, but he listened quite, quite calmly, and only interjected once, to ask what had become of Art.

'I do not know,' I said sorrowfully. 'I pray that Jack and his friends were able to keep him safe, and that he is still with them aboard their aether-ship.'

Mr Burton nodded. Then he said, 'For some weeks now I have made it my business to keep watch upon The Beeches. Dear Ulla has sent me many valuable reports about the comings and goings there. We knew that Sir Waverley Rain was "up to something", but we knew not what, until last night.'

'He is an automaton!' I cried. 'At least, he *was*. I believe I broke him when I fell on him. There was one of those dreadful spiders inside him – a little one. And another bigger one.'

Mr Burton said, 'There was a whole ship full of the creatures, we believe. A black, spiny ship, which landed in the desert near The Beeches a few days ago. It took off last night, soon after we found you. Those spiders undoubtedly removed the real Sir Waverley some time ago. I dread to think for how long his manufactories may have been controlled by that mechanical facsimile.'

'But why?' I gasped. 'To what end?'

R. B. drew his dark brows together, and his eyes glittered. 'I cannot say, Miss Mumby, but it occurs to me that Sir Waverley's company has been constructing the new Crystal Palace in Hyde Park. What if the false Sir Waverley and his many-legged masters have tinkered with the plans somehow? Or installed an explosive device within the structure?'

I declare I almost fainted away again as I contemplated the full horror of what he had said. Even now, my hand shakes as I try to write this. Can it be true? Our own dear Queen in mortal peril? Oh, it is too horrible! I said at once, 'We must raise the alarm! We must travel at once to Port-of-Mars and demand an audience with the Governor himself!'

'Regrettably the Governor is a major shareholder in Sir Waverley's company,' said R. B. with a sardonic smile. 'So are all the rest of the Colonial Government. Without clear proof, I doubt they would wish to take any action which might affect the reputation of Rain & Co.'

'Good Heavens!' I cried, unwilling to believe him. 'Surely no British gentleman would put commercial interests above those of his country, and humanity at large?'

'Little wonder, is it, that my Martian friends laugh at our famous Empire?' said R. B., with that same unsettling smile. 'Their own empire fell long ago, and they do not expect ours to last long.'

He stood up, and pointed towards the canal shore. We were passing a place where one of the ancient Martian ruins stood, an old temple of translucent porcelain, cracked and decayed yet still very pretty. '"Look upon my works, ye mighty, and despair!"' he exclaimed, quoting Mr Shelley. 'Do you know, Miss Mumby, Ulla's people have legends of how their ancient empire passed away – in a war with a race of titanic spiders? I wonder if ours is about to go the same way. Perhaps every race which gets above itself and travels outwards across the deeps of space arouses the ire of those white devils . . .'

'Oh, Mr Burton,' I cried, 'we must do something!'

'Indeed we must,' he said. 'Fear not, Miss Mumby. I have a chum whom I believe I can persuade to transport us directly to the Earth, and there, I hope, we shall be able to confound these spiders, and frustrate their knavish tricks.'

How I pray that he is right!

Later

This evening our paper ship carried us into a small but bustling Martian town, whose paper houses crowd close about the walls of a fort where the British flag flies.

Troopers of the Martian Light Infantry came striding along the canal banks aboard their mechanised fighting machines to ask our business, and when they learned that Mr Burton was aboard they turned and raced back to the fort to announce his arrival.

By the time we drew in to the quay beneath the fort's walls the district officer had put on his hat and come out to greet us, and a Martian band struck up a stirring if discordant tune, which made me suddenly homesick for Larklight and my own dear pianoforte. (It is so long since I practised, and I was growing quite accomplished at playing *Birdsong at Eventide* – I do hope these interruptions will not have made me grow rusty!)

But I digress. Mr and Mrs Burton stepped ashore, and as I followed I saw a naval gentleman standing among the welcoming committee on the quay. He was staring at me in such a strange way that I imagined for a moment prolonged exposure to the Martian sun had deranged his wits, but it turned out that he recognised me! 'Great Scott!' he cried. 'It is the lass whom I saw in the clutches of that wretch Havock and his mutinous dogs!'

It turned out that this was the chum whom R. B. had brought us here to see: Captain Moonfield of the HMS *Indefatigable*. Of course, he had the advantage of me, for I was in a swoon when his ship caused the *Sophronia* to 'Heave To' (as we aethernauts say). It seems that he and his men had been most concerned for Arthur and I, but since they did not know our names, or where we came from, or where Jack Havock had taken us, there was nothing they could do for us, and after the *Sophronia* evaded their trap they had been forced to return empty-handed to Mars, where the *Indefatigable* was stationed. 'I am glad to see you escaped safely, miss!' said Captain Moonfield, bowing most elegantly.

I was able to put him right on one point. 'Jack Havock's crew are not mutinous,' I said. 'Nor are they dogs (with the possible exception of Mr Grindle). They would follow Jack Havock to perdition if he asked them to, and I confess that during my time aboard his ship I found him a perfect gentleman. I believe he has been entirely misrepresented. He may have caused a little mischief, and stolen a few insignificant items from people who can well afford to lose them, but there is no harm in him, no harm at all.'

'No harm?' said Captain Moonfield, very much surprised. 'But what about all the ships gone missing with all hands since he began to prowl the space lanes? The HMS *Aeneas*, for instance?'

'Not Havock's doing, Davey boy!' boomed Mr Burton, coming to my aid. 'From what Miss Mumby and others have told me Havock's a good lad, quite after my own heart. Indeed, if Government don't soon up my pay and start to recognise dear Ulla's contribution to my work, I've half a mind to join the *Sophronia*'s crew myself! No, the real threat out there isn't from the Havock boy, but from those spiders.'

'Spiders?' said Captain M., not following. 'Nasty creatures, Dick, I quite agree. Too many legs entirely – but how can they be a threat? Poisonous, are they?'

'Poisonous, highly intelligent, and bent upon the destruction of the British Empire,' said R. M., and proceeded to illuminate him as to our adventures at The Beeches.

'By Heaven!' cried Captain M., when he had finished. 'We must inform the Governor!'

'No time, Davey,' Mr Burton replied. 'I was hoping rather that you could take us straight to Earth. Time is of the essence if we are to avert disaster'

I saw at once why he had chosen to turn to Captain Moonfield for help. That good gentleman did not waste time with any more questions, or dither about informing his superiors or waiting for written orders, signed in triplicate. Instead he sent straight to his ship, which was moored behind the fort, and we were soon joined by his chief alchemist, an elderly man named McMurdo.

'How long before we can be over London?' he demanded.

McMurdo, a Scotsman of the gloomy sort, shook his head and opined that it would take at least ten days, and only then if his stocks of something called Rufous Mercury held out and his 'main cogs' had not been 'nobbled' by the Martian Metal Worms.

'We shall do it in four!' declared Captain M. 'To your station, McMurdo! We take flight at midnight!'

Mr McMurdo hurried off, muttering, 'I cannae do it, Captain. I'm an alchemist, not an engineer.' But I could see that Captain Moonfield has total confidence in his abilities, despite his uncouth manner.

I write this in the District Officer's residence, where Ulla and I have been invited to recuperate. Night is falling fast upon the desert, and the moons are rising. In a few days I shall be on Earth, at the Great Exhibition which I so longed to visit when I read of it in Larklight all those weeks ago. But my mind is filled with a turmoil of anxiety. Will we be able to put a stop to the spider's machinations? And whatever shall I wear?

➤✦←

And that is quite enough of Myrtle for the moment. She does nothing but blather on about frocks and dresses for the next few pages anyway, so I am sure you would rather read of ME; of how I went to Saturn, and what I found there – A. M.

CHAPTER FIFTEEN

IN WHICH WE FACE FRESH PERILS 'MID SATURN'S
DESOLATE RINGS.

To tell you the truth, I don't remember much about our voyage to Saturn. Days and nights upon the Golden Roads, with nothing to look at but the swirling, shining stuff of our alchemical bow-wave wafting past the *Sophronia*'s portholes. I had tried to reason with Jack about the locket, which you may recall he had stolen from me, and was proposing to deliver to the spiders. But Jack would not talk to me, and I pretty soon gave up. Why had I ever trusted him? I wondered. Why had I ever thought him good, or admirable, or anything but a robber and a cad?

Grindle and Mr Munkulus and the Tentacle Twins were all too wary of their captain's anger to say much. They busied themselves with their work about the ship, casting worried glances from time to time at Jack. As for Ssil, she was shut in the wedding chamber, tending the great alembic and painstakingly calculating our course to Saturn. I don't believe any of them liked Jack's plan, but they were all too used to following him to try and talk him out of it. When Mr Munkulus tried to question him he said, 'Fear not, Mr M. The old spiders have been tearing all around the Solar System hunting this trinket. I think they'll be willing to do business.'

In the end I crept into the little cabin which was mine alone now that Myrtle had been taken from us, and snuggled myself down in her bunk. I convinced myself that the bedclothes still held a comforting trace of her scent, but really they just smelled of mildew.

Nipper came in later with a globe of broth for my supper. 'Best keep your head down, Art,' he said. 'I've never seen the young captain in such a strange taking.'

'He robbed me!' I sniffled. 'He picked my pocket!'

'Well, that's his trade, ain't it? You must see that. Maybe these spiders will pay so well for that little locket of yours that we'll all be able to retire and set up our carriages, and go no more a-raiding.'

'Thunderhead said we shouldn't give it to them,' I muttered. 'What if they don't pay us? What if they just murder us all, and take it?'

Nipper had no answer to that. Trusting Jack Havock's judgement had become a habit with him; it came as naturally as breathing, and I don't believe he cared to entertain the notion that his young captain might be wrong. But talking to him cheered me a little. It reminded me that wherever the spiders were, there I would have a hope of finding Myrtle. Jack might care for nothing but gold, but once he delivered me into the domain of the white spiders I would find a means to slip away from him and search for my sister, or for some clue as to her fate.

Comforted by these thoughts, I slept, and dreamed I was at Larklight, walking down the winding staircases into the heart of the old house. I found myself standing in the boiler room, and out from among the maze of old machinery there shone shafts of light, flickering and twisting like ropes of gold. And in their midst, a golden keyhole. Was this the lock the key would open? I stooped to put my eye to it, but before I could do so a ghastly shadow moved upon the wall, and I looked up to see Mr Webster dangling above my head, his clawed feet slashing at me like bony sickles . . .

I woke with a cry, and found that the straps which held me into the bunk had snapped and that I was floating near the cabin ceiling. The whole ship was shuddering and lurching beneath me as if it was riding on a rough sea. I stumbled up and opened the door. Out in the hold the crew were flapping about, Grindle in his night attire with the long tassels of his nightcap flapping, Mr Munkulus hollering, 'All hands on deck!' The song of the chemical wedding was fading as Ssillissa doused the elements in her alembic.

Nipper blundered past me, swimming through the fuggy air to help Jack, who was struggling with the wheel. 'Aether storm!' he said as he passed. 'Or else some sort of gravitational tide-race . . .'

'Ssil!' hollered Jack Havock angrily as the blue girl emerged from the wedding chamber. 'What have you landed us in?'

'Ain't her fault, Jack,' said Mr Munkulus wisely. 'There ain't no charts to warn us of the tides and shoals out here in Saturn's aether. Ssil's been flying blind, haven't you, Ssil?'

Ssil nodded, blushing terribly at Jack's harsh words. Jack turned away angrily. He knew that he was in the wrong, I think, but he was too proud to admit it. 'At least we're here,' he said, glancing from a porthole as the *Sophronia* slowed and slowed.

I looked too. Outside, a huge, dirty yellow world hung like a lamp against the star fields. A thin line of light seemed to have been drawn across its equator, stretching out into the blackness on either side. Ssil, still blushing, ducked back inside the wedding chamber and set us moving again, at low speed. As Jack started steering us towards the planet our view changed: the line of light broadened, and I saw that it was really a vast ring of glimmering dust, striped with concentric rings of darkness.

We moved slowly now, our aether-wings flapping at the dark. I pressed my face against the glass and cupped my hands around it to block out the distracting reflections of the work going on behind me, where Grindle and the Tentacle Twins were preparing the space cannon. Outside, drifts of space frost glittered, and shoals of iridescent Icthyomorphs shot past. I did not recognise their species, and wished that Father was there to marvel at them. What wonders must await discovery in that uncharted ocean of aether!

Slowly, slowly, that lonesome world drew closer, and the rings which had looked like nothing but dust started to reveal their true nature. Boulders of ice as big as comets and hunks of stone as large as moons mingled with the smaller particles, tumbling end over end, sometimes colliding one with another, but all held in their stately, circling dance by the iron grip of Saturn's gravity. A soft shushing sound filled the *Sophronia* as she dipped into the outermost ring, nosing her way through clouds of tiny particles. *Bomp, bomp*, went larger bits, pebbles and drifting boulders, striking gently against the hull. Mr Munkulus ran aloft and started calling down directions to Jack, who had taken the helm. 'Starboard half a point! Port! Port!' the Ionian shouted, and Jack responded instantly to each instruction, steering us past huge, pitted chunks of space rock and shards of ice that could have split the ship in two.

Things like blue stingrays flapped around the craters of a floating boulder; things like transparent tube worms wriggled through the dust, and reached up their blind heads to gulp down drifting animalculae. I saw no sign anywhere of spiders. I wondered what their home was like, down beneath the saffron clouds of Saturn, and whether they had set these rings here themselves to defend the approaches to their lonely planet. And then, as we crossed a band of open space and plunged into the next ring, I understood how wrong I was. The spiders did not live on Saturn's surface, but among the rings themselves!

'Cobwebs ho!' bellowed Mr Munkulus, and Grindle and the Tentacle Twins ran out their cannon and stood ready to fire them.

Stretching across the face of Saturn I could see great bands and strands of gossamer, tying the larger of the drifting rocks together, sometimes binding great clusters to form enormous tents of web whose pale walls were pimpled with the captive boulders. The *Sophronia* edged closer, Mr Munkulus calling out constantly. I peered upwards as we slid beneath an arch of web. It was thick and tattered, encrusted with space dust and small, parasitic plants, and here and there amid the strands hung the rusty, web-enshrouded wrecks of other aether-ships, caught like flies in the snares of the white spiders.

The ship's hoverhogs began to squeak and twitter nervously, as if they sensed the danger she was sailing into. Jack flapped irritably at the plump, pink bodies which wheeled about his head. 'Stow these somewhere,' he ordered. 'Ain't there a hutch or a hamper we can put 'em in?' There wasn't – Mr Munkulus had not thought to buy one – but Nipper gently caught the hogs and tied a thick length of string around each one's middle, then tethered the whole lot to a brass ring in the wall, well out of Jack's way.

The webs grew thicker. We were sailing into the heart of the spiders' domain, and yet still nothing moved except for the tumbling particles of dust and ice. I told myself that I wasn't frightened, and almost believed it for a while, for although I was scared I was also excited. Jack Havock and I were the first human beings to visit this awful place since the *Aeneas* expedition. We alone knew what fate must have befallen poor Dr Ptarmigan and his people, blundering into these nets of web.

And as I watched I saw the bridges and funnels of cobweb ahead of the ship come suddenly to life, crawling with the white forms of the spiders. At the same moment Mr Munkulus dropped in through the star-deck hatch shouting, 'They're all round us! It's an ambush, Jack!'

Jack spun the wheel, apparently thinking better of his plan, but it was too late. For as the *Sophronia* came about I saw that the spiders had been busy astern, and that the gap of open space we had come in through was now barred by a mesh of fresh webs.

'Full speed astern!' called Jack, and the aether-wings began to flap hard, the old ship's timbers creaking as they jerked to and fro in their mountings. We struck the webs at speed, and for a moment I felt hopeful, remembering how the lifeboat had punched its way out through the shroud of webs which had enveloped dear old Larklight. But the webs *Sophronia* faced were stronger, and wherever a strand broke, there a score or more of the horrid spiders appeared, scuttling in nightmarish regiments along their gossamer bridges to mend the rent.

Groaning, shuddering, the *Sophronia* slowed and came

'Full speed astern!' called Jack, and the aether-wings began to flap hard.

gently to a stop. The Tentacle Twins fired off their cannon, and gave a joint tweet of triumph as a strand of web parted and the spiders clinging to it were hurled off scrabbling into the aether. But before they could reload we all heard the awful *scritch scratch* of claws hurrying over the star deck and the outside of the hull. Jack and the others primed their pistols, their upward-looking faces ghastly in the dim light which filtered in through our web-blind portholes. Even I armed myself with a cutlass from one of the weapons racks, and vowed that the spiders would not take me alive.

No one spoke. We were all waiting for the spiders to begin stoving in our hatches and smashing the porthole glass to grope for us with their long, pale legs.

Instead there was silence, and then a brisk, businesslike knocking at the main hatchway. A voice spoke, muffled by the thickness of the hatch, yet still familiar.

'Step from your guns,' it said. 'Stand peaceful-like. You got that Mumby boy on board?'

A few heads turned to look at me. Nipper pushed himself closer to me, and put a protective pincer around me. I said, 'That's Mr Webster!'

'Better do as he says, Jack,' said Mr Munkulus. 'There's dozens of 'em out there, and some are monstrous huge!'

Jack motioned for Nipper to step in front of me, so that I was concealed behind his shell. 'Art ain't aboard!' shouted Jack, looking intently at the hatch, as if he could discern the shape of the monster who squatted outside it. 'We left him on Io. But I've got what you've been seeking.  They key to Larklight. You can have it, in exchange for Myrtle.'

'For Myrtle?' I gasped. 'I thought he would want gold, or ships, or something . . .'

Nipper's eye-stalks bowed down so that all four of his big, sad eyes were looking into mine. 'Oh, Art,' he whispered, 'don't you know why he came here? He thinks the spiders are keeping your sister captive, and he thinks that he can talk them into letting her go.'

I gaped at him. 'No,' I said. 'Jack does not care about Myrtle. He hates her. They never stopped arguing. He wouldn't do that for her. Anyway, he would have said something.'

'He thought we would not follow him if he told us it was for her sake we were coming here,' said Nipper. 'He thought we would laugh at him if we knew that he loves her.'

'*What?*' I said, quite confused. 'He loves *Myrtle*? But she wears spectacles, and snaps at people . . .'

Outside the hatch, Mr Webster seemed to have finished considering Jack's offer. 'Sounds fair enough,' he said.

Glancing at the rest of us to make sure that I was out of sight behind Nipper and the rest were ready with their weapons, Jack unlocked the hatch and heaved it open. The huge white spider poked his front end into the *Sophronia* and considered us, his many eyes a-glitter. 'Where's the key then?' he asked. 'After all, I've only got your word that it's here at all.'

Jack held up Myrtle's locket, which floated on its golden chain like a tiny, tethered moon.

Mr Webster's banks of eyes gleamed greedily. 'So that's it, eh? Very tasty.' Squeezing a limb in through the hatchway he reached out to take it, but Jack snatched it away. 'I want Myrtle safe first!' he warned.

'Oh dear,' said Webster, all mock dismay. 'I've just remembered. She ain't here.'

'Then where?' cried Jack. 'What have you done with her? If you've harmed her I shall . . .'

'Last time I noticed, she was on Mars,' said Webster. 'I think the cacti finished her off, although I had to leave before I had a chance to make certain. She caused us no little inconvenience, your Myrtle. But it's of no account. Things are moving now. The trap's been set, and nothing can stop it being sprung. Oh, and while we're on the subject of traps . . .'

Webster shot out his foreclaw and snatched my sister's locket from Jack's hand. In the same instant, through every hatch, his spider-warriors came storming in at us. I saw Jack draw his pistols and discharge them both into the eyes of a spider who came whirling down through the entry port above him. I saw the Tentacle Twins' crowns flashing with electric fire, and Grindle laying about him with his cutlass, and the pale slime bubbling from severed spider legs, but the whole cabin was filled with legs by then; a forest of twitching, scuttling spiders, and however many my brave shipmates cut down there were always more behind.

It was Ssil who saved me. Snatching me from behind, she dragged me towards the wedding chamber. Behind us Jack was shouting, and the Tentacle Twins were frying attacker after attacker with their electric haloes, filling the ship with the stench of roasted spider skin. In all the confusion no one noticed Ssil and me as we plunged into the darkened wedding chamber. Shivering, whispering softly to herself, Ssil heaved up a brass plate in the floor and pushed me down into a tight, sulphur-smelling place beneath. As she climbed down after me and pulled the plate back into place above us I understood that we were in one of the exhaust-horns of the *Sophronia*'s alchemical engines.

'But –' I protested.

'Shhhh!' hissed Ssil, her claw touching my mouth. I shhhhed. Around us, above us, we could hear the scratch and stamp of the battle, the bark of Jack's pistols, the crackle of Yarg and Squidley's tentacles. But the hissings and screeching of the white spiders were louder. Soon they were the only sound, and we guessed that our friends had been beaten. There was more scrabbling, and the scratching of claws, and the sound of things breaking. Then silence.

We edged together along the exhaust-horn until we reached its broad mouth, where the brass was still warm, stained green and blue and other, nameless colours by the exhalations from the great alembic. Peering out into the aether, we saw that we were moving. The spiders were hauling us through their worldwide web much as horses tug narrow boats along the canals of England, except of course that there were more of them, and they had more legs than horses, and the ropes were made of web, not hemp.

'Where are they taking us?' I asked.

'Sssssshhhh!' said Ssil again.

On and on they dragged us, for half an hour, an hour . . . I began to find it hard to breathe in the thin aether. Around us the webs grew denser. I could see more and more wrecked ships snagged in them, wound about with mummy-shrouds of web. Some looked to be of Jovian design, some were more like the ancient Martian aether-ships whose images have been found in the ruined temples of that world, and others were like none I had ever seen or heard of – ships from other stars perhaps, or from long-dead Mercury or the frozen outer worlds.

Soon the *Sophronia*'s progress began to slow. More webs enwrapped her, tethering her tight in a great cat's cradle of gossamer. We were in a place where the strands were woven so dense that they blotted out the face of Saturn entirely, forming one of those planetoid-studded tents which I had noticed on the way into the rings, except that this one was far, far larger than the rest, and somehow brighter, as if it were being lit up from within by many lamps. After a while we heard Mr Webster and his m y r m i d o n s making their way off the *Sophronia*, and a while after *that* we saw them creeping away along a bridge which led to a gaping entrance in that castle of web, carrying a number of bulky, white parcels between them. Some of the parcels were still struggling.

'They have captured Jack!' whispered Ssillissa. 'They have captured everyone! Everyone but usss!' Tears drifted from her eyes and wobbled away into space.

I found that I was crying too. 'Oh, why did he come here?' I asked aloud. 'Is it true what Nipper said? Does he love Myrtle?'

'Jack loved your ssisster from the inssstant he sssaw her,' said the lizard-girl. 'How could he not? She is ssso sssweet and pretty . . .'

'*Myrtle*? Sweet?'

'How could Jack fail to fall in love with her? As soon as I sssaw her I knew that he mussst.'

She waved her skinny hands about, as if she were trying to draw diagrams of love in the aether. As for me, I just crouched there staring at her and feeling foolish. Jack Havock, in love with *Myrtle*? At first it seemed impossible, but then I began to remember things. Certain things that Jack Havock had said about my sister. The way that he had looked at her on that headland, before the spiders came for her. How he had bought those hoverhogs to clean the ship up. And I had to admit that it might be true. After all, Jack had lived a long time without human company. He had probably never met a girl before. Maybe, to someone as lonely as him, Myrtle *might* seem sweet and pretty . . .

And if what Mr Webster said were true, she was lying dead upon the planet Mars at that very moment, and she would never know what Jack had felt for her!

'My poor Jack!' sighed Ssilissa. 'We musst go to him. We musst sssave him from these ssspidersss.'

'But how?' I asked. 'They are so strong, and we are not strong at all. We don't even know where they have taken Jack and the others . . .'

But as I looked out at the towering walls of the cobweb castle I realised that it did not matter. The spiders had taken Father from me, and Myrtle too. I could not let them take Jack without a fight. Somehow, Ssillissa and I would have to enter that fortress of web, and bring him and our other shipmates safely out.

CHAPTER SIXTEEN

IN WHICH I ENTER THE GREAT FORTRESS OF THE
FIRST ONES, AND MAKE SEVERAL INTRIGUING
DISCOVERIES.

'

Ssil unlatched the plate above us and heaved herself
out of the cramped tube. I followed. All was still.
The door of the wedding chamber stood open. The
hold beyond was shadowy, lit only by the twilight glow of
Saturn pouring through the portholes. All sorts of objects
turned and tumbled there – discarded swords, spent pistol

balls, plates and beakers from a smashed-open chest and the clenched, twitching corpses of dead spiders. The hoverhogs pooted about on the end of their strings, still tied to the wall, but happy enough, for the battle had overturned lockers and upset biscuit barrels and all manner of morsels were pirouetting about in mid-air. The attackers had left the hatches open when they departed. We shut them, and refilled the ship with air, and breathed deeply, refreshing ourselves after our time in the thin, oxygen-starved aether.

'We shall require firearms,' I decided. And so we busied ourselves upon that melancholy battlefield, finding pistols, blunderbusses, powder and shot, and securing them about our persons.

I was just heaving aside a swag of tarpaulin that had fallen across the cover of the shot-locker when a movement in the shadows beneath startled me, and brought Ssillissa to my side, snarling fiercely. But I stayed her hand before she could bring her cutlass down on the twitching white thing that lay there. It was not a spider, as I had thought at first, but one of the Tentacle Twins.

'Yarg!' cried Ssillissa. She cast her weapon aside and went down on her knees to comfort the injured anemone. Yarg's crown of tentacles stirred softly, like a bush in a gentle breeze, and a few mournful colours flickered there.

'Is he very badly hurt?' I asked nervously.

Ssillissa shook her head. 'I think he was stunned in the fighting, nothing more. But he is without his twin. Oh, poor Yarg. He and Squidley have not been apart since they were spawned.'

She stroked Yarg's tentacles, and the poor creature made plaintive, twittering sounds and little mews. I felt desperately sorry for him. After all, I knew how painful it felt to lose a mother, or a father, or even a sister. I could only guess at the grief Yarg must feel, bereft of the twin he had known all his life, whose very thoughts were linked to his.

That gave me an idea. I shook Ssil by her bony shoulder. 'Ssil, he can find the others for us!'

She looked round at me with a lizardy frown. 'What do you mean?'

'On the Moon he and Squidley found Myrtle by sniffing out her thoughts! And Myrtle hardly thinks at all. Surely Yarg can sense his own brother's thoughts up in that web-palace, and the others too, maybe. He can sniff 'em out like a bloodhound!'

Ssil saw at once that I was right. She stared at me with what the poet Keats calls 'a wild surmise', and Yarg must have picked up our thoughts, because the colours flashing through his crown became more hopeful – red and pink and flaming yellow. He twittered urgently at us, as if to tell us that he could already sense the minds of Squidley and our other shipmates, away among the spiders' webs.

We helped him up, and finished arming ourselves. Then, creeping out through a hatchway, the three of us began our assault upon the castle of webs.

We began by climbing a
steep strand which led
to that bridge
across

which
we had seen
our bound and
shrouded friends conveyed.
We had barely gone twenty feet
before a spider came running down to see
what we were about. I trained Mr Grindle's
favourite blunderbuss upon it, and when I pulled the
trigger the brute flew to pieces in a most gratifying manner.
Cheered by this reminder that our enemies were not
invulnerable, we climbed onwards, and were not troubled
again. It seemed that the spiders, imagining that the whole
of *Sophronia*'s crew were in their power, had not troubled to
leave any sentries on guard about the abandoned ship, and
that the brute I had shot had been no more than a straggler,
left behind by the main force of spiders as they withdrew
into the castle with their prisoners.

We crept on, and made our way to an opening in the castle's side which looked old and somehow disused. Thin wisps of web trailed from its edges, thick with space dust. Yarg leaned in, his tentacles quivering warily.

'He can hear them inssside,' said Ssilissa. 'Or feel them, I mean . . .' She frowned and touched her brow. 'It is strange, Art; I can almosst hear his thoughtss. Just fragmentsss of them. They come apart like dreamss when I try to ssseize upon them.'

'Does he think it's safe?' I asked.

Ssil concentrated, as if Yarg's thoughts were a distant whispering she would hear if she strained her ears hard enough. 'There are no sssspidersss near. They are few.'

'There seemed quite enough of them earlier,' I replied with a shudder, remembering the horde which had poured aboard our ship.

'But not like other racess,' Ssil insisted. 'Yarg can only hear the thoughtss of a few hundred sssspidersss. That is all that are left. Very few, and very old.'

'Older than all the worlds of the Sun,' I whispered, recalling something that Thunderhead had told me.

Yarg turned towards us, beckoning with his tentacles, and we crept to the entrance and made our way inside. It was warm in there, and soft, like a maze of cotton wool, and I felt the gentle tug of gravity, perhaps one-tenth of British Standard. Thin filaments of web, no thicker than the finest silk thread, were strung along the winding tunnels. I touched one to test its strength, and at once my hand leaped back, and I felt as if someone had struck me hard upon the elbow with a hammer.

'Ow!' I complained, rubbing my numb arm, and Ssilissa put her own hand close to the thread and said, 'Electrical currentss run through thiss one . . . Through all these thin onesss. They are clever, these ssspidersss.'

We went on warily. There is not room in this little book to tell of all the strange sights we saw in that place. Many of them I could not explain anyway, like the objects which we found woven into the strands sometimes, as if placed there by the spiders as trophies or ornaments – a six-eyed skull, a curious sword, a great many glass bottles of all shapes and colours, and once, surprisingly, a jar of Mr Keiller's Celebrated Dundee Marmalade. Sometimes we found ourselves in great open spaces, floored and walled and roofed with web, where lamps hung overhead, casting a bright, white light. We had passed through several of these marquees before I noticed that the lamps were also spiders, clinging to strands high above us, with light shining from their fat bodies.

As we crept on, and hid, and crept on yet again, I started to see that the spiders came in many forms. There were the great brutish soldiers we had already met, who trooped about in bony battalions, and the living lamps, who seemed brainless and rooted to one place, but we also saw swift-moving servant-spiders, who scuttled along on their back sets of legs, using the front ones to carry heavy, web-covered packages and parcels. Twice we saw pairs of these strange creatures bearing litters on which crouched smaller spiders – tiny by the standards I was now used to – their bodies no larger than a man's fist, their legs like many-jointed fingers. I began to wonder if the First Ones were like our earthly ants and termites, whom God has made in different forms, for different tasks.

And yet there were not many of them, just as Ssilissa had said. Often we passed through vast halls which seemed deserted, apart from the patient lamp-spiders clinging on in their high posts.

Yarg seemed to know where he was going, and Ssil and I were quite content to follow him, feeling certain that he was homing on Squidley's thoughts. Sure enough, after a half-hour or so, we found our way in through a triangular opening near the top of a chamber shaped like a funnel. Its floor was many feet below us, a red-brown, lumpish thing which I took to be the surface of an ancient planetoid which the spiders had incorporated into their web-castle.

'He iss here!' hissed Ssil, sensing another of our bloodhound's thoughts, but I did not need her to translate. Yarg had began to bounce up and down excitedly, and cheerful glimmerings of orange and maroon flickered across his crown.

It was not hard to clamber down the funnel's sloping wall, for the webs which formed it were soft as lambswool, and we kicked footholds in them as we went. Below us, rows of dark shapes showed among the pallid webs. Ssil, who was nimbler than yours truly, was the first to reach one. She looked up at me and said, 'Art!'

I hurried to join her. The dark shape was a sort of alcove or basin woven in the web, with a thin veil of gossamer stretched across its mouth, like a dusty window. Behind this gently stirring veil, also enveloped in a thin wrapping of web, lay a man's body. He was a short man, with bushy grey hair sprouting around his ears, dressed in a rather expensive-looking frock-coat and a brocade waistcoat. He looked familiar, though I could not at first think why.

Yarg hurried straight to another of the alcoves, and his little chirrup of joy told us that he had found his twin inside. Ssil moved on, peering into one alcove after another. There were about ten of them in all, and she looked into each one and then said, 'They are all here but Jack! Where is Jack?'

Slower than Ssil, I followed her, and peered as I passed into the second alcove. The web which covered this was dustier, so that I had to push my face close to it before I could see inside. Even when I did discern who lay there, I did not believe it.

'Ssil!' I cried, too loudly. Echoes of my voice went bounding away up the web-funnel, making Ssilissa shush me furiously. But I could not help myself. You would have cried out too, gentle reader, if you had been confronted, in that awful place, with a face so dear to you, which you had not expected to see again before the Last Trump sounds.

For in that sarcophagus of web, pale and beautiful and lifeless, lay my mother!

Then Yarg, who had been trying to awaken his twin, suddenly straightened up and flashed a bitter green.

'Sssssomeone issss coming!' warned Ssilissa. Fright made her hiss more than ever; we both knew that what she really meant was, 'Sssssome*thing* isss coming!'

Yarg darted in beside his sleeping twin. Lizardy-quick, Ssillissa hid herself in an un-tenanted alcove, drawing a veil of web across herself and hissing at me to do the same. But I could not tear my eyes away from Mother's face, nor move a muscle in my body, even though I knew I risked discovery. Was she alive, or was she dead? I kept wondering. She looked as cold and pale as a crusader's marble wife upon a tomb. But if she were dead, why would the white spiders have taken all the trouble to bring her to Saturn and keep her in this curious cabinet of trophies?

I was still pondering these questions when the webs about me began to bound and lurch with the scuttling fall of feet, and I turned to find myself facing Mr Webster and a pair of spider-servants.

'So!' chuckled Webster. 'The Mumby boy sees fit to join us after all!' And as the servants advanced on me, reaching out with their forelimbs, he added, 'Bring him too! Bring him to the master!'

There was no point in struggling. They stripped me of my weapons, and I let them heave me up and carry me helter-skelter down the funnel of their webs to a dark opening in the red-brown floor. As we reached that doorway, and they carried me through it, I realised that it was not a cave mouth in a captive planetoid, as I had thought. It was too regular, and the walls of the passageway beyond it were not of stone, but timber, neatly planked and fastened with good Sheffield steel. I was aboard an aether-ship, larger and finer than *Sophronia*, but no less earthly. I could even guess its name. It was HMS *Aeneas*! Those impudent spiders had captured it and woven it into their nest!

Cabins and staterooms passed me in a blur as I was hurried through that web-bound hulk in a knock-kneed scurrying of white legs and feelers. And then, suddenly, we were in the great cabin at the stern, where the face of Saturn shone in coolly through a spread of windows lightly fogged with web.

Jack sat there, looking pale faced and purplish around the lips, recovering, I guessed, from a dose of spider venom. And before him, in a fine wing chair, the spider's master waited.

I had expected something monstrous, for it stood to reason that this spider-general must be vast and wicked indeed if even Mr Webster called him 'master'. But our captor-in-chief was no monster at all; just a man. A small, slight man, with an apologetic sort of face and no chin to speak of, dressed rather eccentrically in clothes which had been woven for him out of spider web.

'The Mumby whelp,' said Webster, by way of introduction, as his minions let go of me and I drifted slowly down to the deck.

'*Arp?*' said Jack. His mouth was too numb yet for him to speak clearly, but he had a good try. '*You rebebber be pelling you bout optor arbigan?*'

'Jack is trying to tell you that he and I are old friends,' said our host, with a kindly smile. He stood up, and walked towards me, holding out his hand. 'Doctor Phineas Ptarmigan at your service.'

CHAPTER SEVENTEEN

IN WHICH SOME PROJECTED IMPROVEMENTS TO
OUR SOLAR SYSTEM ARE DESCRIBED.

I declare, you could have knocked me down with a feather, had I not already been lying on the deck. Dr Ptarmigan picked me up and dusted me down, and as he did so I saw that he was wearing Myrtle's locket around his neck. It hung against his spider-web cravat as if it were brand new and rested on a bed of cotton wool in a jeweller's case. He saw me look at it, and his hand went to it. 'The key, Art, yes. Jack was kind enough to bring it to me.'

'But . . .' I said, and then could not think of anything to add, so I said it twice more, thus: 'But . . . But . . .'

Dr Ptarmigan smiled modestly. 'I can see that my presence here confuses you, Art. Jack too, perhaps?'

'*Ib bubby bib!*' agreed Jack.

'You were assuming that I had perished along with my expedition, lost somewhere upon the trackless aether between Saturn and the moons of Jove?' asked Ptarmigan. 'Well, I confess that pleases me. You see, that is exactly what I hoped the great world would assume. When you knew me, Jack, I was just a humble toiler in the vineyards of natural philosophy, but even then I was preparing this plan. Shall I tell you everything, so that you may see it plainly?'

Neither Jack nor I showed any great enthusiasm, but that did not trouble Dr Ptarmigan. He was one of those villains who likes to explain his plots and machinations, in case his victims have failed to understand how fiendishly clever he is.

'Many years ago,' he began, 'the manager of a comet mine sent me a specimen he had unearthed from the ice in one of his shafts. It was unlike anything else I had seen.

Well, perhaps I exaggerate. It was somewhat like a spider.

'Sensing that this was the discovery that might make my name, I began to investigate. I travelled to Mars and the lesser asteroids. I made the acquaintance of the reclusive Sir Waverley Rain, and was allowed to inspect his unrivalled collection of Martian antiquities. And slowly, "through a glass darkly" (as St Paul would have it), I began to see the truth.'

He turned and strolled away from me towards the window, moving with great ease in that faint gravity. His cobweb clothes billowed in the breezes that blew through cracks in the panes, and all the time he kept declaiming like an actor on the stage. I began to see a truth myself: Jack's Dr Ptarmigan was not entirely right in the noddle.

'Boys,' he said, waving his arms about so that the lacy webs around his wrists flip-fluttered, 'you must understand that this solar realm which we inhabit is not ours at all. It does not belong to Britain's Empire, any more than it belonged to the Martians in their time, or the lost race of Mercury in theirs. These planets which we call our home, and upon which we build our little, petty, squabbling nations, should not even be here! They had no part in our Creator's plan! Look, I shall show you. Observe, my friends, the wizardry of the First Ones, whose machines are as far beyond ours as ours are beyond the simple stone tools of the Tasmanian aborigine.'

He pointed to a nasty big cobweb which stretched across a corner of the cabin, spun between two of the wooden buttress things which we old aether dogs call 'knees'. I glanced towards Jack, thinking, 'This fellow is as mad as a milliner,' and I could see by the look in Jack's eye he thought so too. But just then an amazing thing happened, which you would need someone far wiser than me to explain. The web Ptarmigan pointed at began to shiver and shimmer, to glimmer and to glow. And like a magic-lantern slide being projected on a curtain, a picture appeared there – except that I am quite certain there *was* no magic lantern in that cabin, and what is more, this picture moved!

I gawped at it, so entranced that I did not stop to wonder what it was a picture of, till Dr Ptarmigan set me straight.

'You are looking at the Sun,' said he, pointing to a fiery orb that burned most prettily at the middle of a vast, slow-turning, milky ring or disc. 'But as you will note, it is a much younger, brighter, whiter sun that the one we know today. And around it the aether sea is not ruled by planets, but is filled instead with slowly circling bands of rubble and ice. Strange eddies sweep through these rings of ruin; planetoids collide one with another; some are destroyed, others flung out of the slow dance to wander for ever as lonely comets. Boys, this is an image of a time before the worlds were formed, when the whole of the Solar System had no more form than the rings of Saturn, enlarged to a gigantic scale! This is the world that the Creator built for his chosen ones!'

And the picture changed, showing the whirling rocks and planetoids which he had mentioned, and the skeins of web which tied them all together. From the places where fleet-foot Mercury now orbits all the way to the realms of Uranus and Pluto, all was under the dominion of the white spiders! On plains of web as broad as continents, palaces of silken thread arose. On silken parachutes the spiders' young went soaring outwards on the solar wind to colonise clumps of lonely stone still further from the Sun. Spider musicians stretched harps of web across the sky, and filled the aether with their music. Spider artists caught sunlight in great discs of web, and broke it into rainbows. It really was all quite pretty.

'This is the world that was ours,' said Mr Webster, who had been watching the moving pictures over my shoulder. 'For a million years we ruled here. Great were the cities we wove, the gossamer machines that we devised. Our web-ships sailed to other stars, and on towards the island galaxies. And then . . .'

'And then the Shaper came,' said Dr Ptarmigan, and shook his head, and used a cobweb handkerchief to wipe away a tear.

The moving pictures filled with destruction now: webs crumpled and tore; spiders went tumbling into the night. The rocks and planetoids which had been their home began to collide faster and faster, clumping into stony fists. The bigger they grew, the harder they were bombarded by smaller rocks, by ice mountains which burst and spilled water across their dry surfaces. Huge swirling clouds of gas which had been the backdrop to the spider cities tightened into balls and began to spin. And in the midst of all of it, I thought I glimpsed a strange craft riding the blasts of world-shuddering explosions, sending out pale rays which caught and steered yet more rocks into collision with the new-formed worlds. Fleets of spiny, jet-black spiderships flung themselves across the aether to do battle with it, and it swept them aside with a lash of light and sculpted their wreckage into the core of a minor moon.

A thousand million years passed like a sigh. The spiders were gone now. Where their lacy cities had once circled

were
the worlds I
knew: Mars and Earth
and Jupiter and all their fleets of
moons.

'The First Ones cannot live long on worlds like these,'
Dr Ptarmigan told us. 'Gravity pulls too strongly at them
there; their legs grow weak, their webs are warped. Once
the Shaper built these worlds, the First Ones began to die.
And on the new worlds, all kinds of vermin crept and
crawled. Where once there had only been the purity of the
First Ones, soon all kinds of beings raised up their ugly
heads and thought themselves the masters of Creation. The
First Ones took to weaving their webs among the asteroids,
among lonely comet clouds in the dark beyond the outer
worlds. But even there the new life grew, displacing and
destroying them. They fought back when they could,
destroying the space empires of Mars and Mercury. But

slowly, one by one, they died, or left in search of new suns. Now only a handful survive; poor lonely outcasts among these Saturnian rings.'

Really, the way he went on, it was almost enough to make you blub. I had to keep reminding myself that what he was telling us was all fibs. Everyone knows (I thought) that the worlds of the Sun were made by God, in six days, like it says in Scripture.

Anyway, Dr Ptarmigan seemed to have concluded his lecture. He took Myrtle's locket from around his neck and toyed with it, smiling at Jack and me all the while.

'All this I learned from the ancient texts in Sir Waverley's collection,' he said proudly. 'And the more I discovered, the more clearly I saw the truth. The First Ones are the true masters of the aether, and ourselves and the other races merely interlopers, the puppets of that wicked Shaper who stole the First One's realm away from them.' (Mr Webster purred in agreement at that.) 'So I decided to make amends. I began to petition the Government about an expedition to Saturn, and volunteered myself as its chief naturalist, thus giving myself the chance to speak with the First Ones, whom only I knew we would meet here. I was not disappointed! The rest of the ship's company were seized as soon as we sailed into the web-maze, but the spider-general, the noble creature you know as Mr Webster, was impressed enough by my knowledge of his ancient language to stay his stinger, and we soon became firm friends.'

'Ptarmigan has promised that he will help us to reclaim what is ours,' said Mr Webster.

'Quite so,' agreed Dr Ptarmigan. 'There are few of the First Ones left now. This web-city is a mere feeble echo of the glories which once were theirs, and they live a sad life here, devouring space moss and the creatures they trap in their nets. They had quite lost hope, till I arrived to cheer them. But with my encouragement Mr Webster has salvaged one of their ships, the only one of the First Ones' spine-ships to have survived from the olden times. It is far superior to our gimcrack earthly aether-ships. We repaired it using some bits and pieces from the *Aeneas* and I used it to travel in secret to Mars, where I tried to convince Sir Waverley Rain to join our cause. Alas, he lacked the vision to see our point of view, and we were forced to remove him. He is sleeping peacefully in the web-chamber above us, and his place in the great world was taken by a cunningly crafted automaton, controlled by one of Mr Webster's smaller colleagues.'

'A little tiny chap,' agreed Webster, holding up a foreleg with the pincers about six inches apart. 'Bred him special for the task, we did.'

'So *that's* why the old fellow in the alcove looked familiar!' I said to myself. I had seen his portrait many times, in the advertisements which Rain & Co. put out.

'Alas, your troublesome sister and her friends smashed the false Sir Waverley,' said Dr Ptarmigan.

'*My* sister?' I asked. '*Myrtle?*' For I could not imagine Myrtle smashing automata. (Nor having friends, for that matter.) But Dr Ptarmigan was not to be distracted from his speech.

'It does not signify,' he said. 'Our plans are well advanced, and little petty acts of human vandalism cannot upset them now.'

'What plans?' asked Jack, speaking much more clearly as the effects of the spider sting wore off.

'Ah!' cried Dr P., looking pleased that he'd asked. 'You see, Jack, while studying the books in Sir Waverley's unrivalled library I was able to confirm what Webster here has long suspected. *The vessel which brought the Shaper here still exists!* It hangs abandoned in space, its power forgotten.'

'Larklight!' said Jack.

'That is what they call it now,' Ptarmigan admitted.

'But Larklight's just a house!' I cried. 'No, it is more than a house; it's a home! It is my home!'

Ptarmigan ignored my outburst. I suppose he did not want little things like people and their homes spoiling the grandeur of his great scheme to improve the Solar System.

'Larklight!' he said. 'If I could control it, I might use it to undo everything the Shaper did. So I sent Mr Webster and some of his soldiers to secure it. And now, Jack, thanks to you, I have the key!' (Here he paused to look fondly at Myrtle's locket, which dangled from his long, pale fingers.) 'I shall travel there at once, and go aboard and use the vessel's gravitational engines to split apart the gimcrack worlds the Shaper made and spread a ring of ruin round the Sun where my friends may weave a new world for themselves. And in that world I shall live with them, and study their arts and their society.'

'But the British will stop you!' Jack shouted, and I thought it quite cheering that even a rogue like he put his faith in our Royal Navy when the chips were down. 'They have hundreds of ships,' he told Dr Ptarmigan. 'Thousands of soldiers. They'll never let you!'

'Ha ha!' Dr Ptarmigan chortled, in the fake sort of way that people use to laugh at vicars' jokes at Harvest Supper. 'We have plans under way to deal with *them*. Why, you yourself, with your crew of vermin, have run rings around the British Empire, Jack. Do you honestly believe that the First Ones will be troubled by them? By the time our great work begins, Britain will be in ruins, and all its fleets and armies leaderless.'

I put up my hand to ask a question. All this talk was very interesting, no doubt, but not once had Dr Ptarmigan said anything to explain what my dear departed mother was doing asleep in his webs upstairs.

'Yes, Art?' he said, with a patient smile.

'You've got my mother asleep up there,' I complained.

'Of course,' said he. 'Sir Waverley as well. I would not let harm come to any of my really useful captives. Who knows when I might need them? I keep them close at hand, in the chamber above this ship.'

'But why Mother?' I demanded. 'What makes her useful to you? She is just . . . just Mother!'

At that moment there was a great commotion just beyond the doorway. Spider-servants were twittering and chittering at each other, and Mr Webster's eyes flashed with angry light as he turned his fat body to hear what they were saying.

'What?' cried Dr Ptarmigan, listening to the spider language. 'They can't have! You said you had caught them all!'

I had been so busy listening to Dr Ptarmigan expounding his dreams that it had not occurred to me to wonder had become of Ssillissa and Yarg, last seen darting into those alcoves in the web. Of course, as soon as the spiders had dragged me away they had set to work waking the rest of the crew, and cutting away the webs that bound them, and naturally the first thing they all did upon recovering their wits was to come and rescue Jack.

Poor Dr Ptarmigan looked quite taken aback at the thought that a party of assorted pests could outwit his First Ones. 'Well, stop them!' he cried, springing to his feet, as terrible Grindle-ish curses and spidery squealings echoed down the companionway outside. I heard the familiar,

rather cheering sound of Yarg and Squidley's electric tentacles smiting spiders. Mr Webster shot out a claw to snatch Jack up, and I think he might have dashed him against a wall or bitten off his head, but just then I saw, all fogged and ripply through the cabin windows, the broad, reassuring shape of Mr Munkulus swinging towards us on a rope of spider silk, his big flat feet held out in front of him like a ram.

'Look!' I cried.

Mr Webster lowered Jack and turned himself to see. Dr Ptarmigan turned too, and as he did so Mr Munkulus came crashing into the cabin, filling it with a slow storm of shattered glass and splintered woodwork as his size-twenty-four space boots smashed the old stern-window to fragments!

Old Webster made a grab at him as he somersaulted through the cabin, but Munkulus was ready for him.

Drawing a cutlass, he hewed off the spider's forelimb, and it went backwards in a tangle of legs and a lazy spray of blood globs. Then Mr Munkulus drew another sword and tossed it towards Jack, who plucked it from the air as it cartwheeled past him. Together they turned on Mr Webster, but Mr Webster was already scrambling to escape, calling out in his own twittery tongue as he forced his way out through the cabin door.

'What about the Earthlet?' asked Mr Munkulus, looking towards Dr Ptarmigan, who was cowering behind his desk, his face as pale as his cobweb clothes.

'Leave him,' said Jack. 'He was very good to me once.'

I had just enough of my wits left about me to run and snatch my sister's locket from the fellow's shaking hand. Then we plunged out all together into the dim passageways of that ghost ship, and found Ssillissa and Grindle waiting there, among a heap of clutched white baskets that had been spider-soldiers. 'Come on!' they hollered, and 'Jack!' and things, and we followed them back up the passage that Mr Webster and his myrmidons had dragged me down, until we burst out into the space and light of the web-chamber. The rest of the crew were there, looking down at us from that line of alcoves high above, and with them was Mother.

'Heavens, Arthur!' she said when she saw me climbing towards her up the webs. 'Is that you?'

'Oh, Mother!' I cried. 'I am so glad you are not dead, but we must leave now. There are a great many spiders after us!'

And sure enough, when I looked behind me, I saw them pouring out of the hulk of the poor old *Aeneas*. They were spider-soldiers, and every one of them looked more adept at climbing those walls of web than us mere humans. Mr Munkulus turned and emptied his pistol into the approaching horde, then flung it at them and climbed onwards, but the spiders climbed faster, scrambling over the bodies of their fallen comrades.

I looked up, and it seemed such an awfully long way to where my mother waited. I thought how sad it would be if I were caught before I reached her, and what a disagreeable awakening she would have had if she had to watch her dear Art ripped to bits by vengeful arthropods before she had even had breakfast or a cup of tea. And an idea came to me, as ideas sometimes do at moments of great desperation. I ripped a curtain of web from the entrance of an empty alcove close beside me, and then, holding it tightly beneath my arm, I groped in the pocket of my jacket, and tugged out my box of lucifers. I had remembered, you see, the way that handful of web had burned so well when I was fighting the Jovian squid, and it seemed to me that the spiders might be wary of fire, living in a place made of such stuff. I hoped to try and make a burning torch, with which I might keep them at bay.

My first match failed; my second too. My hands were shaking so badly that I could barely grasp the box. The third match flared, but as I raised my handful of web to try and light it the whole lot, web, box, and all, flashed into a bright sheet of flame and I screeched in pain and dropped it. Down and down it drifted, trailing smoke and handfuls of eager sparks. The spiders scrambled over each other to get out of its path.

The floor of the chamber, where anchors of thick web tied it to the hulk of the *Aeneas*, caught light like a dry leaf in a bonfire. Heat brushed my face, and the screech and pop of roasting spiders filled the chamber. Black smoke stung my eyes as I climbed to where my mother waited. Already the threads which formed the walls on either side were beginning to smoulder and glow red. I didn't spare them a thought as I hugged Mother, and she hugged me.

'I woke them all,' Ssillissa was telling Jack, as she reached down to help haul him up, and presented him with some of the weapons we had brought with us from the *Sophronia*. 'I woke them all and told them that the spiders had you aboard that old hulk, and we hatched a plan to save you.'

'Brave Ssil!' said Jack, and kissed her. It was just a quick, friendly kiss on the cheek, but it made poor Ssil blush purple as an aubergine. Behind her, the reunited twins were hugging one another, their bright crowns woven together in a great knot of happy light.

'There's another one here,' said Grindle, who was trying to tug the slumbering form of Sir Waverley Rain out of his alcove. 'He won't wake up, the great lump. Do we need him?'

'Poor Sir Waverley!' cried Mother. 'He has been here longer than any of us; no wonder he cannot shake off his sleep!'

'Bring him!' ordered Jack, climbing nimbly past us, and Mr Munkulus heaved the slumbering industrialist over his shoulder.

There was no time for me to talk to Mother, or to ask her any of the thousand questions which were buzzing about like hornets in my head. I took her hand, and we scrambled together up the sloping web, while the hot updrafts wafted flags of blazing web past from the inferno below. Twice, bold spider-warriors, scrambling up through the smoke and flames, almost reached us, but each time Ssillissa, who was bringing up the rear, dislodged them with a swipe of her tail and sent them tumbling down again before they could do us harm.

Gasping and half choked with smoke, we reached the chamber's upper entrance, and there we halted, bunching up behind Jack and Grindle, who were leading the way. Ahead of us the web-tunnel was full of spiders, their bright masses of eyes filled with hate and firelight.

To everyone's surprise it was my mother who said, 'This way!' and began tearing at the tunnel wall. Strands and clumps of web began to come away beneath her fingers, and Jack soon saw what she was about and set to work with his cutlass, hacking and slashing at the thick cross-hatchings of silk. 'Why, thank you!' said Mother sweetly, and Jack replied, 'Don't mention it, missus.' I wish Myrtle had been there, for it would have pleased her to see that despite our grim predicament we had not forgotten our manners.

The wall tore through at last. In the widening gap I saw a gleam of Saturn-light, and then the warm, yellow face of the planet herself. She hung before us like a ripe, gigantic peach as we squeezed out one by one to cling to one of the spiders' spindly bridges in the open aether. After a moment we were joined by Ssilissa, who had been holding off the spiders in the tunnel, and we all looked together for an escape route.

Yet none did we see. The great web-fortress flickered like a fire-balloon, venting panicky spiders from every entrance. Squads of spider-servants were hurrying off towards another web-castle, bearing in their forelegs wobbling, bean-shaped bags of jelly which I guessed were spider eggs. I thought how disappointed Father would have been in me, that I had not bothered to try and find out how the spiders were born, or what monstrous spider queen had laid those eggs. But I did not have time to grow regretful, for at the end of the bridge we were all clinging to, patrols of spider-soldiers were busy severing the strands with their sharp mandibles, cutting the blazing castle adrift to stop fire spreading to the rest of their web.

'I am afraid we find ourselves in a rather trying situation,' said my mother. 'Should escape prove quite impossible, I should just like to say thank you to you all for rescuing me from that horrid prison, whoever you may be.'

'Jack Havock, ma'am,' said Jack, a little startled, I think, by the cool way she was taking our predicament.

'Well, Jack Havock,' said she, 'I congratulate you on your pluck, and on the loyalty of your friends. Now, how are we to extricate ourselves from this maze?'

'We've got a ship,' said Nipper, 'tangled in those webs yonder.'

We all looked to where he pointed, and there, like a blot of dark ink soaking through the sheets of gossamer, we discerned the form of our dear old *Sophronia*. We did not know if we might free her, but she seemed a better place to be than out there among the spiders in the aether, so we each took the deepest breath we could of that thin element and jumped from the bridge, bare seconds before the spider demolition squad chewed through the final strands and the whole thing snapped in half like a broken fiddle string.

We were all well used to propelling ourselves about in zero BSG, so it was not difficult for us to flap our way across the aether to the web-mass where the ship was caught. But I confess I was surprised by how expert my mother seemed. Ssillissa's crinoline made her faff and

flounder, but Mother, despite her fashionable clothes, swam through that nothingness as gracefully as any Aetheric Icthyomorph, and made it to the *Sophronia* ahead of all of us.

The ship was still unguarded. Either the spiders had not realised which way we had gone, or they were too busy fighting the fire inside their cobweb castle, which cast long rays of ruddy light and sombre shadow through the nets of web and drifting rock about us. Mr Munkulus and Grindle began hacking with their cutlasses at the webs which tethered the *Sophronia*. The rest of us dived in through her hatches, and set to work heaving them shut and starting the air generator, while Ssillissa scrambled down into the wedding chamber and set about stoking the alembic. I helped the Tentacle Twins carry Sir Waverley to a hammock and strap him in, and then went to wait beside my mother, who was looking about with great interest at the ship. I felt a little self-conscious at bringing her into such a cluttered, scruffy place, but when Nipper lit the gas lamps I saw that the hoverhogs had been hard at work, and that most of the crumbs and crusts which had been drifting about before had vanished. (The hogs themselves were fast asleep, hovering in a cosy pink clump at the end of their strings.)

'This is the *Sophronia*, Mother,' I said, clearing a few severed spider limbs from a locker to make a space where she might sit down. 'She is a good ship. Captain Havock took Myrtle and myself in after the spiders seized Larklight.'

'The spiders have Larklight!' cried my mother, and for the first time since she was restored to me I thought I saw real alarm in her eyes. 'Tell me they do not have the key!'

I remembered the locket, and, reaching into my pocket, drew it out and showed it to her, whereupon she kissed me and ruffled my hair and called me a clever boy. I would have given anything to understand what was going on, and wished that she would explain herself, but at that moment the *Sophronia*'s engines started, and Mr Munkulus and Grindle came plunging inside, the Ionian bellowing, 'All hands to battle stations! Those nasty insects are upon us again!'

All hands meant me, I supposed, so I left Mother and ran to help the Tentacle Twins run out one of *Sophronia*'s big, antique space cannon. Through the gunport I could see the nearby webs silhouetted in the glow of the great fire that still burned off the shoulder of Saturn. Every strand was crawling with the spiders.

Sophronia groaned and shuddered, trying to heave herself clear. The Tentacle Twins trilled at me to stand aside and Squidley pulled the lanyard of our cannon, setting it off with a great roar and severing a thick, spider-creeping bridge of web a few hundred yards away. I opened the shot-locker and heaved out a fresh round, which Yarg shoved into the smoking breech. Grindle's gun went off on the far side of the ship, and he gave a shrill squeal of victory – 'Got the ————!' and then noticed Mother watching and said, 'Pardon my Martian, ma'am.'

But the *Sophronia* was still trapped, and now we could hear the scrabble and scratch of white claws on the hull above our heads. A hatch burst open, and Jack emptied a blunderbuss into the horrid face of the spider who pushed through it, the recoil throwing him across the ship. Bouncing from the bulkheads like an India-rubber ball, he shouted, 'Ssil!'

Ssilissa poked her head out of the wedding chamber, looking more inhuman that ever in her smoked glass goggles. She was in time to see Nipper snatch a cutlass and slice the foreclaws off another spider as it groped in through the hatch. The *Sophronia* was pitching now with the weight of spiders scrambling over her, and all the hatches were bowing inwards under their fierce, incessant blows. Grindle fired his gun again, but didn't waste time watching where the shot had gone, just flung the breech open and ran to reload.

'Get us moving!' Jack ordered. 'Full speed, Ssil!'

'But Jack, among these rocksss and websss . . .'

'The wedding, Ssil! Begin the wedding!'

She stared at him a moment longer, then turned and fled back to her work. Another hatch gave way, and another spider tumbled in, scrabbling and clawing, until my mother, of all people, snatched up the cleaning rod from Grindle's gun and pinned the monster to the wall as if it were a specimen in a collector's display drawer. 'Good Heavens, Mother!' I cried. 'Please do not overexert yourself!'

The *Sophronia* shook herself like an old dog waking. From the exhaust-trumpets beneath her stern burst the bright, uncanny clouds of wedding fire. Still the webs held tight, although those astern were already parting and bursting into flame. Suddenly a spiky ship loomed up huge in my porthole, driving towards us as if intent upon impaling *Sophronia* upon its spines. It was the very ship I had seen off Larklight on that first day, and again on the night the spiders stole poor Myrtle, and I knew somehow that Mr Webster was aboard it, determined to destroy us all.

And then, before I could so much as cry out a warning, we were moving, and moving so fast that everything was a blur, a rush of fire and gossamer and spider legs that brightened and faded and vanished into gold.

Thus we made good our escape from the webs of Saturn, which is a horrid place, and one that I pray I may never have cause to visit again!

CHAPTER EIGHTEEN

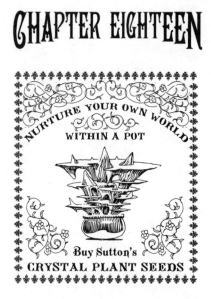

NURTURE YOUR OWN WORLD
WITHIN A POT
Buy Sutton's
CRYSTAL PLANT SEEDS

IN WHICH I DISCOVER THE CURIOUS
TRUTH ABOUT MY MOTHER.

Safe on the seas of space, we licked our wounds. Jack had a dozen claw cuts on his hands and arms, and his coat hung in bloody tatters. The Tentacle Twins had each lost several arms, and Mr Munkulus had been badly nipped by spider pincers. Yet all of them made light of their injuries, and said that they counted themselves lucky to be alive.

'We must go to Larklight,' said Mother, when everyone's wounds were bandaged, and my own poor, scorched fingers had been smeared with soothing balm.

'No,' said Jack firmly. 'Myrtle's on Mars. That's what Ptarmigan and Webster said. In danger on Mars. Dead, maybe. But we've got to go to her.'

'No, Jack,' said Mother.

'What, don't you care about her at all, missus?' he cried angrily. 'Your own daughter? I'd have thought –'

'I care exceedingly,' said Mother. 'But if she is dead we are already too late to help her, and if she is not she faces a greater danger. We all do. The spiders control Larklight, and even without the key, they may do terrible harm there.'

'What *is* Larklight, Mother?' I asked.

She turned to me, looking troubled. 'I suppose I must tell you,' she said. 'Larklight is what you would call a ship. A ship of a most uncommon sort. It's real name is . . .' (and here she said something in a flutey, musical language that I shall not even *try* to spell) '. . . which means the *Lantern of Creation's Dawn* in the language of my people.'

'Bit of a mouthful,' grumbled Grindle.

'But I thought your people came from Cambridgeshire?' I asked.

'Dear Art!' cried Mother, smiling at me, and reaching out to take my hand. 'How can you forgive me? I am afraid that I have been less than honest about my past. I do not come from Cambridgeshire. I was born – or rather, I *came into being* – four and a half billion years ago, far from your sun, out among the island galaxies. I am – or was – a Shaper. My people have existed since the first morning of the Universe. We travel among the stars, giving new solar systems the helping hand they sometimes need to bring forth life. For we do love life, in all its infinite variety.'

I remembered the moving pictures that Dr Ptarmigan had shown us. That strange vehicle, half-glimpsed, dragging planetoids together with its flickering rays and swatting the First Ones' ships aside with fans of force. Jack must have been thinking of it too. He said, 'What about the spiders,

Mrs Mumby? You don't seem too fond of them, nor they of you.'

Mother glanced at him. 'The First Ones. Yes. Were it not for them, there might be no need for Shaping. Left to themselves, most stars stir up planets out of the clouds of dust and gas which gather around them in the aether. But the First Ones drift through space on their gossamer threads, and when they find a solar system in the early stages of formation they bind it, and tie it, and wrap it in their knots and cradles, and make sure that no worlds can ever form, and no sort of life but their own can ever thrive.'

'Until you Shapers come along and slaughter them all?' asked Jack.

'The Shapers only destroy in order to create,' said Mother. 'Though I am afraid it *is* rather hard luck on the spiders.'

'Serve them right,' said Grindle, rubbing his bruises, and most of us agreed with him. But I could see that Jack felt a sort of sympathy for those spiders. He was no friend of the British Empire, remember, and I believe he saw the Shapers as just an empire of another sort, sticking their cosmic noses into other beings' business and moulding the Universe to reflect their own notions of right and wrong.

'If it is you Shapers who make everything,' Mr Munkulus asked, 'what place is there for God?'

'Think, dear,' said Mother. 'Who made the Universe and lit the suns? Who shaped the Shapers? For Shapers are not gods, just servants of that invisible, universal will which set the stars in motion.

'Usually,' (she went on) 'when a Shaper vessel has done its work, it dies, and the Shaper aboard it dies too. At least, they *choose to cease to be* – we are not alive in the same way you are, so we can never really die. But I chose another course. After all my hard work, I longed to stay and see what grew in the gardens I had made. Oh, I slept for the first billion years or so, for these worlds were no fun at all till they had atmospheres and suchlike. But once I awoke . . . ! How jolly it all was! Life popping up everywhere! I flew about aboard the *Lantern of Creation's Dawn,* peeking down first at this planet, then that. But I could not imagine what it would feel like to be one of the creatures who lived on them, so I began taking on corporeal forms. (That means, inhabiting living bodies, Mr Grindle, dear.)

'I was a Dinosaur for a while – so invigorating! And the Age of the Great Slime Moulds on Venus was awful fun. Then, for centuries and centuries, I tried being a Martian.

Ah, the morning sun upon the porcelain pinnacles of Lllha Ahstellhion! Wind harps playing in the perfume gardens at Oeth Ahfarreth! It seems like yesterday. And then I was an Ionian, but four arms didn't suit me. I could never think what to do with all those hands. But when humans arrived . . . Oh, I simply *loved* being a human! I parked Larklight in orbit out beyond the Moon, and visited Earth every century or so. And . . . Well, I'm afraid I did something rather silly.

'I met a man named Isaac Newton. An odd sort, but *so* clever. It was sweet to watch him puzzling over gravity and so forth. How could I resist giving him a helping hand? Just little hints at first – hiding in that tree and dropping apples on his head, that sort of thing. He worked out the rest all by himself, you know. Perhaps I should have just left it at that. I admit, I got carried away. But he was such a dear.'

'What are you saying?' asked Jack. 'You mean *you* told Sir Isaac how to make the chemical wedding?'

'It's such a simple thing,'

she said. 'I thought it would amuse him. He was very keen on Alchemy, you know, and I thought he would be pleased to see some genuine transformations going on in his smelly old oven, so I suggested certain elements he might try combining. I was quite surprised at what it all led to: aethership, and the expansion of your empire into space. I confess, I was a little embarrassed. I retired to the *Lantern of Creation's Dawn* and lived quietly for a while, growing my flowers and making a few improvements to the old place. But I could not resist popping back to Earth now and then; I have grown so very fond of it. And on one of my visits I met dear Edward Mumby. Such a gentle man. He made me realise that I could not truly hope to understand your species until I had been in love, and had children . . .'

'So are Art and Myrtle human?' asked Nipper, eyeing me curiously. 'Or are they Shapers like you?'

'Human, quite human,' said Mother. 'To all intents and purposes I am human now too. I turned my back entirely on my old existence. I shut down my vessel's mighty gravitational engines, all except for a few tiny parts of them, which provide what gravity we need to keep our feet upon the floors. The rest I immobilised and locked, and hid the key in a trinket which I gave to my first-born child. You see, I was aware that a few First Ones might still exist among the nooks and crannies of the system, and I knew that it would spell disaster if ever they were able to control the *Lantern of Creation's Dawn* – Larklight, as I had come to call it.

'Little did I know how advanced their plans were! When the *Aeneas* expedition vanished I suspected the worst, and set off for England to warn the Government. Alas, the spiders seized the ship I was travelling on. They devoured my poor fellow passengers, and hid me away in their webs so that I could not interfere with the great plot they were weaving with that renegade Dr Ptarmigan.'

'But without this key they can't do any harm?' asked Jack.

'Without the key they may do a great deal of harm,' my mother cautioned him. 'They will not be able to use Larklight's power, but in their attempts to turn the gravitational engines on without the key they could trigger an explosion that would have all manner of calamitous effects. And who knows what other plans they have laid, to divert and dismay the British Empire while they struggle to set Larklight working?'

'What must we do?' asked Ssil.

'My dear, if you could use that clever brain of yours to steer us quickly to Larklight,' said Mother, 'I shall be eternally grateful. Larklight is where we must begin. Then we shall endeavour to find out the rest of their plans, and frustrate them. And we shall find dear Myrtle too,' she promised, turning to smile at me.

But I was not sure that I wanted her smiles any more. It is strange. You would think that I should have been beside myself with joy at being reunited with my dear mama. Yet all I felt towards her was anger. I was angry that she had left us, and let us grow up without her. I was angry at her for being all those billions of years old and not really human; not really my mother at all. I don't wish to sound like some fellow in a gloomy play, but I felt as if my life up until then had all been lies.

And as if she sensed my doubts, Mother came and put an arm around me while the rest of the crew began getting *Sophronia* under way. 'I am sorry I lied to you, my dear,' she said gently. 'Please believe me when I say that of all the things I have seen and done and been, there was not one that gave me so much happiness as my life with you. Shapers appreciate beauty and order, but we do not feel. I had to become a living being before I could begin to do that, and I don't think I truly understood what it meant until I knew you and Myrtle . . .'

Well, I am sure can imagine the rest; I won't go on. I don't know about you, gentle reader, but when I am reading a book and people start to blub and talk about love and such I generally think it is time to skip a few pages to the next exciting storm or gory battle. So I shall save you the trouble by skipping there myself. But I should say that I felt quite at ease with Mother again by the time *Sophronia* sailed into the trans-lunar aether. I think the rest of the crew did too, for she was a model passenger, quite unlike Myrtle. She helped us tidy up and heave all those nasty old dead spiders overboard, and never once complained of anything. And when she tucked me up in my hammock and sat and sang to me at night, I sensed my shipmates gathering close outside the cabin door to listen to her pretty voice. Poor orphan monsters, I expect they wished they could have found their own mothers among the First Ones' webs, don't you?

Ssillissa steered us swift and true across the leagues of space, and we slowed into the trans-lunar aether on the morning of the 1st of May, 1851. At first I thought Ssil must have brought us to the wrong quarter of the sky. I barely recognised the white ball of cotton wool which hung in space ahead of us. The spiders had shrouded Larklight in webs so thick that barely a rooftop or a chimney stack was to be seen, although after I had stared at it a while I spotted a familiar weathervane poking out of that cat's cradle of silk.

'It looks just like a gigantic chrysalis!' Mother said when she saw it.

'But what manner of trouble is going to hatch from it?' asked Grindle.

Jack began calling out his orders, and the rest of us jumped to obey him, even Mother; for although she might be very clever at shaping new worlds out of the raw matter of creation she could tell that Jack was the master when it came to battles, boardings and assaults from space. Grappling hooks and sidearms were readied, the cannons double-shotted, and the Tentacle Twins warbled a cheerful space shanty as they briskly sharpened cutlasses and boarding axes on a grindstone. I stood watch on the star deck while Mr Munkulus donned his armour and stuffed four cutlasses through his belt. I could see Larklight looming larger and larger as Ssilissa brought us up upon it from below. Away to my left the huge crescent of the Moon half-filled the sky, and I stared at the lonely mountains there and shuddered as I recalled my meeting with the Potter Moth.

A flash of light blazed in the corner of my eye, but when I turned it had already faded. I wondered if I should cry out to the others, but I did not want to raise the alarm until I was sure, so I used Mr Munkulus's spyglass to scan that region of the aether. I saw a dense shoal of Red Whizzers swooping and turning in perfect unison, their scales flashing with moonshine. Had they been the source of the light I'd seen? But no; for as I watched they scattered, and through them came rushing a huge, dark, thorny shape which I knew all too well. It was the spine-ship of the First Ones! That flash I'd seen had been the light of its engines as it swung towards us!

'Ship ahoy!' I shouted, not certain of the correct aethernautical term. 'Help! Help!' I added, as I scrambled to climb back inside, but I feared I was too late. Already big, prickly balls from the spine-ship's guns were whooshing past me, drawing faint, pale trails across the aether. As I dropped back into the main cabin I felt the *Sophronia* lurch and shudder as the broadside slammed into her stern, filling the air with smoke and sparks and cartwheeling splinters and the shrieks and shouts of my shipmates . . .

CHAPTER NINETEEN

ANOTHER EXCERPT FROM MY SISTER'S DIARY, CONTAINING
A TRUE ACCOUNT OF HER PART IN THE RECENT
UNPLEASANTNESS AT HYDE PARK.

May 1st

What an extraordinary day! I shall write down quickly all that happened, in case I do not live to speak of it. Oh, how my hand does shake! Outside the windows of the building in which I am sheltering I can hear the crash and clatter of collapsing masonry, and the afternoon sky grows dark with smoke . . .

How different it all looked this morning! As we slowed over the polar regions and began our descent we saw that the skies above the British Isles were quite clear, (apart from a pother of factory smoke above the mill towns of the north country and the potteries). The rising sun shone brightly down on our dear green homeland, set in its silver sea, and I doubt that there was any heart aboard the *Indefatigable* left unstirred as we approached the cloud of aether-ships which clustered about the orbital terminus of Mr Brunel's great space elevator.

There we left the ship, Mr and Mrs Burton and myself. Captain Moonfield suggested that we take a party of his space marines with us, and I wished we had, for they looked very splendid in their red coats and white cross belts. But Mr Burton explained that speed was of the essence, and that we should reach London more quickly if we went alone.

There was some delay at the elevator station, but when Mr Burton waved his repeating-pistol in the air and announced that the safety of Queen and Empire depended on our reaching London forthwith we were soon permitted to descend, and emerged after a half-hour or so in early morning sunlight at the elevator's base, which is built at a squalid spot called Shoeburyness, near the mouth of the river Thames. There, Mr Burton at once commandeered a swift-moving steam packet, which carried us upriver in great style, past little villages and docks and warehouses and through the clusters of shipping in the Pool of London. I looked with delight upon the sights: the Tower, and St Paul's Cathedral, and the new Houses of Parliament, still wrapped up in scaffolding.

I wonder how many of those great edifices will still be standing by this evening?

Once we left the water our progress grew slower, for crowds of people were making their way to Hyde Park, intent on seeing the opening ceremony of the Great Exhibition. It was late morning before we reached the park, and saw the roofs of the magnificent Crystal Palace rising above the trees ahead.

I shall try to forget what happened later, and record my first impressions of that wondrous building. It is – or rather it *was* – like nothing so much as an almighty greenhouse. Indeed the original design was done by a Mr Paxton, gardener to the Duke of Devonshire, and famed formerly for designing the great hothouse at Chatsworth, where that gentleman's collection of extraterrestial flora is housed. The palace is so large that whole groves of elm trees are enclosed within it, and the gleam of sunlight on its many windows so bright that on a clear day it may be seen from the Moon!

But although we could admire the wonders of Mr Paxton's design, as we disembarked from our carriage among the throngs outside, our hearts were filled with gloomy forebodings, for we all knew that the actual building of the place had been carried out by Sir Waverley's company, using prefabricated sections shipped from his works on Mars. Did some infernal machine lurk hidden in one of the iron cross-trees which held up that enormous arched roof? And if so, how might we contrive to find it?

Mr Burton had already sent several warnings by telegraph, advising that the opening ceremony be delayed and the palace and its surrounds cleared. However, his messages had either gone astray, or been dismissed as the ravings of a crank or madman. As we hastened through the turnstiles we heard fanfares sounding, and when we had recovered from our awe and surprise at the great hall of sunlight in which we found ourselves we saw, upon a podium in the heart of that great space, the Queen, her children, and Prince Albert, surrounded by as great a gathering of Bishops,

Generals, Lords and Members of Parliament as I imagine I shall ever see!

'Stand aside, in the name of Her Majesty's Secret Service!' cried Mr B., and made a path for us through the throng. People turned to stare at us, looking askance at Ulla's rusty elfin face and borrowed trousers; looking at me too, I fear, for to my shame I still wore my old brown dress, and although the *Indefatigable*'s laundry had done their best with it, it was sadly stained and faded by all that it had been through!

We hurried past displays which seemed to come from every world of the Sun and every nation on the Earth, as if Science, Art and Labour had all poured out their horns of plenty in that mansion of glass. Somehow we managed to draw close to the podium, where a clerical gentleman in a white surplice with big, puffed sleeves was intoning a long and somewhat dreary-sounding sermon.

'Please! Clear this place!' shouted Mr Burton, and Ulla cried, 'There may be an infernal machine close by. We expect an explosion at any moment!'

Some of the ladies and gentlemen about us reacted in horror, and a sort of eddy swept through the crowd as they began shoving their way towards the doors. But the Royal

Family did not appear to have heard. I stared at the Queen. She was much smaller than I had imagined her, and although she wore a splendid gown of pink silk with sprays of lace at the sleeves and bosom, and a broad blue sash, and a tiara, she was not beautiful in her own face or person. Indeed, she seemed rather plump, with a beaky nose and slightly bulging eyes, and the look upon her face was one of mild boredom rather than the noble and gracious expression which one expects of one's monarch.

A horrid thought came to me then. What if the white spiders had exchanged Sir Waverley Rain for an automaton simply so that he might affect a still more dastardly exchange? I clutched at Ulla's sleeve and whispered, 'Mrs Burton! That is not the Queen!'

'Now, steady on,' I heard Ulla warn me, but my mind was made up; I was perfectly convinced that my dreadful surmise was correct. As fabricator of the Crystal Palace, Sir Waverley had doubtless been invited to visit Her Majesty at Balmoral, her new estate in Scotland. In that remote spot he must have overpowered her and set up this replica in her place! For how better to smuggle an infernal device into the heart of our island home than to conceal it in the person of our own beloved monarch? No doubt in an instant more, when the clerical gentleman had concluded his address, this facsimile queen would turn upon her family and the assembled Members of Parliament and rend them limb from limb with an arsenal of concealed weapons!

Horror overcame my natural meekness and good breeding, and I pushed my way past several gentlemen who stood between me and the podium and ran quickly up the steps. I believe I shrieked, 'She is not the Queen!' or something similar, and I heard a great rush of astonished

voices echo all about me as I lunged at the demure shape in front of me and threw her to the floor. 'You'll see!' I cried, tugging off her tiara and pulling at her glossy hair. 'Her head opens! There will be one of *them* inside!'

Except, of course, that her head did *not* open. She was not an automaton at all, merely a small, startled woman, staring up at me, while all around me men shouted and women screamed, and Prince Albert drew his ornamental sword and brandished it at me, demanding to know the meaning of this outrage.

I believe it was the most embarrassing moment of my entire life. I am quite confident that, even if I live to be one hundred, I shall never be quite so humiliated again.

Of course, it is hardly likely that I shall live to be one hundred. Indeed, I am unlikely to see tomorrow morning. For as I sat there on top of our dear queen, wondering how I might begin to apologise, a terrible rending noise came from the massive iron frame of the palace, and the white spiders' master plan became all too horridly apparent.

It was not the Queen who was an automaton, nor Prince Albert, nor the Duke of Wellington, nor any other person present. The infernal machine which the spiders had inveigled into our midst was *the Crystal Palace itself*!

A thousand windows shattered and crashed down as the iron frame stirred. It is only due to the great goodness of God that nobody was impaled upon the brilliant daggers which rained down all around. Of course, panic was spreading fast, and most of the onlookers had already turned tail and were fleeing out into the park. One by one, the iron pillars which supported the palace began to uproot

The infernal machine which the spiders had inveigled
into our midst was the Crystal Palace itself !

themselves, to fold and turn and twist about. The entire palace was changing itself, transforming itself from a giant greenhouse into the semblance of a colossal metal spider! Trailing torn flags and the rags of calico sunblinds it crouched above us, blocking out the Sun, and still, with clashes and crashes, the metal girders kept folding and combining, strengthening its monstrous limbs and forming a spiky, armoured body between them.

Mr Burton discharged his pistol, but it had no effect, other than to wing one of the sparrowhawks which the Duke of Wellington had introduced into the Palace to keep down the pigeons. 'Bullets just bounce off it!' I heard him cry, and at once he and Ulla began herding the Royal Family and the startled ladies and gentlemen of the court towards a stand of trees which had been safe inside the palace until a few moments ago.

For the great iron spider was moving, creeping forwards slowly, as if testing its own strength. One forefoot crushed the boiler house which had stood behind the palace, and a flare of white steam gushed up into the sunlight. Sobbing with fright, I hurried through the swooping shadows as the huge feet stepped over us. I found myself running for a moment beside the Queen, and managed to say, 'Ma'am, I am most dreadfully sorry,' but at that moment a clawed foot tore apart a display of steam engines and other devices which had stood in the Hall of Moving Machinery, and I doubt she heard me above all the racket.

We were almost among the trees when, with a deafening 'WOOF!', they burst into flame. The *Indefatigable*, swooping down from orbit, had trained her Phlogiston Agitators on the iron spider, and one had missed and almost roasted us. The others played across the spider's armoured body, causing it to glow red hot, but before any real damage could be done it reached up with one limb and swiped the *Indefatigable*'s wings and engines off. The poor ship veered away. I heard someone say that her crew had managed to bring her down in the Thames.

When I finished watching this aerial calamity I looked around, and realised that I had become separated from the royal party. For an instant I caught sight of the Burtons. I was horror-struck to observe that poor Mr Burton had been struck by a shard of twisted metal flung out by the exploding steam contraptions. It had gone clean through his leg, pinning him to the lawn. Dear, brave Ulla was struggling to free him, but above them one of the Crystal Palace's huge iron feet was descending! 'Ulla!' I screamed. I will never know if she heard me – she did not look away from her husband's face. Thankfully I was spared the sight of their dreadful end, for the park was full of running people (many of them a very common sort). I was swept helplessly along with them, and the Burtons were lost to my view just before the foot came down on them.

At last I reached this small red-brick building which I take to be the hut of some park keeper or other menial. There is, at least, a teapot here, and a calendar with engraved views of London in happier times, and a copy of this morning's *Times*, and a stub of pencil with which I am writing this. If I peek from the window I can see that the spider is moving ponderously away towards St James and Westminster. I have heard the boom of big guns, and seen shells burst upon its body and limbs, but all to no avail. From time to time it raises one foot and quite deliberately stamps upon some great public building or other place of interest.

I wonder what has become of the Queen? I wonder if I shall be charged with High Treason, for attacking her? Oh, I only ever wanted to be genteel, and now I have sat upon royalty, and am trapped in a park keeper's hut, likely at any moment to be crushed to atoms by that giant automaton!

No. No: I must not give in to despair. After all, is it not

partly my doing that this terrible machine has been unleashed upon our capital? I do not understand it, but the spiders' plot all has something to do with Larklight, and Art, and poor Papa, and me. Now that Mr Burton and his Ulla have been squashed, I am the only soul on Earth who knows about the white spider which must lurk within that greater spider somewhere, directing its rampages. It must fall to me, mere weak maiden though I am, to put an end to it. I may die in the attempt, but I must not let my fear get the better of me. No, I must gird up my – whatever one is supposed to gird in such a situation, and put my trust in GOD and be as bold and resolute as some Christian martyr

of the olden days!

The machine has paused in its wicked work, and one of its sturdy iron legs has come to rest not far from where I hide. I think that if I could reach it unnoticed I might climb up to the lower joint, and from there to the upper joint, and from there creep inside its iron body, where I suppose the controlling spider lurks. And if it is no larger than the little brute which crept out of the false Sir Waverley on Mars . . .

I shall arm myself with whatever weapon I can find, and then venture forth to do my duty.

But, oh, how I wish dear Jack were here with me!

CHAPTER TWENTY

WE RETURN HOME (HUZZAH!), BUT DISCOVER THAT IT MAY
ALREADY BE TOO LATE TO SAVE DEAR OLD ENGLAND FROM
THE VENGEANCE OF THE FIRST ONES (BOO!).

I spun backwards, head over heels, and saw that a vast
and raggedy hole had appeared in the hull, up near the
stern. All sorts of things were whirling out through it
– kettles and cannon balls, enamel mugs and shards of
shattered planking – and in the inky aether beyond I saw
the spiky black shape of the spiders' ship go swooshing by,

trailing a wake of smoke from the broadside she'd just unleashed at us.

'D——d clever bugs, them spiders,' said Mr Munkulus, catching me before I could go the same way as the mugs and kettles. 'They've followed us all the way from Saturn's rings!'

'Dr Ptarmigan is insane, but he is no fool,' said Mother, training a fire-hose on a coil of smouldering ropes while Yarg and Squidley worked the pump handle. 'He guessed we'd be bound for Larklight, and trailed us here.'

'Go about!' Jack was shouting, half choked with smoke. 'Ssil! Bring us about!'

But the song of the great alembic had died. Lilac smoke was billowing out of the *Sophronia*'s wedding chamber, which had borne the brunt of the spider's attack. Through the swirling smoke came Nipper, carrying Ssillissa, who hung limply in his pincers, leaking clouds of purple blood.

And outside, between the pale horns of the crescent Moon, the spider-ship was turning, turning, making ready to swing back on a second pass and empty another broadside into our poor, crippled *Sophronia*!

Just then, with a soft, yielding sort of crunch, our drifting ship crashed against the veils of web which covered Larklight, and her bowsprit snagged fast in the strands. My mother shouted, 'Into the house, everyone! Let us go into the house! I believe "Abandon Ship" is the proper term.'

'Leave the old *Sophronia*?' howled Mr Grindle. 'Never!'

'Dear Mr Grindle,' explained Mother, who was already opening the forward hatch, 'If we stay aboard her the First Ones will most certainly blow us to smithereens, whereas if they see that we have gone into Larklight they will leave the *Sophronia* be and follow us inside. And there, perhaps, we may have a better chance of defeating them. Mr Munkulus, be a sweetheart and bring poor Sir Waverley along.'

So Mr Munkulus unstrapped the insensate industrialist from his hammock and untied the hoverhogs' strings from their ring on the wall, and we all went after Mother, out of the hatch and along the bowsprit netting. Sure enough the looming spider-ship turned aside, and a few shots went whooshing past us as we reached the wall of web. But Jack and the others had their cutlasses out, and quickly hacked a way in for us through the gossamer. As luck would have it the *Sophronia* had struck just above the main entrance; indeed, the tip of her bowsprit, poking in through the web, had gone through Father's dressing-room window. It was quite easy to climb down and heave open the big front door, which those foolish, overconfident spiders had left unlocked!

We all stumbled into the hallway. It was dark, and a few long strands of web blew about in the breeze from the open door, but otherwise it looked much as it had on the day of Mr Webster's arrival. Bits of our smashed auto-butler bobbed about under the ceiling, and the hoverhogs who had come in with us went swooping about among the pieces, snuffling up floating  crumbs and specks of fluff and looking like pink party balloons with their strings a-trailing. I recalled what Dr Ptarmigan had said about the First Ones not liking our earthly gravitation, and guessed that they had left the gravity generator switched off for their own comfort.

'Where are all the spiders then?' wondered Mr Munkulus, leaving Sir Waverley Rain adrift in mid-air and drawing his cutlasses.

'Maybe they aren't here,' said Jack. 'They've been busy shooting about the system in that ship of theirs. I suppose they just left a skeleton crew to guard this place until he found the key.'

'So where are they?' asked Nipper.

'Lurking,' said Grindle darkly. 'They're first-class lurkers, that lot.'

'Waiting for their chums to come aboard so they can all tackle us together, no doubt,' said Jack, and Yarg and Squidley flashed their agreement with sprays of flickering tentacles.

Mother went over to where poor Ssil was floating and tried to staunch the flow of blood from her wounds. 'Oh, how fragile you all are!' I heard her murmur sadly.

At the sound of her voice Ssil woke, and stirred, and moaned with the pain of her injuries. Her face was a pale lilac colour, most unhealthy looking. She clung to Mother's hand and said, 'Oh, Mrs Mumby, tell me one thing before I die. Do you know what sort of being I am? For I hatched from an egg found drifting in space, and no one knows what laid it. Have you seen others like me ever, on any of the worlds you made?'

Mother smiled down very kindly at her, and said, 'I have never seen your like, Ssillissa. Not on any of the worlds of my sun. I believe you must have come from some other star. But you are not going to die. You will get better, and one day, I am sure, you shall find your people.'

'Oh, my people are here,' Ssil replied, looking round with a weak smile at her shipmates, and most particularly at Jack. 'I was only curious, that is all . . .'

She slipped back into unconsciousness, and at the same instant the engines of the spider-ship moaned loud and low, bringing her to a stop outside, and reminding us what peril we were in.

Mother nodded at Nipper to take over the job of nurse, and seized an umbrella which had drifted out of the stand at the foot of the stairs. 'Come, Art,' she said. 'Jack and his friends can hold those creatures off. We shall go down to the heart of the house.'

I took her hand and we propelled ourselves together down the stairways of Larklight. I was not sure what she was planning, and before I had a chance to ask her we found ourselves confronted by a particularly big and ugly spider, who had been lurking in the shadows on a low landing, just as Jack had warned. 'Rarrrhhh!' exclaimed the brute (or something similar) and lunged at us with his foreclaws. My mother neatly avoided the scything talons and darted nimbly in between his legs, where she wielded the umbrella like a rapier, poking and prodding the creature in his unprotected under-parts until he retreated, whimpering, into the dark mouth of an airshaft.

'How tiresome,' Mother complained, looking down at the globules of spider blood which were tumbling through the air, bursting against the ceiling and soaking into the carpet. 'As soon as we have saved the Solar System, Art, we shall have to redecorate.'

Just then, the boom of pistols and the clash of cutlass against spider claws began to echo down the stairwells from the hall, where Jack and the others were trying to hold off the boarding party from the First One's ship. At the same moment we heard whisperings and leggy scrabblings emerging from the air shaft. The spider which Mother had bested must have climbed off to find reinforcements from among the other creatures left to guard our house, and now they were returning!

'Quickly,' she said, pushing me past her. 'To the gravity engine!'

I suddenly understood what she was about, and as the white legs of another spider appeared out of the shaft and Mother turned with her umbrella raised and cried out lustily, '*En garde!*' I scrambled as fast as I could into the heart of Larklight, pulling myself along by means of banisters, gas mantles and the ducts which snaked along the walls towards the boiler room. After all my odd adventures that strange place, with its mysterious air currents and ever-shifting patterns on the floor, felt quite homely, and I greeted the huge, antique bulk of the gravity engine like an old friend. Lots of strands of web were hung about it, and there were many spidery claw prints in the dust on the floor all around it, but no actual spiders, thank Heaven! A few panels had been removed, exposing the intricate workings of the old machinery, but I paid them no heed, just rushed

to the main controls and heaved on the levers as I had done a hundred times before to start the gravity working again.

This time, though, I adjusted the dial so that the humming machine produced two and a half times British Standard Gravitation. 'If those First Ones don't care for the gravity upon the Earth or Mars,' I said to myself, dropping heavily to the floor, 'let us see what they make of this!'

I began to wonder if I had been quite wise as I climbed back up the spiral stairway outside the boiler room. Walking in two and a half BSG makes you feel as if you're wearing a lead suit, and granite socks, and carrying a knapsack full of flat irons on your back, while trying to balance an anvil on top of your head. By the time I reached the top of the stairs I was puffing and panting as if I had just conquered Mount Victoria. But there I was rewarded with a sight that bucked me up exceedingly. Mother was stood triumphant over the dead body of a spider which she had run through with her brolly, while two more appeared to have tumbled from the air shaft and now lay quivering and helpless on the floor, their spindly legs unable to cope with the sudden increase in their weight.

'Jolly good work, Art!' cried Mother, quickly binding up

their legs with handy lengths of web and running to kiss me (the extra gravity seemed to trouble her not a bit). Together, we made our way back upstairs towards the hall. The sounds of battle had ceased, and we could hear Mr Grindle singing a boisterous victory song, so we no longer feared for the safety of our friends. This was a good thing, as the anvil on my head seemed to be getting heavier and heavier, and Mother kept having to pause and wait for me to catch my breath.

It was during one of these pauses, as we stood on the landing below the hall, that I happened to look round and noticed a strangely shaped bundle dangling from the ceiling in a web-strung corner. I knew at once what it was. 'Oh dear!' I cried. 'Oh no! It is poor Father!'

Mother ran to him, and I hobbled after her. By the time I reached the place, she had already tugged away enough of the webs for me to see his face, which was very pale and dead looking.

'Is he . . . ?' I asked, but I could not bring myself to say, 'alive': it seemed too much to hope for.

'I believe so,' replied my mother, stroking his dear face and setting his spectacles straight. 'No doubt the spiders felt he might be useful to them.'

She stood on tiptoe then, and
kissed him. And whether it
was because she was a
Shaper, or whether
it was simply the
Power of Love,
like in a fairy
tale, the spider
venom seemed
to lose its hold
on him, and he stirred, and mumbled something, and
opened one eye. 'Amelia!' he said. 'Aha! So this is another
dream. Or, rather, an hallucination, produced by the venom
of those intriguing *pseudo-arachnidae*. I must say, this one is
more agreeable than the others.'

'Edward, my dear, I am not an hallucination,' Mother
told him, and explained, while helping him out of his
straitjacket of cobwebs, that she had not died, but merely
been captured and imprisoned by the First Ones. Of
course, they went in for a great deal of kissing and stuff
too, and calling each other by silly baby names and suchlike,
which I think was a bit unnecessary really. I'm surprised
they don't know better, being grown-ups.

All in all it was a great relief when Father felt well enough to free himself from Mother's embrace and come and greet me. 'Art!' he said, taking my hand. 'I'm glad to see you well! I feared those beasts had – well, I shall not say what I feared. They are fascinating specimens, but one does not really want them loose about the house. There was one who wore a hat, you know, and woke me up to ask me about a key . . . No, surely that must have been another dream. But, I say, where is Myrtle? I hope you have kept her safe, as I instructed.'

I did not know what to say. I know that it is wicked to tell lies, but I was afraid that if I told him the truth it might shock him into a decline.

Luckily, Mother saw what a bind I was in, and came to my rescue. 'I fear we have mislaid poor Myrtle,' she said gently. 'Finding her must be our next act. As soon as we are certain that the First Ones are defeated I shall prevail upon Jack Havock to take us to Mars, her last-known whereabouts.'

'Myrtle is on Mars?' cried poor Father, quite bewildered, as we began to follow Mother upstairs to the hall. 'And who, pray, is Jack Havock?'

'He is a very brave and personable young man,' said

Mother sweetly, 'and I believe he has formed a sentimental attachment to our Myrtle.'

'But is not Myrtle somewhat young to be forming sentimental attachments?' asked Father plaintively. And then he stopped, for we had emerged into the hall, and quite a scene of devastation it was.

Spiders lay all over the floor, some dead and clenched up on their backs, others flattened by the weight of gravity and feebly struggling. Our pirate friends were suffering the effects of two and a half BSG too, but they took it cheerfully, sitting about on the hall furniture, binding up their wounds and cleaning their cutlass blades. Jack Havock heaved himself to his feet when he saw Father, and nodded, which is as close as I ever saw him come to showing respect to his elders and betters. But he was spattered from head to toe with spider juice, and I do not believe he made a good impression upon Father. Father stared at him, and then at the gang of monsters lounging about our hall, and at last his eye lighted on Ssil, who lay on the floor near the foot of the stairs, moaning piteously while Nipper and Grindle tried to nurse her.

'That poor creature!' Father exclaimed. 'What species does she belong to? And what in all the worlds has happened to her?'

'Nobody knows what she is, Your Honour,' said Nipper, touching his shell with a respectful pincer.

'And she got blowed up by a dirty big cannon shell, begging Your Honour's pardon,' explained Grindle. 'It would have cut her right in half, it would, if it hadn't been for these prodigious great thick skirts she's took to wearing, which preserved her against the worst excesses of the blast.'

'You must bring her at once to my study!' Father cried, and I believe he was rather relieved to have an injured Xenomorph to tend to, for it saved him from having to make conversation with Jack Havock.

Nipper gathered Ssil up again and he and Grindle hurried off after Father. Mother turned to Jack and asked, 'What of Mr Webster?'

Jack shook his head. 'He was stronger than the rest of 'em, Mrs M. This gravity was too much for him, but he still managed to make it out the door, and that spiky ship of his took off with him. Gone back to Saturn's rings to lick his wounds, I reckon, and good riddance.'

A cooing and a fluttering of brightly coloured tentacles alerted us to Squidley and Yarg, who had been keeping watch on Sir Waverley Rain. The industrialist was stirring, frowning, opening his eyes at last. He looked about, and cried out at the sight of the Tentacle Twins stooping over him solicitously. They startled him so much that he rolled right off our hall table and fell crash upon the floor, where he found himself surrounded by dead and disabled spiders.

'Help! Help!' he wailed.

I waded to his side through the treacly gravity, and he seemed reassured by the sight of a normal, human boy. 'What is going on?' he cried. 'Do you know who I am? I demand to see a representative of the British Crown!'

'It's all right, Sir Waverley,' I promised. (He was being jolly rude, I thought, but I was patient with him because I remembered how startled I'd been myself when I tumbled out of that moth-pot and found myself surrounded by all Jack's crew.) 'You were a prisoner of the spiders, but we've rescued you and . . .'

I was just wondering whether it would be polite to mention that some sort of reward was probably in order when a look of ghastly horror dawned upon Sir Waverley's phiz. 'The spiders!' he cried, gripping me rather painfully by both arms. 'That traitor Ptarmigan! The Queen! The Empire! We must warn them at once!'

'Have no fear, Sir Waverley,' said my mother. 'The spiders' plan has failed. Larklight is safe.'

'Larklight?' said Sir Waverley. 'What the D—— is Larklight? Who said anything about Larklight? It is my Crystal Palace you need to be worried about! Don't you know what that unspeakable tergiversator Ptarmigan intends? He means to turn the whole building into some sort of dangerous automaton! Quickly, we must hasten to my manufactory on Phobos and stop the work at once.'

'Of course!' Mother said brightly, taking this latest instance of the spiders' villainy quite in her stride. 'We were about to depart for Mars in any case.'

I shook my head. Mother and Sir Waverley had been senseless prisoners of the First Ones for so long that they had rather lost track of time. I said, 'But Mother, it's too late! We cannot hope to stop the Crystal Palace being built!

It has already been assembled, and stands in Hyde Park. There is to be a grand opening ceremony on the first of . . . Oh, golly! Today!'

CHAPTER TWENTY-ONE

Excerpt from Lord Tennyson's

Ode Upon the Emergency in London

Onward raged the iron titan,
Onward stormed the crystal beast,
Proud London, crush'd before it's mighty wake,
Pandemonium unleash'd!

But in the blackened heavens,
A flash! of golden sun,
The batteries fall silent,
All hands are raised as one.

What apparition springs upon my sight?
Abode of Angels, borne on wings of light!

IN WHICH A GREAT MANY SENSATIONAL THINGS OCCUR.

I will say this for my mother; she is not easily disheartened. Most people, upon learning that an evil automaton may be stomping about London, laying waste the heart of Britain's Empire, would have been inclined to fret, or even dither. Not Mother. I suppose when you are billions of years old and have helped bring the Solar System into being and watched whole species rise and vanish, you learn to view these little setbacks philosophically.

'Jack, dear,' she said, turning to him, 'how long would it take us to reach London aboard that ship of yours?'

Jack shook his head. 'Can't be done,' he said. 'That broadside from the spiders knocked out our wedding chamber. It'll take weeks to repair it, and only Ssil knows how.'

'Very well,' said Mother, as if this were no more than a minor annoyance. 'I had hoped,' she sighed, 'to keep Larklight a secret, but I see there is no other way of bringing this affair to its conclusion. Have your people make the *Sophronia* fast to the outside of Larklight. Arthur, might I trouble for you for the key again?'

I fished inside my shirt, and drew out Myrtle's locket, which I passed to her. Then, with Jack at our side, and Sir Waverley following, we all went back down the long stairs, careful to avoid the hoverhogs, who were swimming laboriously about at ankle height, weighed down by the gravity.

Upon reaching the boiler room, Mother opened a panel which I had never noticed on the flank of the old gravity generator, revealing a heart-shaped hole, into which she fitted the locket. At once that blue glow began to shine from it. The gravity engine shuddered, and its sound changed, rising from a hum to a deep, rumbling, musical note, like the voice of a huge church organ. I pushed a little closer to Jack, who was standing next to me. I knew Mother would let none of us come to any harm, but I was scared all the same. I could not help it; it was as if every nerve in my body sensed that there was something ancient and powerful and unearthly about that sound.

And away in the dark recesses of the boiler room, bits of the gravity engine which had never moved, and which I'd thought long since rusted up, began to turn, and twirl, and tremble, and glow with light, and add their own notes to the rising song. The room was huge, I realised; far bigger than I'd ever guessed. It was no wonder the air currents seemed strange there. Breezes were blowing at me down aisles of singing enginery that looked a hundred miles long. And on the floor beneath our feet those curious tiles began to change their patterns faster and faster, and I started to imagine that they might be numbers, written out according to some system that was not of Earth, and that their movements were the working-out of some enormous, complicated sum. 'So this is how the Shapers travel about the Universe . . .' I thought.

I had a sudden sense of falling, and clutched Jack's hand.

Then, all at once, the song of Larklight began to die away, fading by degrees to a murmur, a sigh, an echo. The light of the strange machines died too, and we were standing in the same old, cramped, draughty boiler room, looking at the same old, dusty gravity engine.

'What's wrong with it?' asked Jack.

'Nothing's wrong,' said Mother, taking the locket from the keyhole and replacing it about her neck.

'But it didn't *do* anything!' I complained.

'Indeed it did,' said Mother.

'Coloured lights and foolish tootlings,' said Sir Waverley Rain crossly. 'I have seen better stage effects at Drury Lane. Really, my good woman, we do not have time for these diversions. The Empire is in peril.'

'Come and see,' said Mother.

We started up the stairs, and as we went I noticed that something had changed after all. Larklight's gravity was no longer pressing down upon me like a lead-lined quilt, but had returned to something like British Standard. In the hall, Mr Munkulus and the Tentacle Twins were busy tying the legs of the surviving spiders in case they took advantage of the reduction to try and fight again. But I hardly noticed them. What I saw, as we came up the stairs, was that the webs which had screened the windows had been torn away, and that a soft, pale yellow light was streaming in through the dusty glass.

I ran down the hall and pulled the front door open. I could hardly believe the vista which stretched before me as I brushed aside a few torn-off, flapping strands of web and stepped out on to the platform outside. The sky above was blue, streaked with feathery white clouds. The Sun, filtered by this kindly atmosphere, gave out a light as gentle and golden as elderflower wine. Below me the green Earth curved away into a haze, and a silver river which I guessed at once was the Thames snaked its way through the heart of an immense city.

Looking back, it's a bit of a bore in some ways that I was stuck down in the boiler room all through that miraculous journey, and didn't get a chance to peep out of a window as we sped across thirty thousand miles in the space of a few

seconds. A pity too, that I wasn't down on the ground to witness the sudden appearance of Larklight over London. It came with a flash of light, they say, and a huge thunderclap, much to the surprise of people on the ground.*

But even if I missed the journey, the *arriving* was glorious. Opening that door and stepping out, and finding England underneath me . . . Well, I wouldn't have swapped *that* for anything!

Of course, it didn't take long for the others to join me: Mr Munkulus and Jack and Mother and the Tentacle Twins,

*Some people claim to have seen mysterious pinions of golden light sprouting from the airborne house. The Poet Laureate mentions them in his 'Ode upon the Emergency in London', the one where he writes, 'What apparition springs upon my sight?/Abode of Angels, borne on wings of light!' But he was hiding under an old tin bath in Hyde Park Gardens at the time and can't have seen it for himself, so yah and boo to him.

Sir Waverley, Grindle and Nipper. Even Father emerged to tell us that Ssillissa was out of danger and sleeping peacefully and could we please tell him what in all the worlds was going on? His face was a study when he looked over the rail and saw London below.

By then the rest of us had already noticed that all was not well in the capital of Empire. Over to the west, dense pillars of smoke were climbing into the sky. The bells of St Paul's Cathedral and all the other churches were ringing out, and it did not sound like peals of joy, but rather as if they were warning all London of some terrible danger, and perhaps asking for God to intervene. The streets beneath us looked like rivers in spate, but instead of water pouring through them it was crowds of frightened people, all hoping to escape the stricken city!

And there! Oh, look! Westward, among that stand of green trees, where the smoke coils thickest! –

A crooked metal leg glinted in the sunlight; then another.

I had not stopped to think till then what Sir Waverley's Crystal Palace might look like if it got up and started ambling about. But there it was in all its horrid glory – a spider the size of St Paul's. I pointed it out to the others, and as we watched it reached up and knocked a passing aether-ship out of the air.

'I believe we must do something about that,' said Mother calmly.

'But *what*, Emily? What *can* we do?' cried Father, staring in horror at the thing as it demolished a tall building in Mayfair.

'Nothing, that's what,' said Jack Havock darkly. 'I ain't risking my skin in a fight with that thing, and I won't ask my crew to risk theirs, neither.'

'But the Empire!' cried Sir Waverley.

'I don't care twopence for your empire,' said Jack. 'It's Myrtle I'm worried about. Instead of standing here staring at that machine, we should be making for Mars, and finding her.'

'Then I shall have to see what may be done without you, Jack,' said Mother.

In St James's Park, little puffballs of smoke were rising from a battery of field-guns. Larklight drifted towards them, soaring over Coram's Fields and the rooftops of Bloomsbury like an immense hot-air balloon. We passed over the Royal Xenological Institute, low enough that if Jack had wished he might have dropped a pebble down the chimneys of his old home, but he was sulking, so I did not

suggest it. I had no idea what was powering our house on its strange flight, but later, looking back, I remembered seeing Mother frowning to herself, and fingering Myrtle's locket, which she was wearing around her own throat, and I wondered if she was somehow controlling Larklight remotely through that strange key.

The auto-spider did not see Larklight coming, or, if it did, it did not care. It was busy kicking down Buckingham Palace, much as a rough boy at the seaside might kick down the sandcastles built by smaller children. Larklight came to a halt above the battery in St James's Park, and Mother ran back inside and emerged soon afterwards with a bundle of ropes and wooden bars which turned out to be a rope ladder. She tied one end to the balcony rail and let the other drop, down and down until it was brushing the lawns. People gathered behind the guns looked up and gawped at us as we descended, Mother going first, then Father, then myself, and then, to my surprise, Mr Munkulus and the rest of the crew. Jack shouted at them to climb back up, but they shook their heads, or pretended not to hear, all save Mr Munkulus, who said, 'There's work to be done here, Captain Jack, and we shall help if we can.'

Jack stared down at him, startled and a little hurt, I think, by his disobedience. Then he said, 'I'm going to check on Ssil,' and went back inside.

How that ladder jerked and jerked about as we climbed down out of the sunlight into the gritty haze of gunsmoke! And how the guns boomed, and how the falling masonry crashed and rattled as the auto-spider ignored the shells that burst about it and trampled down No. 1, London, the Duke of Wellington's house at Hyde Park Corner!

The first person I saw when I jumped down on to the grass was the aged Duke himself, whom I recognised by his big beaky nose. He was standing behind the barking guns and looking very cross indeed about having his house trod on. He shook his cane at us new arrivals and accused us of being all sorts of dreadful things – anarchists and aliens and French spies and I don't know what else. Luckily, although he kept on shouting for the soldiers to clap us in irons, they

were all too busy aiming and
firing their guns and trying
to control their horses,
which I'm afraid had been
rather badly spooked by the
sudden appearance of a
large house a few feet above
the treetops.

While my mother was
trying to calm the Duke,
another chap came limping
out of the smoke at the
western end of the park. This one wore civilian clothes and
a curious moustache and his right leg was bandaged in tatty
lengths of blood-soaked calico. He was leaning on the arm
of a pretty Martian lady. 'It's quite all right, Your Worship,'
he said, approaching the Duke. 'I'm Burton, of the Secret
Service, and these people are known to me.'

The Duke subsided, muttering.

Next, to my amazement, the stranger turned to me and
said, 'Art Mumby, I presume?'

'Yes, sir,' said I. 'And this is my father and mother.'

The stranger tried to make his bow to us, but almost

collapsed, and his companion made him settle himself on the grass while she fussed with his makeshift bandages. His leg was in a very poor way, I think, but he bore the pain manfully and said, 'I am dashed pleased to find you still alive. Your daughter, Myrtle, gave me to understand that you had all perished horribly through the machinations of these beastly spiders.'

'You have seen Myrtle?' asked Father.

'She travelled with us from the planet Mars,' said Mr Burton. 'We were separated when all this hullabaloo began. But I am sure she is all right.'

'How can you be sure?' I cried. 'How can you be sure of anything, upon this battlefield? Where is she? Where did you see her last?'

Mother caught my arm and said, 'Never fear, Art. If Myrtle has any sense* she will be hiding somewhere; we must put a stop to that automaton's tricks, and then begin to search for her.'

Meanwhile, Mr Burton shielded his eyes against the smoky sunlight and peered up at the house which hung

---

*Which is a very big 'if' if you ask me, but nobody did, so I politely held my tongue.

above him. 'I take it this is Larklight? I guessed that there was something special about it when Myrtle told me what lengths our arthropod friends had gone to to try to secure the key to it. I should dearly love to know how you managed to bring it here with such admirable dispatch.'

'It has an engine of unearthly origin,' said Mother cautiously, though I could tell by the glint in her eye that she liked this gentleman, and felt inclined to trust him. 'I believe it works by an arrangement of shaped gravitational fields.'

Mr Burton nodded thoughtfully, glanced behind him as the rampaging palace crushed Marble Arch 'neath one foot, and said, 'I wonder if these shaped gravitational fields might not be used to put an end to the Crystal Palace's games? It appears annoyingly impervious to all our shells and bullets.'

'Alas,' said Mother, 'it would be far too dangerous. Larklight's machineries are designed for manoeuvring planets and moons about, not squashing spiders. I risked ripping the dear old Moon in half when I used them to bring us here. To unleash them upon Hyde Park might lead to a most terrible disaster.'

Mr Burton looked grave. My father wrung his hands and

asked if anyone had tried to reason with the Crystal Palace and whether that might not be better than all this rowdy gunfire.

Grindle looked up, cocked his head on one side, twitched a leathery ear and asked, 'What's that?'

A moment later we all heard it too: the whine of alchemical engines. Over the rooftops an aether-ship came tearing. It was a ship we all knew; spiky as a chestnut and black as sin, still smoking with the heat of its over-hasty descent through Earth's atmosphere.

The men at the guns stopped firing and looked up as the ship descended on to the grass nearby. The crowd behind them had thinned out a bit, because some of the spectators had noticed how little effect the guns were having and had decided to leave before the Crystal Palace came and stamped on them, but the few who remained all pointed and cooed as the unearthly ship came to rest upon a patch of singed lawn not far off, and a hatch yawned open in its flank.

I had expected spiders, but instead a human form emerged, nattily dressed in cobweb clothes. I'd half forgotten Dr Ptarmigan. He raised his hands to signal a truce, and came walking across the grass towards us.

'Good afternoon, all!' he called, and bowing to Mother, added, 'Good afternoon, Mrs Mumby. I was up in high orbit, watching the fun, when I saw your house arrive. What a surprise! I'd almost given up hope of getting hold of it after you overcame Mr Webster and his friends this morning, but now you have brought it right to me, like a homecoming present! Sweetly kind!'

'You'll never have Larklight,' said Mother, soft but very fierce.

'We shall see what all these gentlemen have to say about that,' chuckled Dr Ptarmigan. He raised his voice, addressing the men at the guns, and the Duke and his staff, who still lingered behind them. 'I am Dr Ptarmigan, late of the Royal Xenological Institute. I built the automaton now trampling your city. I can stop it. I could stop it in an instant, if you wish. But there is a price to pay. I want *that.*'

He pointed with one skinny hand straight up, to where Larklight hung above the smoke. Some of the gunners looked up too, but the Duke leaned on his cane and watched Dr Ptarmigan intently.

'Don't listen to him!' I shouted. 'He's in league with the spiders who built that automaton! He wants to smash up the Solar System, and he'll use Larklight to do it if you let him!'

Dr Ptarmigan laughed. 'Oh, what stuff,' he said. 'Dear Art, that sob story I told you among Saturn's Rings was mostly for Mr Webster's benefit. I let the First Ones think I was on their side, but I've really no more time for their empire than for yours. I just needed them to help me set my plan in motion. What other race could provide me with an aether-ship, and willing warriors, and the help I needed to bring all these things to pass? No, I don't want to smash the worlds apart; simply to rule them. With Larklight at my command, and devices like this to do my bidding' (he flung his hand out to indicate the Crystal Palace, which had sidled closer while he spoke and now towered silently over the ruins of Buckingham Palace, as if listening to him) 'there will be *nothing* I cannot achieve! Spiders and humans alike shall be my slaves!'

'The poor fellow's as mad as a bucket of eels,' said the Duke of Wellington gruffly.

'So be it!' cried Ptarmigan.

Then – it all happened so fast that I am not sure how he managed it, but somehow he lunged out and caught me by the collar and dragged me close to him, and reached into his cobwebby pocket and took out a pistol, and poked the cold, hard muzzle in beneath my chin, and held me like that while he said, 'Give me the key, Mrs Mumby! Give me the key, you Shaper witch, or the boy will die!'

'Oh, Art!' my mother cried. 'Oh, Art!' She clutched the locket tight, and tears ran from her eyes. It must have been agony for her, to have so much power at her command, yet still be powerless. For what could all the engines and contraptions of Larklight do against one small pistol in that madman's hand?

Mother reached up and

undid the clasp of the locket chain. She started forward, holding it in her outstretched hand. I felt Dr Ptarmigan quiver with pure pleasure at his victory, and hoped in his excitement he wouldn't accidentally let his finger tighten on the trigger.

'Don't give it him, Mother!' I managed to say. I did not much want to be shot, but I couldn't bear to think that the whole Solar System might be given into the control of potty Dr Ptarmigan on my account!

'Now don't be hasty, ma'am,' Mr Burton cautioned her.

'That's easy for you to say, sir!' snapped Father. 'He's not *your* boy!'

'Shoot 'em!' shouted the Duke of Wellington, losing patience with us all. 'Shoot the whole d——d lot of 'em!'

But nobody obeyed him. Mother and I stood between Dr Ptarmigan and the soldiers, and they none of them wanted to shoot a woman or a boy. Mother kept coming slowly forward, and the locket glittered in her hand, and her grey eyes were fixed on Dr Ptarmigan's face, as if she were trying to hypnotise him. Or (I suddenly realised) *as if she were trying to keep him from noticing something that was going on behind him* . . .

With a wild, piratical cry, Jack Havock came down upon

the demented doctor from above. Looking down from the
windows of Larklight, he had seen what was happening,
and he had found that he hadn't the heart to leave us to our
fate after all. He had come to rescue me! He hadn't time to
make the long, slow climb down that rope ladder, of
course, so he had jumped. But above his head to ease his
descent flew all the *Sophronia*'s hoverhogs in a
squealing, chuffing cloud. Jack held tight
to the ends of their strings like a
peddlar with a fine display of fat
pink balloons, and let the hogs
support him.

His feet flailed, kicking
Ptarmigan's pistol aside so that when
it went off – *Bang!* – it was pointing
up into the sky, and did no harm
(tho' later we found out it had
smashed a box-room window on
the underside of Larklight). Dr
Ptarmigan howled in fury and
tried to twist his gun about to
point at Jack, but Jack was too fast.
He let go of his ropes and dropped

to the ground. Ptarmigan tried to aim at him, but the frightened clump of hoverhogs blundered past him, and the ends of the trailing strings lashed at him. He dropped the gun. Before he could snatch it up Jack was on his feet again. His shipmates cheered. A swift uppercut sent Ptarmigan staggering backwards, and as he staggered a huge white shape burst from the drifting smoke . . .

I had forgotten Mr Webster until then. I had imagined he was trapped aboard his ship, prostrated by Earth's gravity. But Mr Webster was made of sterner stuff than that. Even with two and a half BSG bearing down on him he had managed to creep out of Larklight, and he was easily strong enough on Earth to take his revenge upon the villain who had double-crossed him.

'All for my benefit, was it?' he bellowed, snatching Dr Ptarmigan up in his foreclaws and shaking him. 'Spiders shall be your slaves too, shall they?' (He must have heard everything Dr Ptarmigan had told us, you see, and he wasn't best pleased to find he was just another pawn in the mad doctor's game.) 'You just needed us to set your plans in motion, did you?' he shrieked, throwing poor whimpering Ptarmigan down upon the grass and lifting one great gleaming claw above him like the Sword of Damocles, ready to pin him to the lawn.

But to everyone's astonishment, Jack went haring in between the spider's legs, grabbed Dr Ptarmigan by one foot and dragged him aside before the claw stabbed down. And Grindle and Mr Munkulus and I set up such a hollering and whooping and a waving of cutlasses, and the Tentacle Twins crackled so bright and fierce, that Mr Webster flinched back and missed his chance to impale Jack and Ptarmigan together.

Jack arrived at my side, panting, still dragging Dr Ptarmigan, who looked as pale as unbaked pastry and as shaky as a syllabub. 'I had to help him,' Jack said. 'He was kind to me when I was little.'

Mr Webster, meanwhile, had recovered himself. He drew himself up to his full height, towering over us on his long back legs, claws and eye-cluster a-gleam. He signalled towards the western end of the park, where the Crystal Palace automaton had paused in its rampages, and called out to it in a clattery language of his own, doubtless telling it that there were some insolent humans and assorted Xenomorphs here, waiting to be crushed. It responded at once, raising its great wrought-iron legs one by one and stamping towards us, moving with a lurching, wayward, drunken, galloping gait, as if maddened by the prospect of killing us. As the ground began to shake beneath us with the thunder of its approach old Mr Webster turned and surveyed us all, the whooping space pirates, the gunners frantically turning their pieces towards him, my mother and father clinging together in the shadow of Larklight, and said smugly, 'You have defeated us for the moment, but the First Ones will triumph in the end! Your victory is temporary, and none of you will live to enjoy it!'

Only we did, of course. For at that instant the drifty veils of smoke above us parted, and down upon Mr Webster came one of the huge iron feet of the Crystal Palace. He looked up as it descended, and saw that great weight dropping towards him, and cried out,

'Oh, b—', which I believe would have turned out to be a Very Wicked Word Indeed, had he had time to get the rest of it out.

There was a great squelch as the foot squashed him flat, and then silence. We all stared at the massive, spidery structure looming over us. It showed no further inclination to move. And as we peered up at it we saw a little compartment beneath its body pop open. A small, ragged, human shape came creeping out and began to descend towards us, climbing clumsily down one of the motionless legs.

'It's Myrtle!' I cried.

'Myrtle?' gasped Jack, who of course had believed her still on Mars until that moment.

'The gent with the curious whiskers brought her here,' I explained helpfully, but Jack wasn't listening. He didn't care how Myrtle came to be there, he was just glad that she was.

'Oh, she will fall and break her neck!' Father exclaimed.

'Not Myrtle,' said Jack Havock, grinning at my sister's pluck. 'She can cope with more than you know.'

Nonetheless, Mother touched the key which she still held, and Larklight started moving again, gentle as a summer cloud, until it hung close to the motionless spider palace, and Myrtle was able to reach out and grab a hold of that dangling rope ladder, down which she climbed to meet us.

'That's the lunatic wench who sat upon Her Majesty!' thundered the Duke of Wellington, pointing at her with his cane as she drew close to the ground. 'By G-d, so it was she controlling the palace all along!'

'No, no!' I cried, certain that there must be another explanation, for I knew Myrtle was not the sort of girl who tramples wantonly on public monuments. I think the Duke would have ignored me, but luckily Mr Burton took my side and said, 'I imagine that the palace was controlled by a smaller version of that monstrous spider we have just seen crushed; a brute no bigger than your hand, bred specially to operate in British Standard Gravity. I would have attempted to reach him myself, but it appears this brave young lady has beaten me to it . . .'

And my sister, jumping down on to the turf, said, 'Oh,

dear Mr Burton, I am so happy to find that you have not been trod upon! You are quite right; there *was* a horrid little spider inside, just like the one which steered the false Sir Waverley. I squashed it with a rolled-up copy of the *Times*. Then, as I looked down and wondered how I should make my descent, I saw that horrible Mr Webster menacing you all. I do not know how I managed to steer the automaton towards you and crush him; I suppose desperation helped me to focus my mind. I certainly could not do it again. It is a most unsuitable occupation for a young lady . . .'

And then she looked past Mr Burton, and was astonished to see me, and more astonished to see Father, and yet more astonished still to see Mother standing there, and there was a great deal of hugging and hurried explanations, and it felt very strange indeed to think that we had counted her, and she had counted us, among the dead. And meanwhile the story of how she had saved the day was spreading quickly among the people in the park, and the artillerymen were getting up a chorus of 'For She's a Jolly Good Fellow' and shouting 'Huzzah!' and hurling their pillbox caps into the air, and at last Myrtle turned her attention from us to Jack Havock, who stood shyly watching our reunions with his crew behind him.

'Oh, Jack!' she said.

'Oh, Myrtle!' said Jack.

And I cannot bring myself to describe what happened next. It is one thing to write of giant spiders and man-eating moths, but there are some sights too stomach-turning for even the bravest British boy to contemplate, and the soppy way Jack and my sister ran to cuddle and to kiss each other is one of 'em.

EPILOGUE

And now my tale is almost done (as proper authors say) and it only remains to tell what happened after.

Some weeks have passed now since those extraordinary happenings in Hyde Park. The clearing up and rebuilding of London has begun, and many prayers of thanks have been offered up to the kindly Providence which allowed my sister to stop the Crystal Palace before it laid the whole capital in ruins, and which ensured that nobody was seriously injured during the catastrophe. (The Queen and Prince Albert, about whom Myrtle was terribly worried,

were found hiding under an upturned rowing boat on a small island in the Serpentine.)

Larklight has returned to its own lonely orbit, north of the Moon. It did not travel here in an instant, on mystical wings of light, but slowly, hauled along by space tugs which were loaned by the London Corporation by way of a thank you for our help in saving the city. Never again will it speed about the aether with such haste, and such scant regard for the Laws of Physics, for Mother has had Jack's crew help her break up the strange Shaper machines in the boiler room, and Sir Waverley Rain (who is quite a kindly gentleman when you come to know him) agreed to melt them down for her in the furnaces of one of his factories in the north country.

Everyone was very sorry to see their secrets consigned to the fire, but Mother would not listen to any arguments. 'Now that the world knows such power exists,' she said, 'we should never be able to rest easy. There would always be somebody trying to seize Larklight and use it for their own selfish ends – spiders or anarchists or agents of the Tsar. So I shall destroy those old machineries for ever, and Larklight will be just a house again.'

But of course Larklight will never be *just* a house. It is

our home. We have a new gravity generator now, the very latest patent model from the Trevithick company, also a whole staff of Rain & Co.'s finest auto-servants, given us free and gratis by Sir Waverley. And we are having the roofs repaired, and the old carpets taken up, and the rooms redecorated, and all manner of improvements made. For we are quite well-to-do now.

You will remember how a number of the spiders from Mr Webster's ship were left behind at Larklight, disabled by our gravity, yet still alive. Well, Father has been chosen by the Royal Xenological Institute to make a study of them, and he is to receive a very handsome grant for doing so. He

calls them *Tegenaria saturnia*, and says that he hopes his studies may one day enable us to make peace with their strange race. But for the moment we shall remain very wary of the First Ones.

As for Dr Ptarmigan, he has been confined in the Bide-A-Wee Sanatorium for the Criminally Deranged, which stands upon a lonely island in a Scotch loch. There, amid the heather and the porridge, we must sincerely hope that he comes to see the error of his ways.

Jack and his crew are staying at Larklight for a while, until they finish the repairs to the *Sophronia*. When it emerged who they were there was a great uproar. Gentlemen stood up in Parliament to demand that they all be arrested for piracy. The *Sophronia*'s owners insisted that their property be returned. Sir Launcelot Sprigg announced that he would sue for damages, as the hullabaloo that Jack and his friends caused when they fled Russell Square had led to Sir Launcelot being dismissed from his position, and becoming the subject of satirical cartoons and a popular music-hall song.

But Mr Burton (who is Sir Richard Burton now, on account of all his fine work on Mars) calmed them all down. He pointed out that, contrary to popular belief, Jack and his crew had never harmed anyone. He reminded the shipping company that the *Sophronia* had been headed for the breaker's yard when Jack stole her. He told Sir Launcelot not to be such a d——d bad sport. And then he took Jack aside and suggested that he might consider remaining captain of the *Sophronia*, but working for Sir Richard as an intelligence agent. 'For mankind is spreading ever outwards, Jack,' he said, 'and who knows what threats and perils we may encounter in the wilds of space, which you and your brave crew could help us foil?'

Jack looked sullen at first. He has a rebellious nature and has always thought himself the enemy of Britain, so it must have come as a surprise to him being asked to serve her. But he understands that it is in no one's interest to let monsters like the First Ones rove about unchecked, and besides, he wants to keep the *Sophronia* aetherborne and his crew together, and now that their pirating days are over they need some way to make a living. So he agreed, and shook Sir Richard's hand, and became Jack Havock of the Secret Service there and then.

→>-←

So here I sit at Larklight, with a huge full Moon shining in at the drawing-room windows. Mother and Father are talking quietly together in the corner. They have a great deal to talk about, of course. Poor Father was quite distressed to learn that his dear wife was really a four-and-a-half-billion-year-old being from another star, but he seems to be

growing used to the idea, especially since it means that Mother can explain to him all sorts of secrets about the nature of life. Currently he is terribly excited about something he calls 'Evolution'.

Meanwhile, Mother's space flowers sing softly in the conservatory, their curious voices harmonising with *Birdsong at Eventide*, which Myrtle is playing on the pianoforte. Myrtle looks very ladylike and demure and almost pretty (tho' I expect we shall see a different side of her when she finds out I have copied all those passages from her secret diary). Even her piano playing has improved somewhat, no doubt because she is in LOVE. It certainly seems to please Jack, who is leaning on the pianoforte listening to her, and reaching out to turn the pages when she asks. But it does not please Mr Grindle or Mr Munkulus, whom I can see waiting impatiently to get their own hands upon the instrument and treat us to a rousing aether shanty.

Ssillissa, who has quite recovered, sits toasting muffins and Mars-mallows by the stove, occasionally throwing a crumb to one of our hoverhogs, who have emerged from whatever cranny they hid in while the First Ones were here and resumed the task of keeping Larklight tidy. (They got on swimmingly with the hogs from the *Sophronia*, and we now have several litters of fat pink piglets too.) Ssil looks quite fetching as blue lizards go, for Mrs Burton took her to a good dressmaker in Knightsbridge and had some clothes made up which better fit her saurian physique. The Tentacle Twins are up on the roof, catching Icthyomorphs for our supper, and my good friend Nipper is dozing beside me on the sopha – indeed, I am using his shell for my writing desk.

And that is the picture I shall leave you with, of Life at Larklight. No doubt, as Sir Richard says, all kinds of threats and perils lie before us, and who knows what horrors may be winging towards us even now from out the vasty deeps of space? I am sure that I shall pretty soon find other adventures and alarms to tell you of . . .

But first I shall have a hot buttered muffin and a nice cup of tea.

Arthur Mumby
Larklight

The author and illustrator record a new species of ogleweed.

Two Gentlemen of Devonshire

Mr Philip Reeve was born and raised in the bustling seaside slum of Brighton. Like all residents of that vile town he fled as soon as he was able, and now lives in a secluded cottage on Dartmoor, where frequent encounters with gigantic house spiders and fruitless efforts to preserve his tweed and serge against the voracious moth have given Mr Reeve a deep understanding of Art Mumby's plight. He is the author of the bestselling *Mortal Engines* quartet.

Mr David Wyatt was expelled from the Pre-Raphaelite Brotherhood for being 'a bit weird', but remains one of the finest illustrators of the present age. He lives and works in an ancient house in a Devonshire graveyard, where he is much troubled by restless spirits who knock upon his door to complain about his late-night lute playing and other Bohemian excesses. He has illustrated books for such authors as Mr Tolkien, Mr Pratchett, Mr Pullman, Mrs Wynne-Jones and many others of the finest pedigree.

ACKNOWLEDGEMENTS

Mr Reeve and Mr Wyatt wish to express their thanks to the Three Graces of Soho Square: Mrs Val Brathwaite, who inspired their joint venture, Miss Elena Fountain, who guided it to fruition, and Miss Helen Szirtes, who spied out all the spelling mistakes.*

*Except this wun.